Tongue in Cheek

When I showed up at St Matthew's College Marcus didn't conceal his pleasure as an older man would. He was happy and that was that. I hoped the teachers thought we were long-lost cousins or something. I actually said hello to some of the students as we walked away. I loved watching his arse when he walked ahead of me, and his taut back muscles beneath his flimsy white shirt. I had the whole scenario planned out: as soon as we got home I wanted to hold each bottom cheek in my hands. I was going to tie him to the bedposts with his stripy St Matthew's college tie and ride him into the clouds.

Tongue in Cheek

TABITHA FLYTE

Black Lace novels are sexual fantasies.
In real life, make sure you practise safe sex.

First published in 2000 by
Black Lace
Thames Wharf Studios
Rainville Road, London W6 9HA

Reprinted 2000, 2001

Typeset by SetSystems Ltd, Saffron Walden, Essex
Printed and bound by Mackays of Chatham PLC

ISBN 0 352 33484 3

Chapter One

*T*he sun comes down on us thickly, like great globules of honey on our burnished backs. We are the only ones on the beach – the only people for miles in our private alcove. The rocks conceal us from behind and, in front, a green-blue sparkling sea protects us for as far as I can see. I stretch out languidly on the towel; I can feel his eyes wandering hungrily over my body, seeking out my breasts, like a traveller searching for a room for the night.

'Sally,' he murmurs. 'You look beautiful. Please, let me give you a massage: just a massage, I promise.'

He puts his sandy fingers to my neck, across my shoulders. He undoes my bikini strap slowly, too slowly, and then pauses to drip suntan lotion into those big hands of his. His hands are capable, like a labourer's: he can do anything with them. The huge, soft palms are as wide as a baseball mitt. His thumbs alone are the length of my sunglasses. He can circle my waist with his hands, and my waist is not small any more.

He massages my back efficiently. He knows how to do it perfectly: long, strong slopes follow spine-tin-

1

gling caresses. But he leaves me begging for more. I want him to touch me more. He snaps at the elastic of my bikini bottoms and then helps himself to my arse.

'I thought this was just a massage.'

'This is,' he croons, his breath hot in my ear, 'a very special massage.'

He is a con man, but I love him for it.

He moves between my legs and pulls aside my weenie bikini bottoms, allowing himself untrammelled access. I feel his finger tremble inside. I am wet, an embarrassing puddle of arousal. His exploring finger grows increasingly confident. He probes and discovers my clit. I bray up against him, rocking on his fingers, feeling his thumb come in to join the others, to stroke the narrow passage of my tender clit. He masturbates me, harder, straighter and more satisfyingly. His other hand creeps around to stroke my buttocks. I purr, swaying back and forth, meeting his hands with my arched body.

I turn over to take a look at him. His penis is rigid, erect to the sky, and it's white as the moon. It's the only part of him still untouched by the holiday sunshine. I want him inside me now. He opens my legs still wider with his mobile fingers, and then in goes his hard cock. It is big, squeezing against the walls of my cunt, bashing against my tight vestibule. My vagina can't help but clench around him as he launches forward. Poor bikini, caught up between us, stretched uncompromisingly tight. I feel the fabric rise against me, coming to rest in the crack of my arse.

He kisses me. At first our lips knock together, almost accidentally, but then the pressure becomes firmer, more demanding. My mouth struggles open, and his tongue rides in: I feel him explore the hollow of my mouth, mirroring his cock. I kiss him back as

2

hard as I can, till the sides of my mouth scrape against the sides of his.

I grip him tighter around his hot back. My hands slide around on his damp skin. My legs move, wrapping around him on either side. The top of his cock produces an almost agonising pressure against my clit. He breathes heavily into my neck.

He doesn't move. He is a master at keeping still, at waiting for the right moment. He can go for hours like this: the best sleeping lion in the world. His penis shoved rudely into my fanny, enjoying just being there. The fuck without the fucking. The stealth intruder, the meditation expert, the sodding Tantric master. I am so wet, so soaking, that if he weren't so huge, so concrete, he would have slipped right out of me. But he is locked firmly, tight as a cork in a wine bottle, and his rough hands are massaging my big arse. He is as in control as I am out of it.

I can feel all my nerve endings zing. I want to turn myself inside out. Have him rub against me harder, harder, scrape himself against me. I work at him wildly, bouncing up against him, pulling him into me, drowning his cock with my juices, tearing at him to fuck me.

'Yes, now.'

As if by magic, he grows inside me. I am coming. I scream with pleasure just as the chaos of spurts begins against the wetness of my hole.

I ploughed myself until I felt as dry as the Arizona desert. It wasn't working. Masturbation was boring. I couldn't get into it, no matter what tales I whispered to myself. No matter what pictures I drew in my eager imagination. No matter what I did to my deprived sex, I couldn't tip myself over the edge. Sometimes I couldn't help wondering if there was something wrong with me.

3

I got up and gazed morosely at the fridge. I had bought croissants and strawberries the day before, ready for our usual lie-in. (Will always said that I was the best in bed – at breakfast in bed.) It wouldn't be much fun by myself, though, so I decided to have cornflakes instead.

I usually spent Friday nights and Saturday mornings with Will, but he had cancelled our date. It wasn't that disappointing any more: Will was always working late. If there were brownie points to be won at his company, Will wanted to scoop them all up. I guess he knew he had earned enough brownie points with me, so he didn't bother about doing overtime in our relationship. I know it sounds daft, but the day I met him, I told my mother that I had found the guy I was going to spend the rest of my life with.

I called him.

'I was just about to phone you,' Will stammered. He sounded surprised.

Even then, after all those years, I felt a *frisson* of happiness at his voice. I could picture him there, the cordless jammed under his chin. He would be padding around his flat, barefooted, tiger in the jungle. I imagined him switching on the kettle (that I bought for him), his suit flung carelessly over a chair. I imagined his penis peeping out from his boxers, tortoise head under his white T-shirt. Will had more white T-shirts than anyone I had ever met. I tried to get him to branch into different colours, but he had to sleep in white. I used to laugh that he was like a virgin bride.

'Were you?' I asked playfully.

'Yes,' he said abruptly. He was in a bad mood. I hoped I hadn't woken him up. He was not at his best in the mornings. He must have worked very late.

'Did you speak to Sharon?' he asked.

'No, why?'

4

He didn't reply.

'I was lying in bed thinking about you,' I continued seductively. 'Shall I tell you what we were doing?'

'No . . . I . . . there's something . . . I mean, the thing is, I can't see you today . . . I'll call you later.'

Will didn't usually talk in riddles. He prided himself on his clear and concise speaking. I heard a voice in the background. Not a voice, but a murmur. He must have been watching TV.

'Is anyone there, Wills?'

'No, it's the radio,' he said. The radio erupted into giggles.

'Who's that, Will? Is there someone there?' I thought for a moment that it might be his sister. Although why she would be there early in the morning, giggling, was beyond me.

'No one.'

More laughter. Will's voice sounded croaky.

'Look, I'll ring you back. I can't talk now: I have to go to the bathroom.'

The giggling continued.

Have you ever done that? Have you ever fucked someone while you were on the telephone to someone else? I wouldn't do that to my friends, but I had had no qualms doing it to his. I once kissed his balls while listening to his friends invite him to a football match. And now, now I was certain he was doing it to me. It was the hurried quality of our conversation. Plus, I definitely heard something suspicious: that gasp of enjoyment that inadvertently escapes your mouth when someone touches a sensitive place. I couldn't be sure they were fucking, but that's what it sounded like. I may have been naïve (no, I definitely was naïve), but I knew there was someone there with him.

Almost as soon as I put down the receiver, Sharon called, and I suggested that she came over. I didn't say why, and she didn't ask. It was only as I was

5

getting the mugs of tea ready that I realised that she had said she was coming anyway. I wondered why. Although we were close, Saturday mornings were usually strictly reserved for the men in our life.

'I'm so sorry, Sally: he was such a bastard,' she said as soon as she arrived. She actually tried to hug me.

'What do you mean?'

I didn't want to admit that something was wrong. Not yet. I still had to pretend I was in a wonderful relationship, having the time of my life. I was my mother's daughter. Standards had to be kept high. All disorder hidden from the twitching net curtains.

'He did tell you, didn't he?' Sharon persisted.

'Tell me what?'

Sharon hesitated and then plunged in with her usual frankness.

'He's met someone else.'

'I don't think so,' I replied, and laughed hollowly. She looked at me knowingly as if to say I was in denial. It killed me, that look.

'Sally, I saw them together last night.'

'Who?'

'Will. He was with a woman.'

'Maybe it was his sister,' I said, clutching at straws.

The look on Sharon's face was enough to make me lose my grip. I felt suddenly shattered, broken up. I wanted to rewind this morning, back to where I was lying in bed with my fantasies. I wanted Will to telephone and say, 'I'm coming to see you,' and 'Get the breakfast ready.'

'It's over, Sal.'

'Why should it be?' I protested. All over? Five years all over: just over because of this.

'Of course it's not finished.'

'But Sally, he was with someone else.'

'What did she look like?' I whispered.

6

Sharon looked at me, pained. I could always tell when she lied.

'Not as pretty as you.'

I started crying.

'No, she wasn't,' Sharon insisted. 'She had no personality; she looked, umm, different to you, a different type.'

They say that in grief there are many stages: disbelief, anger, sadness and acceptance. When grief comes in the shape of rejection, there is just one: incomprehension. You are thrown down a black pit while the person you love shovels mud all over you. Whatever you do to make yourself a nicer, prettier, skinnier, better, cleaner or funnier person makes no difference: they pour mud all over you. And it's not even their fault. It's never their fault: it's the alcohol, it's the time of life, they are only obeying orders. They can't control themselves, any more than they can fall back in love with you. And the worst thing is that you can't understand why.

Will refused to answer my calls. I talked into the barren coldness of his answering machine. I wouldn't speak to anyone else. Will was a shit. Will is a shit. Will will always be a shit. Repeat. It seemed to me that week that everyone had known for years that Will was a wanker. Everyone else had had him sussed, while I had wandered around in a contented, yet cloudy, oblivion. Until now.

He was a shit. He is a shit; he will always be a shit. But there was a reason, there is a reason, and there will always be a reason why I fell in love with him. His telephone voice, the way he walks, the way he sat on my sofa with his legs up in the air. You don't fall in love with people because they are shit. You fall in love with them because they laugh at your jokes (or pretend to). They let you bleed over their bed when

7

you have a heavy period, they buy you Kettle Chips and Toffee Crisps and, after you drink too much, they mop your forehead and clear the sick off the toilet rim. They hold your hand in the movies, but don't mind when you pull away to scratch. However much I persuade myself, there will always be a corner in me that is for ever William.

Every time I thought about him that morning, I could hardly catch my breath. I gulped awkwardly. I thought I was going to die. I saw their life flashing before me. Him with her, whoever she was. Them in bed together. Him doing the most intimate, the most precious, the most explicit things to her. Exploding inside her! They were our things, our secret loving things.

'Calm down, baby,' Sharon said. 'Take deep breaths.'

But deep breaths weren't working.

'What about something to eat?' She found my cereal in the kitchen. She brought out the soggy flakes obliterated by milk. They looked how I felt. I started crying again.

'This woman . . . I'll forgive him. If it's a one-night stand, it's forgotten. Everyone makes mistakes. You know what men are like. One mistake. It's not such a big deal.'

In fact, Will had already made his 'one mistake'. He had used up his extra life a couple of years earlier. A girl at work 'threw herself' at him (Will's words), rendering Will 'incapable of resisting' (ditto). Fortunately, the *femme fatale* was Spanish and, after Will broke it off, she disappeared into the mists of the Mediterranean.

Kindly, Sharon didn't mention the incident that had caused us endless wine consumption in a local bar. What she said though, I would remember for ever.

'Sally, baby, you've got to accept that he's gone

from your life. You will meet someone else, I promise.'

She was too much of a friend to say the old 'plenty more fish in the sea' line, but I knew she was thinking it.

'I don't want anyone else,' I groaned. 'What did I do wrong? Why wasn't I good enough?'

'It's not you. It's him. Listen, one day, someone will make you feel like – like the most amazing woman in the world.'

'I want him,' I said sullenly, like a three year old offered vanilla when she wanted raspberry.

'He'll get what's coming to him: people always do,' she said darkly. 'What goes around, comes around. You can't treat people like this and expect to get away with it.'

I suddenly noticed how tired she was. Poor Sharon, she was four months pregnant, and the undersides of her eyes were glazed with black. She didn't want to leave, but I told her to. Seeing her, especially with that bump in her stomach, seemed to be evidence of her success against my failure. She had craved her man, caught him, and caressed him, conceived with him. And me? I was dumped on. Although I was thrilled for her, since she and Hugh had been trying for so long, and although I definitely wasn't ready for motherhood, it made me uncomfortable. Sharon was relieved. After two years of trying, they had finally done it. She said that now they could start fucking again, instead of baby-making.

'You won't do anything stupid, will you?' she said, hugging me at the door.

'Like what?'

'Like, I don't know, cutting off your lovely hair. That's what women do when they split up from their men, so I heard.'

'Very funny.'

9

'No, seriously, I'll kill you if you do,' she warned.

I suppose I did do plenty of stupid things. All day long, I left calls on Will's various answering machines. I left my tears on his mobile, the one at home, even the shared one at work.

I left a trail of melancholy behind me. I talked into thin air until the tape filled out and told me there was no more room. 'No one will love you as much as I do,' I threatened him.

I demanded information. 'Just talk to me, Will: I need to know the truth.'

'It doesn't matter about this: we can work it out.' I forgave him for his mistakes. I was the most forgiving person on earth.

'Are you listening to me?' No reply. This was a test of faith. He was probably screwing her, but I believed in him. I believed he was there.

Maybe he was stroking her clit as I soothed him with my silver tongue.

'Wills, I still love you.'

Maybe he was telling her that he loved her as she jerked up and down on top of him.

'Please call me back. We had five years together: you can't throw it away just over this.'

That night, I couldn't sleep. I put my hand down my pyjama bottoms and felt the warm comfort of my pussy. The hottest part of my body was also the loneliest. Stroking myself, I got up and stood over the answering machine. There was a stream of messages from him: my favourites, the messages that I could never bring myself to erase. Although they snarled up the machine, I kept them there, savouring him and his love for me.

I sat on the floor next to the machine, with one finger curled up: a soft, velvety hook shape inside my warm hole. I worked my clitoris, my thumb in front, massaging my way down the damp skin. As I exercised my sex, his voice caressed my heart, and I remembered.

It was our first anniversary, and Will had arranged a weekend away for us. We hadn't had sex for the two weeks before (his idea), so that by the time we got there, I was craving him madly. (We were still at the 'gagging for it' stage of our relationship.) We had a large room with an *en suite* bathroom and balcony, but the best thing about it was the huge bed. It was a genuine four-poster, with huge wooden pillars at each corner and velvety curtains to enclose us. We bounced around gleefully on the mattress. The quilt was silky under my legs and invitingly smooth. It was a fantasy room: a place overflowing with secret promises.

'I'm having you on here, baby,' he said, and then he got up and started unpacking his clothes.

'Not now?' I lay back with my legs and arms spread like a starfish.

'I'm going to make you wait.'

'I can't wait.' I lolled on the bed, in a fashion I thought might be construed as inviting. 'Let's do it now.'

'You have to wait,' he instructed. He looked at me mischievously, like one of those villains in the old movies after they tie up their woman on the railroad.

'Why?'

'Waiting is good for you. Tonight,' he added extravagantly, 'I am going to make you come like you never have before.'

'Promises, promises.'

I changed into a black lace underwear set. The bra fastened at the front, and the high-cut knickers elongated my thighs. As I did it up, I couldn't resist feeling myself, just to feel what he was going to

11

experience later that night. The whiteness of my flesh looked unusually erotic.

We had dinner in the crowded hotel restaurant. On the other tables, bored-looking women sat with boring husbands. I was glad I was with Will. Just looking across the table at his handsome face made me want to hold him, have him hold me. I crossed and uncrossed my legs. I could feel a heavy warmth emanating from the tops of my thighs. It had been a long time.

Wills fed me. Each time his spoon wobbled across the table I licked it clean, curling my tongue into the cold metal. He had mussels, and I watched him lick out the shell, trembling with anticipation. I took the asparagus, licked it, and held its length in my cheek. He told me to stop, please: he was getting too excited. The serviette that he had put down to protect his clothes was now fluttering, hovering over his lap. Between courses, we held hands. Will fondled my knuckles, and I could feel my lace knickers growing wet. I was sweating, and was glad that I was wearing perfume. My vagina seemed to twitch with antici-pation. He smiled conspiratorially at me. He knew what I was thinking.

Dessert would be too slow, too painful: as soon as we could, we dashed upstairs. But Will insisted that we had a bath: he wanted to delay the inevitable as long as possible.

While the bath – a large china tub set in the middle of the room – was running, Will undressed me slowly. He unzipped my dress, and it slid down onto the black-and-white tiled floor. He gazed at me reveren-tially as I stood in my black skimpy underwear. He unclasped my bra, and then fingered my panties down. I stepped out of them, leaving the cotton parcels dishevelled next to me. I waited, frozen, with my arms down my sides; look at me.

Will pulled me closer to him, and we hugged each other tightly. I deftly tugged his shirt from his trousers, and squeezed my bareness against his. Our skin met, warm and inviting. My naked breasts pressed against his chest. I couldn't wait any longer. I yanked down his trousers with curious, trembling fingers. I pulled down his pants and watched his shaft spring up against me. I loved to watch his penis unfold, the way it turned straight and solid. I was shorter than he was, so his extended prick came right up to my stomach. He caught my breasts in his hands and thumbed them confidently. Then he put his penis there, rubbing up and down in the valley between my engorged tits. My nipples were hard and red. I was already breathing fast, and I knew that if only he dared put his fingers down there, to my soft crack, he would find how desperate I was. The two weeks' waiting had taken a heavy toll. I was shocked at my own appetite for him. I was ravenous: I wanted to fuck him there, standing in this beautiful bathroom, the gushing water from the tap complementing the stream of excitement inside me. I sat back on the side of the tub. I wanted him to pump his hardness up me, right into me, right there, right now.

'Not yet, not yet,' he said, as I manoeuvred myself around him.

'Yes, now!' I was panting. Two weeks was a long time in celibacy. I massaged his penis. I kissed its glorious crusading head.

'Sally,' he warned, with just a hint of threat. But I refused to take a naked man with a hard-on seriously. I knelt down and took his balls in hand. They were soft, tight walnuts, compact and sensitive.

'Sal,' he repeated, this time with a whimper that seemed to negate all protest.

'I won't do anything,' I lied blatantly. First, I kissed the long shaft of him. His penis sprang out at ninety degrees to the rest of him: a good towel rack. It had been so deprived: we both had. We must never go without sex this long again, I resolved. Never again. Not even for Lent.

The head of it was already moist. I massaged the top skin back and forth, tracing the small protruding vein that ran down the back of it. I loved watching his face change when I did this. The tight muscles around his mouth began to loosen, and I could see his expression change to fear that I would stop. Then I went lower, kissing his golden balls and the little crinkly hairs that sprang from there. His balls tightened, responding to my lips, and his cock swelled further, seeking my mouth. I loved holding the whole of him, making my mouth into a toothless ball and moving his penis in and out. I enjoyed making his cock wet with my saliva. He filled my mouth. The tip reached down my throat hungrily. It was going to fill me up. I continued my rhythmic sucking, and I kept a hold of his darling, appreciative balls, weighing them with my fingers, moving the skin around. I wanted him to fling me back against the tub and take me there.

'Let's get in the bath,' he whispered. It was a pale resistance that turned me on, even more than I would admit.

I stepped into the tub. The water turned my skin strawberry red, but I love it scalding hot. Will had tipped in some bath oils, and a sweet scent had taken over the room. The windows and mirrors were already steamed up. I leaned back, feeling the water suspend me. Opposite, Will held my feet firmly; he massaged my pressure points, taking care over each toe. He stimulated each one individually, and my legs started to shake. He nibbled at my toes, and my vagina filled with arousal almost like a reflex. My toes had turned into conduits of pleasure to my clitoris.

14

Will felt his way along the trajectory of my legs. He smoothed a route across my calves, gripping the backs of my legs tightly. He risked higher and higher. I willed him to go up, up into my thighs and beyond. I wanted him to steal into my nest of hairs, to feel my wetness within the wetness of the bath.

He soaped my breasts. He went around and around, circling me with his soap. I liked the flannel's roughness against my skin. My nipples hardened even more with appreciation. I could hardly wait. I needed some release from this tense excitement. I leaned forwards to kiss his face. He locked his lips on mine. Sometimes he nipped me with his teeth, or slipped his tongue into my waiting lips, just for a second.

'Not yet, not yet,' he whispered when I lunged for more.

I got out first, lazily, allowing him to glimpse my glistening body. Little droplets of water fled to the floor, and I shook the wetness out of my hair over him. I massaged myself dry with the towel, quickly rubbing over my shoulders and breasts, then more slowly lowering it, lowering it, and snaking it down my thighs, between my legs. Wills stayed in the bath, playing in the fading bubbles. His thing came out of the water, like a curious sea animal. I looked in the mirror, demisting it with my hands. My face was red with heat or excitement: I couldn't tell which.

I put on one of the hotel's silk dressing gowns and went out to the balcony to wait for my Romeo. I couldn't wait for him to take me onto the luxurious four poster bed. The night sky was filled with stars. The moon was half full. It seemed to curve into a benevolent smile. I held onto the balcony rail, watching the lights of the restaurant below. It was the perfect setting for our love. And I had no doubts that we were in love.

15

I felt like a princess in a fairy tale waiting for my prince. I could hear the sound of a flamenco guitar. Someone was playing, plucking the strings: a melancholy song. Light applause followed, then a tinkle of music from a faraway disco. I felt the back of my gown twitching. He was behind me. He raised my robe, exposing my rump both to the cooling night air and to him. He put his hands on my buttocks. His fingers were tight around my twin globes.

'You have the most gorgeous arse I've ever seen,' he announced to the world. His towel was now discarded on the balcony floor. He was already hard. He stood behind me, kissing the back of my neck and blowing into my ear. His fingers walked around my bottom, feeling the curve from thighs to buttocks, exploring the line that divided the two.

'It's so fucking peachy, I want to eat it.'

I wanted him to know how much I loved it. I arched my back appreciatively, so that my bottom was more exposed to his touch. So what if the neighbours came out on their balconies? We were in love! I wanted someone to see us now. To see us like this, to know what pleasures we could give each other.

Will held me close. He moved his hands around to my breasts, and my nipples saluted him, glad of the attention. I wanted more of that hot pressure on my arse. I stuck it out as much as I could, showing him how willing I was. In return, he pressed his penis needily against me, as if it were trying to find its way home. I felt its hardness against my bottom.

'What about the bed?' I whispered.

'Later,' he mumbled. His mouth was in my hair. 'I can't move now.'

I didn't mind not getting there. I was riveted with desire for him. Still, I couldn't resist pursuing the issue. He had talked about doing it in a four-poster for weeks. It was our mutual fantasy. And the follow-

16

ing day we were getting up at six to take the coach back. I had no delusions about the next morning; the best we would manage would be a hasty smoke-mouthed smooch.

'You brought me all the way to this hotel so you could fuck me on the balcony?'

'Shhhh.' He kneaded me with his thumbs and veered dangerously close to my secret crevice. I wanted him to touch my cunt. I wanted him to feel my wetness. I knew he would be amazed: my arousal was surely a big compliment to him.

'Will!' I warned.

'Just wait a moment,' he said impatiently. He wrapped his arms around me tighter. He moved from my bosom, to land first soft on my belly, then going down, heading towards the Southern Hemisphere. I waited, trembling, wanting so much for him to be pleased with what he found. He had to touch the equator, the hottest line. Gracefully, he moved my legs apart, and for a moment I felt the sweet pleasure of sheer vulnerability.

'Fucking hell,' he whispered, amazed. 'You are a hot little thing, aren't you, darling?'

Realising how excited I was, he darted inside my gaping vagina. With two fingers he finger-fucked me. I felt like a swarm of bees were creeping inside me to pollinate.

'You are so wet, it's incredible.'

I was so wet and proud of it too. It was the external sign of my internal state. I needed him so much, I was soaking. His fingers slid around my warm stickiness with ease.

'Fucking unbelievable,' he whispered, swimming in my ocean. His other fingers were consuming my clit: double pleasure.

I felt the attentions of his penis more direct behind me now. It had unwound and stretched up, hard and

17

impatient. It didn't care about a four-poster bed, and nor did I. It was pressing into me, on a mission, like a plug meeting its power point. Will pushed me forwards slightly, searching for a comfortable angle. I held onto the balcony railings. I felt dizzy and ephemeral, as if I had taken a large quantity of drugs and didn't know where I was.

'Please, please.'

'You are so fucking horny,' he hissed. His tongue snaked a wet route into my ear. 'I can't believe you.'

'It's your fault for making me wait so long.'

He removed his wet fingers. I couldn't wait any more: I was desperate for his cock. My clit was numb without him. I leaned further over the balcony to give him a grand entrance. I wanted him to put something up me. I didn't care what it was, fingers or cock, as long as there was something.

Slowly, he began to caress the outside of my cunt with his rod. He slid the end around my hole, playing with me, teasing me, until I was desperate for the full treatment. I had to reach down to touch him. I felt how wet his foreskin was; I moved the flap of skin over the swelling head. I couldn't distinguish whether the wetness was his or mine.

'Will,' I groaned. My voice felt unfamiliar to me. I sounded husky and oversexed. A girl of easier virtue you could never find. 'Please, do it now.' Without even realising it, I had put my hands to my tits and was holding onto them tight, squeezing them, pressing them together and then apart.

'You naughty girl. Can't you wait?'

'Please,' I insisted. Two weeks of waiting, a whole fortnight of touching but never penetrating, had worn me down. I had to have him inside me. Who cared where or how? Open me up and slot yourself in. Come on, come on. I can't wait forever.

I turned around to face him. My naked arse was

leaning suspended over the balcony, like two unexplored planets white in the night sky. I locked one leg behind his, pressing him into me. We kissed, full on the mouth; I loosened my tongue into his lips and gnawed at him, as wide mouthed as I could. I ran my fingers through his hair and clutched the back of his head.

'Please what?' he quizzed. He pulled his mouth away for an instant, until I swallowed it up again.

'Please, make love to me.' I felt my face burn. I raised my leg higher around him, so that I was open wider onto him.

'What about the lovely bed?' he teased me, with his words as well as his prick.

'Now. I . . . Now.'

'What?'

'Fuck me now,' I ordered, losing it.

'You asked for it.'

With a sudden, almost unbearably fast move, he plunged his cock inside me. I heard a strange howl and barely recognised my own voice. Will's hotness pierced my wetness. He slid up, knocking hard on my vaginal walls, clearing through, screwing me. More, I wanted more. I was taken over, colonised by his dick. He raced up my womanhood with long, full sweeps of his penis. I was swelling with excitement. My other leg slid up behind him, so I was suspended off the ground. I was trembling on the edge of heaven, oblivious to the swimming pool six floors below. My cunt squeezed involuntarily around him. Will sighed and moaned. His hand came round to join mine, working at my bosom, twisting my nipples tight. I moved further over the balcony to accommodate the vast length of his shaft. His cock was right up inside me, hard as iron, hard as heaven. I felt full and complete. I moved my hips up and down, creating as much friction against him as I could. I didn't need to work much to feel wonderful at every slight movement. He was so huge.

'Baby, you are so good,' he murmured. He pumped kisses onto my swollen lips. He dangled his tongue into my desperate mouth. He moved down and dialled on my clit with his sopping fingers, dialling so insistently that I could feel my entire body melting. My whole being was overwhelmed by pleasure, the pleasure of two bodies fucking. I didn't care that I could drop over the edge. I didn't give a damn that they might hear me or even see me.

'You're the best,' he hissed. 'The very best.'

I let him do it to me, the way he liked best. Each movement, each wild pound of his flesh against mine told me that I was loved. I felt gloriously and wondrously powerless. He screwed me so eloquently, so passionately, that tears of happiness cruised down my cheeks, and I had to bury my face in his shoulder for fear that he would laugh at the strength of my emotions.

I was crying again. I walked to the wardrobe and pulled out the gown I had stolen from the hotel as a keepsake. I wrapped myself in its silk layers and crept back to my comforting place in bed. Perhaps it was arrogant, maybe it was plain stupidity, but I couldn't believe Wills didn't love me any more. No one was as good at breakfast in bed as I was. And we still hadn't made it on a four-poster.

Chapter Two

I rang in sick (well, I was sick, lovesick) and took the week off work. I had started at the advertising company one year earlier, but I still felt like the new girl in the office.

The rest of the staff were old hands, cynical know-it-alls. Every suggestion I made was greeted with cries of 'been there, done that'. We were a strange collection of people. I always felt we were like a jumper my mother had knitted: when she ran out of one yarn, she added another, irrespective of whether it matched or not. It wasn't that my colleagues were old. They weren't: they just seemed it. They were masters of complaining, and I didn't like whining (unless it was wining and dining). Still, it probably did them better than it did me. I locked my complaints up inside.

I don't know how I got the job. Apparently, Duncan Moore, who owned the company, liked me. After the interview, in which I faltered throughout, he said I was more in touch with normal people than the rest of them in the office were.

Our office was an open-plan, 70s-style building, like a Californian beach house plumped down in the grisly heart of Britain. To further the image of Americana, there was a gym in the basement. It was full of mirrors and mirror-lovers. For me, exercising was like masturbation: a strictly private matter, and one I wasn't much good at. The only person who used it regularly was Ms Feather, one of two bosses from hell.

On my first day at work, Penny Feather had secured me as her secretary, and I never had the chance to show my creative skill. Ms Penny Feather was about the same age as me, but everything about her screamed maturity and professionalism. That is, she was a hard-nosed bitch from her small pointy breasts to the stiletto, feet-crippling heels. I imagine she was the head girl at school – the one who read Bible stories – smug-smiled and freckle-cheeked. Sharon told me I should complain about the way she treated me, but I suppose I had got used to it. I didn't think I could do anything else now.

Perhaps the person I hated second in the world to Ms Feather was Mr Finnegan. He was a mean bastard. Physically he was the kind of guy I hated. I liked men sinewy, artistic and lean like Will. Finnegan had a body that screamed forty years of rugby playing and nights drinking real ales. I was sure that he would have a hairy chest and a hairy back too, probably. Also, he wouldn't let us call him by his first name. In fact, his first name was a tightly guarded secret, a mystery that antagonised us dull office workers when we had nothing else to complain about.

Our office was in trouble. It wasn't only our financial situation, but also, more dangerously, our reputation. We were no longer innovative; we were middle-of-the-road. Whereas we were once relied on to bring a bit of 'oomph' to a product, now we could only give it an 'Oh dear'. None of us believed in what we were doing any more. We were a company built on insincerity.

The week at home didn't do me any good, though. Sharon came around and, since she was eating for two, I did as well. One for me and one for the memory of Will. When Sharon wasn't there, I ate five meals a day because there was nothing else to do. I didn't get dressed, and I wore my gown until it had dirt on the sleeves and had turned even shabbier and frailer than its owner.

It was spring, and the TV programmes were about romance. There were dramas about affairs and first timers, May to October relationships, policemen and women, doctors and nurses. Or there were talk shows, and it seemed like everyone was doing it, everyone was in love, or two-timing, or three-timing, or had to tell you they were gay. Or there were nature programmes about pollen and flower reproduction, or snakes or hippos mating. Oh, to have a mate, I sighed, attacking towering bowls of cornflakes wearily. Sex was ballooning in everyone's life except mine, where it had withered and died. Was I to be like one of those extinct volcanoes, never to blow again?

About four long weeks after he had dumped me, Will finally responded to my calls. I had been calling him twice or three times a week, even though I had run out of things to say on the messages. I told him I had to see him face to face. (I meant mouth to mouth.) I wanted him to see me; wouldn't he want me when he saw me? How could he want me one day and not the next?

I was going to be strong, cool and undemanding. I would be witty, amusing and beautiful. I wanted him to take one look at me and instantly regret his sins and beg for solace. I was going to outfuck his present girl. I dressed with care. I couldn't ask Sharon for her

23

advice, because she would classify this as 'doing something stupid', so I bought myself a new outfit. I had put on weight (why couldn't I be one of those people who, when stressed, forget about food?), but it was distributed fairly evenly over my body. I would show him I could get by without him (if I wanted to, which I didn't).

Unfortunately, the glamorous outfit proved such a contrast to my apparently drab habitual attire that everyone at the office noticed.

'Been to an interview, Wendy?'

'No,' I said bitterly, 'and it's Sally.'

'What?'

'My name is Sally.'

'Looking good; new job?' they persisted.

Finally, I told them that my boyfriend was coming to meet me, and it was a special occasion. Ms Feather, eavesdropping as usual, was enthralled and asked me many questions about 'lover-boy', as she called him.

'Didn't you split up with him?' she asked.

'Yes, but tonight we're getting back together.'

When I left, she watched me, waving animatedly from the window. The cow.

Will was waiting in a designer suit (we had chosen it together), bright shirt, and expensive leather jacket. He looked wonderful. When I first met him, he only ever wore jeans and jumpers. His hair was floppy, and he seemed to look out from under it. After he got this 'executive' job, his style improved; he talked more about money, and of getting respect, and of earning respect. He had changed, but I would change with him. I could keep up with his new style. I felt a sudden urge to feel his executive tongue in my mouth, his hands on my breasts. I reddened.

I walked up to him and gave him a sedate kiss on the cheek. He received it coolly, the way an eight year old receives the attentions of a whiskery great-aunt.

He didn't compliment me on my new haircut, or the new clothes that had caused the revelation at work.

'Hurry up,' he said. 'I haven't got long.'

He wouldn't let us go to a restaurant. No, after five years together, going to a restaurant would be sending out the wrong signals! We went to a coffee bar near my work. You may have seen me there. I was the girl with her back up against the wall, trying and failing to be seductive, trying and failing to take control of the situation, of him. My lips were heavy with lipstick. My eyelashes were fluttering like the wings of birds.

I prostrated myself. I reached out for his hand, his hand that had once caressed the insides of me, but he shrugged it off. I tried to touch his thigh, the thigh that I used to use as a pillow after sex, but he picked that off too, blowing me off like an irritating insect. He was flirty with the waitress who came over with our teas.

'But Will, I didn't even know you were fed up. We can work it out, I promise. We've been together five years!'

'Four and a half,' he corrected. He couldn't even look at me.

The people on the next table were talking about gardening, and a middle-aged man near the door was telling a woman about the latest catastrophe in the accounts department. The handsome waiter who usually served me was behind the counter, shooting sullen looks around the room. Will must still want me; he must still love me.

'I don't care about this other woman,' I conciliated. 'I love you, and I know you love me, so –'

Will spoke down to me, seriously and clearly, the way you might talk to a foreigner who has difficulty in understanding English. He enunciated his words slowly, only he didn't raise his voice, he lowered it, and he kept his eyes on the other tables. Will hated to make a scene.

The gardening couple had ordered cakes. When the great slabs of chocolate gateau arrived, the woman responded predictably, 'Oh, I can't eat all that.' Although I was starving, I was glad I hadn't ordered a cake. Will would think I was 'letting myself go'.

He droned on about how he felt about the other woman. It seemed, though, that she was the woman, and it was me who was 'the other'. He couldn't help it, he said. He didn't want to hurt me, but it was the right thing to do. It was difficult now, but one day I would surely understand.

I stared down at my plump thighs in their new trendy trousers. Wills used to say I had an hourglass figure. Now he wouldn't even give me a minute.

The one thing that he never said was a simple 'I'm sorry.' It was always sorry with excuses attached. What was so bad about a genuine apology? I asked myself. If he would only say sorry, then I would forgive him. He wouldn't do it, though. He seemed to want me to apologise for putting him through this, after five (or rather four-and-a-half) years.

'I know it's difficult for you, but it's incredibly difficult for me too.'

I stared at the coffee. I remembered Sharon telling me that how you liked your coffee was how you liked your men. I always had my coffee sweet and milky. It felt bitter.

'I really am so much happier now,' he continued. I felt the people around us flap their ears. No one can resist prying into other people's relationships. We were living out our own nature documentary for them.

'I feel so content now I've met her.'

Like I cared about that! What about me and how unhappy I was?

When he wasn't using his hard voice, like a police-man trying not to listen to a suspect's innocence, he slipped back into familiar Will-isms. He forgot he had to keep me at a distance, and he became enthusiastic again.

'Sally, you should see her! Wherever she goes she turns heads.'

I felt my head spinning as if it were about to be sliced off by a guillotine.

'She's like a dream come true,' he finished.

'Does she make love to you like I did?' I inter-rupted. 'Do you remember when we were on holiday and –'

He turned away. His face was gleaming with disgust; his upper lip curled into a snarl.

'You just don't get it, do you, Sally?' He couldn't contain himself. 'I don't love you any more. Perhaps I never did. I'm in love with her.'

The rest of the people in the café waited. I could sense their expectancy. Superficially, they were discussing their gardens and the red in their accounts, but underneath I knew that everyone was waiting for me. They were waiting for me to tell him to go to hell. They expected that. They didn't know that I was back down the pit, and he had thrown all this shit in my face.

'I'll pay,' I whispered politely. But Will was already picking up the bill and heading for the counter, where the pretty waitress was simpering at his approach. I stayed where I was, weeping copiously. My water-proof mascara let me down hideously. The middle-aged gardener and the woman came over to my table to ask if I was OK.

'Don't worry, love, you'll get over him.'

'I want to,' I said, deliberately misinterpreting them. I wasn't ready for the sympathy of strangers yet. 'But he won't let me. He always pushes me off and takes me from behind.'

They shrugged their shoulders and walked away. The waiter looked at me pensively, and then he too turned away. His bottom was like two tight pillows trapped in his fitted trousers. The waitress gave me a smile, as if to say 'we've all been there'. I didn't believe it. She obviously never had.

Back home, I listened to the messages from the days when Will loved me and I dreamed . . .

Will comes around full of flowers and champagne. When he sees me, he sets them down hurriedly on the table and takes me in his arms. I resist, pushing him away, to humble him as he did to me. But he comes at me again, kissing me deeply, his lips on mine, his tongue poking at my mouth. Our tongues meet and travel together. I can taste his spit, his sensual wetness.

He doesn't jump-start my tits like he usually did. He touches my shoulders, as if touching a precious statue. He touches the bone under my neck, the jutting-out one. He feels his way around my sides.

I am hurt, tragic, but benevolent. I push him gently away.

'Wills, can I ever trust you again?'

'Please give me one more chance.'

I play cool. I hold him off again. I don't believe he can make it up to me, but he can try.

'I honestly don't know if I can. Why should I?'

In answer, Will undoes his tie and his shirt; he unbuttons his trousers. The mighty muscles in his legs strain as he reaches over me.

'You've got a cheek,' I whisper.

'Please,' he says quietly. He is almost naked, and I am fully dressed. It is hard to resist, but I am still smarting. Even an Oscar-winning performance in the sack won't obliterate what he has put me through. Or will it?

More kissing. He treats my lips like bone china. I am in my gown and, before I realise it, his hand is making a determined expedition to my breast. To my embarrassment, the nipple immediately hardens like a marble, belying my protests. I see the shadow of a smile on his face, and I smile back just a little to show willing. And then I remove his hand coldly and say firmly, 'No.'

'I'm so sorry,' pleads Will. He tries to touch my breast again, but I slap his hand.

'That's not good enough.'

'Please let me make it up to you.'

'Why should I?'

He takes my hand and puts it against his upstanding cock.

'Because I want you so much.'

I shake my head, but I can't move my hand away. It does feel nice there. His penis is so rigid, so upright, and yet the skin so silkily touchable.

'Oh, baby,' he breathes. He pulls down his pants and holds his knob up to me, like a peace offering. It is purple and swollen. But I come to my senses. I won't touch it again, I won't. He hasn't earned his brownie points yet.

'That's not a good enough reason.' I turn and walk away.

'I love you, Sally.' He chases after me, and stands in front of me blocking my path. I try to avert my eyes, but his cock is compulsive viewing, like a torch lighting the way. Be strong, I tell myself. One touch, and you'll be addicted all over again. My hands flop helplessly down at my sides. I will not touch him.

He works on each nipple with the attention of an artist. His saliva lubricates my nipples, and they come alive in his mouth. Then he pushes my breasts together. I like the sight of them squeezed up like that, like a centrefold, but without the staples. He moves down to my tummy and sneaks his tongue into my belly button. His breath is hot on my waist.

I still won't touch him. I won't, I won't. I am not a pushover. He moves down my body, gliding over my belly, and arrives at my trim mound. He nuzzles my pubic hair, like a horse nuzzling sugar, and then he is under me, and I am over him. He opens my legs skilfully and in goes his face. I am standing, straddling him. I start to touch the hair on his head as he works at me. Then I stop: I will not touch him. My clit is swollen and eager to play. Every touch makes my body twist, yearning for him. He touches me with consummate ease. His face is held horizontal up at me; his fingers are supporting his mouth. More, more, I want more. I am hornier than I have ever been in my life, yet I have not given up. Will licks and licks at me, like a thirsty man. He guzzles at my clit; his nose is buried in my cleft. He is desperate to have me. When he looks up to check that I am OK, I see that my wetness has made his face gleam.

'Marry me,' he says to my moist muff. He inserts his big fingers inside my tight and creamy vadge. I am being stimulated everywhere I like: the front, the middle, all the parts that make me glad to be a woman. His tongue taunts me again, pleads with me, begging me for more of my nectar. I grip his hair hard, holding him firmly in place against me. Rubbing me at the front, he gasps for air, and his mouth is surrounded in white, like pearls. He dives at me again, controlling my writhing with his fingers fearlessly. I start bouncing, twisting up to his face. The pleasure is almost unendurable. His face is pressed against my sex, swallowing my womanhood. Everything seems to be caught up in this great flow of sexual interaction. Nothing outside of my body exists. The world is obliterated. There is nothing, nothing outside of the golden triangle between my legs. Nothing exists, except for him between my legs.

'Marry me,' he whispers again.

My pussy says yes in the only way it can.

However much I rubbed and rubbed, and however much I imagined our euphoric reunion, I couldn't tip myself into orgasm land. Sex *toute seule* was lonely. Besides, cruel reality had a bad habit of interfering. I was beginning to understand that, while I could play my part to perfection, Will would never do any of those things anyway.

Chapter Three

*A*fter my miscarried rendezvous with Will I felt sulky and sullen. Whereas before I had been sad, now I was apathetic. My natural optimism deserted me. The glass was neither half full, nor half empty, but spilt all over my best dress. I had been humiliated completely. My self-esteem could go no lower. I had nothing to lose any more.

At work, my eyes constantly watered. I pretended it was from staring too long at my computer screen. Occasionally, one of my colleagues came over to offer me biscuits or a cup of tea, but I had no real friends. In the early days, I was invited out for lunch, but I had refused, going instead to the supermarket to buy Will his chicken breasts and sweet corn. I didn't want socialising to interfere with my love life. Eventually they stopped asking me. It amazes me how much I give up when I am in love. I dropped everything, but then maybe women always do. Men certainly seem more able to carry on as usual.

Ms Feather was worse than ever. Her already high self-esteem increased further still. I wasn't jealous of her, but I was jealous of the response she evoked in others. It seemed to me that everyone adored her. Everyone listened to her, nodding when she spoke (instead of nodding off), and saying yes. Apparently, she was dating someone, although it was hard to believe she would find time for someone else.

One afternoon, we had a meeting to discuss the progress of our work. Usually someone missed half the meeting sorting out the teas, and it was usually me. Even when a modicum of agreement was achieved, there was always someone ready to throw in a spanner at the last minute. I usually struggled to conceal my yawns. That week, however, as we sat around facing off, I felt uncommonly alert and strangely aggressive. This is my job, my company, I told myself. Why shouldn't I have a say in the running of it? I hadn't had any say in my relationship, and look what had happened to that!

When someone came to tell me that the photocopier was broken, I snapped back, 'Call the engineer.' And although it was I who ended up making the call, it was a step forward from doing it myself and getting black ink all over my fingers with Ms Feather grinning from the sidelines, her perfect white nails covered in layers of varnish like old masterpieces.

We were debating the progress of an advert.

'Hands up who thinks we should go with the first one?' asked Ms Penny Feather: a rhetorical question, she had already made her choice known, and no one would go against her.

Ten hands raised.

'Hands up who thinks we should go with the second?'

No one. It was ridiculous.

'Sally,' said Finnegan, amused, 'you didn't put up your hand for either.'

'Do you have a better idea?' asked Ms Feather haughtily.

'No, it's just that the consumer is saturated with these same old images.'

'Images sell.'

'Well, not these images,' I retorted. One of the staff – I didn't yet know everyone's names – whispered, 'She's asking to get fired.' And I wondered if I was, subconsciously, at least. Maybe I was one of life's victims, pleading for rejection. But I was sure I was right: this kind of work had only earned our company a reputation as staid and uninteresting.

'It's about time we tried something a bit more original.'

I went over to the coffee machine. I had to get away from them for a few minutes to calm down. Otherwise, I really might get fired. No job, no boyfriend, no inner peace. Unfortunately, Finnegan was already there.

'What are you thinking, Sally?' he asked.

'What's the matter with her?' I asked bitterly. 'She's ridiculous: she's so – I don't know – so self-absorbed.'

'I think Ms Penny Feather has just discovered sex,' he said irreverently.

'Ms Feather?' I said, a bit disgusted, but very interested. 'So she really has got a new boyfriend!'

We had all wondered who the poor sod that was lighting that fire was. I only hoped he was using a very long match.

'She loves it,' he said knowingly.

Crude bastard, I thought. I wondered if he could be Ms Feather's prodigal lover. I pictured the two of them, crumbling into each other. Him taking her from behind in the photocopying room. Her working on him, her wrists yanking him up and down as though she were churning butter. That would be a sight for conjunctivitis.

Still, even that old bat had someone interested in her.

I was becoming tearful again. Over the last few weeks, my face had now acquired that washed-out quality, like cheap underwear. I wasn't going to cry again, I wasn't. Screw them all.

Mr Finnegan threw away the disposable cups and said, 'Why don't you tell us what you are thinking about? We could use a bit more input from you.'

When we sat back at the meeting table, I decided to try. Mr Finnegan and his semi-receptiveness to my comments gave me confidence. I imagined that what I was saying not only affected our company, but also my relationship with Will. A success here meant he would come back to me. If I could prove myself at work, then I could handle myself at home.

'The advertising world is stuck up its own arse. Too many big egos. It's time we got back to the grass roots. Find out what people think, what they need and want.'

'Go on,' said Finnegan. He chewed his pencil deliberately. I caught sight of his little pink tongue as it struck against the eraser on top. Ms Feather tossed her blonde locks impatiently.

'What about pensioners?' I suggested. 'Getting some ideas from them.'

A collective groan sounded from the table. One of the old farts got up as if to leave. The two girls opposite me raised their overplucked eyebrows at each other. Here was I, the village idiot.

'Or teenagers, asking them what they think about. Directly, I mean: no surveys, no diluting. Get to the point.'

The old timers gave a sigh.

'How do we do that?' asked Finnegan, flashing his tongue at me again. I decided he would get lead poisoning from the pencil, and he would be replaced by a kind, wizened, asexual geriatric.

'We haven't got the money to commission another

survey: besides, all we pick up is a load of illogical jargon.'

'Yes, I agree, but . . .' I insisted. I was on a roll now. If at first I hadn't believed in what I was saying, I did now. Why shouldn't I have something to contribute; why shouldn't they respect me? 'The teenage world is surreal. It is illogical. It's about being in and not trying to be in. Surely we should try and crack their codes?'

'Rubbish, let's just go with the usual —'

'No, Sally is right,' Finnegan suddenly interrupted. 'What do we know about kids really? We may think we listen to them, but do we hear them, what kind of products they like?'

There was silence. Finnegan and Ms Feather were in joint and unhappy control of all our operations. Duncan saw to it that neither of them got the upper hand and, if they disagreed, they had to take it to him. He had been known to get very angry if they didn't work together.

Ms Feather studied her nails. Then she looked up at Finnegan mercilessly, like she wanted to step on him.

'So,' said Finnegan defiantly, 'that's the plan, that's how we approach the trainers, and the, erh, the . . .'

'The CDs.' Ms Feather reminded him coolly.

'Yes, the CDs,' he snapped back. If they were having it off in private, they were doing a grand job of covering up.

My head was buzzing as we trotted out of the office. Will would have been proud of me. He was always saying I wasn't assertive enough. I imagined him bounding over to congratulate me. 'Sally, you've turned into a real pro. Please let me prove how much I care.' He takes my hand, kisses the back of it, and kisses up my arm to the little hollow of my elbow.

'Baby, I missed you.'

One of the farts grabbed me by the wrist, whispering, 'Fucking hell, Sally. I didn't get this job so I could spend all afternoon hanging out with students.'

He pushed past me to get out of the door. You didn't get this job, I thought sullenly. Your father bought you this job, remember? I wished Will was waiting for me to call, to tell him what I had bought him for dinner, and supporting me. But I knew he wasn't. He wasn't hanging out for me, as I was for him. There was no one supporting me now. I was on my own, and I had never felt lonelier.

In the end, about fifteen of us went out on 'reconnaissance missions'. There was no plan or anything. We were to 'get into the moment', to be spontaneous. We were so used to complaining; we didn't know how to handle the new situation. All the old grumbles didn't seem to fit; still they carried over their scepticism.

'That doesn't mean you spend all afternoon in a coffee shop, does it, Sally?' smirked Mr Finnegan.

Why was he always picking on me? I scowled back at him. I wanted to get a result. Just to show him and Ms Feather exactly what I was made of.

Chapter Four

*F*ired up with a rare breed of professionalism, I took the train to St Matthew's College. St Matthew's was famous for its adventurous curriculums and for being on the receiving end of several damning government inspections. No one doubted that St Matthew's students would either do brilliantly – one sock in the eye to the system – or would end up in mental institutions. That was why I wanted to go there. I figured it would be pointless to go to the nice establishments. I wanted the extremities of youth. A few students were hanging around outside. They were even more self-assured than I had imagined. They looked as though they had been born cool.

I had prepared a few questions on the way, but I didn't take the clipboard out of my bag. I thought of Will and his female friend. I wondered how they spent the evenings. Probably sniffing each other's pay cheques.

A couple of boys asked me for directions, so I interviewed them. I trailed a couple of pretty girls, and they giggled; one boy picked his nose throughout. It wasn't exciting, but it wasn't bad. I wondered how the others were getting on, and I considered going home. I had already collected nineteen specimens in my sample; I was just one man short from my goal. That's when I saw him: the representative of his generation, spokesman for St Matthew's and beyond. He was slim, medium to tall, and he had a shock of brown hair. He was dawdling his way along the main road.

I followed him for ages. I shadowed him past a supermarket, a disused cinema. I didn't really know what I was doing: I was just walking, I suppose, and my legs led me after him. It was almost as though I had lost my mind. I didn't want to talk to him, but I didn't want to lose him. He cast little glances back over his shoulder. Finally, when I caught up with him under the span of a railway bridge, he turned around.

'Why are you following me?'

Sally the stalker. I put on my spectacles to acquire a professional air.

'It's for market research. Do you mind if I ask you some questions about your tastes?'

'I don't mind,' he said cautiously.

My target was even more handsome close up, and he smelled clean and fresh, as though he had showered in lime.

'So you go to St Matthew's?'

'Yes.' His voice was low and I had to move closer to catch everything he said. A police-car siren blared in the distance.

'You're not a teacher, are you?' I asked hopefully. That wouldn't have done for research purposes, although work was rapidly emigrating from my mind.

He laughed. His little white teeth were crisp and even. If he sank them into me, I wondered, would they leave red marks? Stop it, I told myself firmly. What was the matter with me?

'OK, let's see. What fizzy drinks do you like?' I began.

'I like them all really, but I don't buy them: I prefer milk.'

'Milk!'

When he spoke, his brows furrowed slightly. His nose was big; his cheeks were flat and his cheekbones protruding. He had sensual, full lips. I got through drinks, crisps, trainers, chocolate bars and cereals. Like me, he was a cornflakes man.

'Do you like pop music?'

'I don't follow the charts. I like old stuff, folk and things.'

He had long eyelashes. If he kissed me, would they brush against my cheek?

'An old-fashioned boy, huh?'

He looked up, but with his head still lowered. He had huge, puppy eyes. I felt a surge of crazed emotion go through me. Stupidity, probably. I fancied him, and I hadn't fancied anyone like this in years. I loved Will, I really did, but I didn't tremble at the sight of him. I envied those women who fancy anyone in trousers. I didn't: they had to conform to very specific criteria.

'Women?'

'Sorry?'

'Doesn't matter,' I said, ashamed. My giggle sounded almost hysterical. A more worldly man would have heard what I was trying to say. I continued bravely through jeans, films and TV. But I felt compelled to return to the subject of women. I wanted to know him and his thoughts. Besides, I thought, justifying it to myself wildly, I had a job to worry about.

'What kind of woman do you like?'

He wrinkled up his face and smiled. A winning

white-toothed smile, shaking his head. He wouldn't speak.

'Come on, answer.' A few people walked past. Was I being paranoid, or were they looking at us? Or perhaps at him: he was divine looking, a god sent down to show us mortals how to live.

Still shaking his head, he said, 'All women.'

I raised my eyebrows, in what I hoped was an attractive older woman style.

'Cute.' He stared at me uneasily. 'Like you, I guess.'

I took my glasses off. I was glad my hair was loose, tumbling down my back.

'How old are you?' I asked, pretending to be shocked at his familiarity with one so senior.

'Old enough,' he said. It didn't sound cheeky or rude. It was a suggestion, a question. He really was too good looking to be true.

I was slightly under him, so I moved; now I was on the step, the same height as him.

'Thank you for your help,' I said, and then I kissed him. I started by just offering a trembling lip, just a lip kiss, to thank him for the answers. He looked at me quizzically, and it felt wrong to break away, so I moved in again. This time his eyes shut, and I had the most beautiful view of the ridge of his eyelids and his eyelashes. His hands were locked in his coat pockets. I pulled them up and pulled them around me, and pressed myself against him. Two people walked by.

'Shameless,' a woman said. She was pushing a shopping trolley.

Shameless. The word spun around my head, a pleasant tune. Shameless – I was shameless!

'Do you like this?' I whispered. I pulled him closer; he gave a sigh, and his face was like a kitten when you stroke it under the chin. I could feel the growing bulge in his trousers. I slid my hand over it.

'And that, do you like that?'

'I shouldn't do this,' he whispered.

'Why not?' I said. There was no earthly reason why he shouldn't. How dare he act like he would get in trouble? I felt our lips slide together, and our bodies greeted each other almost involuntarily. It was as if I had no control over myself. I could only stand back and watch as my body got further and further involved with this delectable stranger. Once I was inside his mouth, it felt like home. I was nearly fainting. We were squeezing up next to each other. I was standing there, trembling inside his big coat. I rubbed myself against him and felt his penis stir. I nearly passed out.

'Because I have a history class,' he whispered.

A history class! I pulled away from him and his tyrannosaurus prick. Thank God, I had come to my senses in time.

'I – yes.'

One more kiss. We jammed up to each other, and I could feel the size of him through his trousers. Was it a mobile phone in his pocket, or was he pleased to see me? Will, what would Will say? I pushed the boy back. In my mind, Will was laughing at me. He was saying I had gone mad, absolutely nuts.

'Can I see you again?' the boy asked. He stroked my lips, wiping off the present of his saliva. Then he moved closer to kiss me again.

'Sure,' I said cautiously. 'I have to do this research thing; you'll probably catch me around.'

'No, not for work.'

I shook my head. Reality crept in with its icy accusations. I felt as though I was the one being unfaithful to Will, not the other way round. Would I always feel like that with other men? No, only if they had to run off to history class. I was probably like a history lesson to him.

'There's a college party next week,' he said, oblivious to my dismissal. 'Can you come?'

'I don't think so.' I took the ticket anyway and folded it in my back pocket. I tried to think of something to say. Something to neatly finish off this pathetic little dalliance. I had to control the strange impulses that were still ricocheting through me. My nipples were aching, and my palms were wet. Just to stroke his huge cock, just to see it, just to rub myself on it. No!

'You have been very, er, helpful.'

Sharon was right: there would be other men. There was life after Will. But was it the right life for me?

'Where the hell have you been?' Mr Finnegan bellowed across the office when I arrived back at work, totally desexed by a horrible bus journey, and my mind awash with teenagers' attitudes to various brand names.

'I've been interviewing kids. They gave me loads of ideas.'

I was unused to speaking directly to him. Except for that time at the coffee machine, I usually just cowered in the corner and let him roar.

'You know, it is so fascinating to penetrate the minds of young people,' I said daringly.

My afternoon had given me confidence, a new voice. You don't know what I've been up to, I thought happily. I still had the boy's saliva swirling around my teeth.

He looked at me strangely. I thought, You bastard Mr Finnegan, you always make my bubbles burst. He probably didn't believe me. But for once, he didn't criticise me, or put me down.

'Where did you find these right-on kids?' he asked, and his voice wasn't so patronising as usual. It was curious, not quite friendly, more like neutral. That was good coming from him.

'I waited outside St Matthew's College.'

'St Matthew's?' He looked surprised. Ms Feather looked over disdainfully at us. Then she went back to her work, smirking.

'Yes, do you know it?'

'Yes, I do.'

'It's really cool,' I blathered on. 'I've got some fantastic ideas, you just wait.'

'I am waiting,' he said coolly, back to his old spiteful self. He would have to start watching his weight soon. He was heavily built, paunchy even, but he carried himself as though he was Mr Fucking Universe.

I hate you, I thought suddenly. My venom surprised me.

Chapter Five

Sharon and I had been friends since we were eleven, and the thing we had always done together was discuss the intricacies of other people's relationships. Who was suitable for whom? How in love other people were? Who would lose their virginity first? (Her.) Who would fall in love first? (Me.) Who would marry first? (Her.) Who would have a baby first? (Her.) I remember when we were thirteen, we spent the whole night discussing the intricacies of blow-jobs – Did one blow or suck? – until about three o'clock in the morning. Then her father shouted through the walls, 'That's all very interesting, girls, but do you think I might get some sleep now?'

A week after the St Matthew's incident, we were doing an inane quiz from a magazine about ex-boyfriends. Sharon was putting her swollen feet up on her sofa; I was plying her with chocolates and tea.

'How many times a day do you think of your ex?' Sharon asked.

'Never.'

Sharon looked at me sceptically.

I listened nightly to the messages Will had left

when he still loved me. Even if the fire of my love had been dampened by the coffee shop embarrassment, even if I had proved to myself that I could fancy someone else, it still did no good. Time was healing the rejection pangs, but I still wanted him back. I lay on the bed, and I played the tapes of his love over again. I rationalised that since I had kissed someone else, Will and I would, one day, meet as equals. We had both done wrong, we had both strayed, but we would one day be reunited.

'When he clicks his fingers you go running. True or false?'

'False,' I said.

'True,' yelped Sharon incredulously. 'You bloody would!'

'I've never gone running to Will.'

'That's because he hasn't called you.'

'Cow!'

When we were fifteen, Sharon had engineered her hymen-breaking with the married manager of the bread counter at the supermarket where she was working part time. They did it after hours, in the back room where they do the stocktaking. He kept his boots on and told her that she was the best English loaf that he had ever tasted. They did it every other evening, and they did it everywhere: on the floor, on the counter, on the Formica chairs, on the plastic table. He took her away for three days to a caravan park, and it was there that Sharon (and subsequently I) learned that men had an automatic hard-on when they woke up. She called it 'morning glory'. It was Sharon who told me that other things could be inserted up a fanny too, although I never quite believed her. And it was Sharon who hinted that there were ways to have sex during a period without getting bloody. I never quite believed that either. They split up eventually, but from that time on Sharon was full of knowing smiles, and whenever there was a sex scene in the movies, she would nod, and say, 'Yes, that's so-oo right.' Her advanced experiences infuriated me, and I was desperate to catch up.

Looking back, this probably propelled me into having sex a little prematurely. I would have done it with anyone who offered (so not much has changed then!). Eventually, I lost my virginity with a Catholic boyfriend in front of his fireplace, while his ten brothers and sisters were asleep upstairs. I had to get on top because it wouldn't go in any other way. I remember feeling like a blow-up doll. I was floppy, inanimate. However, I loved the smell of his hair, and the surprise on his face when I had finally agreed to allow him in, 'Just once, just for a second: I'll take it out.'

I remember gliding around the next day, wondering how come nobody knew. Wasn't it written all over my face? Even ever-so-experienced Sharon didn't know I had, until I deigned to tell her a few days later.

But I didn't manage to get a repeat performance. After that, he didn't talk to me. Not one word. I threw myself into my A levels. I told myself, if only I had done it better, like Sharon had, he would still like me. After all, her lover hadn't run off after one pat-a-cake, so why on earth had mine?

'Who was the best person you ever had sex with?' Sharon asked. 'Don't tell me it was Will?'

I smiled enigmatically.

'Who do you think?'

In bed, Will was single-minded. He couldn't kiss and fuck at the same time. He could drive and eat a sandwich, he could watch TV and read the newspaper, but he couldn't use his tongue and prick simultaneously. He couldn't mind-read, and we're all looking for a mind-reader, aren't we? Someone who will treat us rough when we want, and smooth when

47

we want. I guess he only read papers and books; he wasn't so good with people. Or maybe he could read me but ignored it. There is always that, I suppose.

'Do you ever fantasise about making love with someone else when you're with Hugh?' I asked her.

'Umm, occasionally,' she said shyly. We didn't talk about Hugh so much now that they were married.

'What about a younger man: I mean, much younger?' I asked her.

'Urrggh,' said Sharon. She looked at me strangely. She had her hand over her bump, and her eyes were lowered. 'How young?'

'Oh, you know, eighteen, nineteen,' I said vaguely.

'Not my thing,' she said decisively. 'I like a man who knows what he's doing.'

Pregnancy had coloured her vision. Sharon may have been the biggest party animal, the royalist drug queen in her previous life, but now she was scared for her son or daughter. She was mentally far away from me now. I couldn't help thinking what bad timing it was. Trust me to want to launch myself on a sexual adventure, just when my best friend had decided that sex was something that other people did.

I tried not to think about the boy. I did try. I didn't want to offend Will, although, oddly enough, the Will in my dreams always looked delighted when the boy made a guest appearance. Trouble was, the boy was there every day. That is, every day I was there chatting with the kids outside St Matthew's. Will may have been locked in my head, but the boy was standing there in front of me, and he had ceased to be so timid. One time, when he gave me back a paper I had dropped, our hands touched. It felt as though neither of us had the strength to take them away. We stood staring at each other, alone in this busy world. He moved his thumb across the back of my hand, pressing me where the veins run blue, and I wondered

48

about kissing him again, but I knew that if I started, I would never ever be able to stop.

It was only a kiss. But a kiss is never just a kiss. A kiss has words. Besides, it was a very particular kind of kiss, not just with tongues, but with real passion too.

There was no way I could see him again.

'You'll meet someone soon who'll take care of you properly,' Sharon comforted me. I smiled innocently back. Quite possibly, I had met someone who I could soon take care of properly.

Chapter Six

*A*t the party, they wore tight T-shirts and drank water from plastic bottles. They looked so young. The make-up was the big giveaway. A bouncer friend once told me he could always spot the underage girls in a pub by their three-legged race to the loos to exchange lipsticks.

Sharon's husband Hugh had come back home with a takeaway dinner. They asked me to stay, but I couldn't bear to be the extra third, and they looked so peaceful and so intimate together. However, I couldn't stand the thought of going alone to my flat. Some nights, I felt as though Will was haunting me there. So, when I found the party invitation that the boy had given me in my back pocket, it seemed like fate was directing me to attend. The paper was crumpled and had already been washed once, but I could read the date and address clearly. Why not go? Mixing with the St Matthew's students would help my work, and (in a long, roundabout way) it was almost on the route home.

I saw the boy, sitting on a sofa. Even the back of his head made me shiver. The nape of his neck was lightly suntanned. He sat with his arm stretched out. I ignored him. I got a drink. I got several drinks. The barman asked to see my identification. I laughed at him, but my mood was stupidly buoyed by that one kindness. He served sour wine in paper cups, and said he would take me somewhere afterwards.

'I'm fine,' I said. Increasingly, I was.

I started dancing. I raised my hands over my head. I knew I looked good. The boy was looking at me. His head tilted slightly to one side, his eyes fixed on me. I couldn't move without being aware of him and his movements. When, for one second, he disappeared from my vision, I felt almost bereft. Then I saw him again, with a girl. The sight of them together made me feel sick, but then she simply squatted down, handed him a drink and then left his side.

The music throbbed in my eardrums. The beats vibrated through my body like an underground train running through me. Small figures bounded around stamping their mark. I watched him. He was public-school good looking. His features were strong and sensual. He watched me back.

I piled everything into the balance. On one side was Will and my job. On the other was this strange giddy feeling I had when he was there, plus the alcohol. *Voilà*. The scales were tilted.

'Ahh, so it is you,' I announced with bravado, and as if I had only just become aware of his presence. His face lit up sweetly. I felt frivolous, carefree. I could smell him; I could feel his breath on me, and I could see the rise and fall of his chest. My arms shot around his back and, before he could say 'history class' my lips were making tread marks on his. For a millisecond he didn't respond, and I feared that I had made a big mistake, but then his tongue was probing inside me.

I reversed the boy against the wall. His tongue

explored the welcoming, warm cave of my mouth, and he kissed the rest of my face too, biting my lips. After you've been with one man for a long time, whatever positions you try, wherever you do it, nothing is surprising. It's like ordering food in an Indian restaurant. You may order Korma, you may order Chicken Tikka Masala, or Lamb Dupiaza, but whatever it is, it all tends to come out with that similar curry flavour. Not that there's anything wrong with that. But going with a different body, a different man, is like trying out a whole new genre of cooking.

I didn't know which way his head would tilt; I didn't know where he would rest his lips next; I didn't know what his hands would feel like on my breasts; I didn't know what his dick would feel like inside me. But I wanted to know. I took his finger and sucked deeply on it. I grazed his nail with my teeth. I rolled it over my tongue. Did he know what I was trying to tell him? If I could perform such delights on his digits, think what I could do with his prick!

'Oh, Jesus.'

His whole body seemed to tremble. He was such a fragile thing. I put my hands to the hollow of his stomach and moved lower.

'We should go somewhere private,' I said, as I started to move my hand somewhere very private. I started to forget about Will, blotting him out temporarily. If you are in St Lucia, you don't start dreaming about holidays in Southend.

I slid my fingers under his T-shirt. His back was smooth and silky. His skin fitted his skeleton perfectly. He had no excess to grab hold of. He was beautifully compact. I meandered lower. I felt my way down his trousers. The groin area was lumpy, hardening up like custard. It wasn't only his courage that was growing; there was definitely something substantial. He tried to stop me two times; I don't know if they were token gestures, or if he was genuinely scared.

'I shouldn't be doing this.'

You shouldn't be doing this? I thought incredulously. Boys are supposed to be doing this. What about me? I shouldn't be doing this! I should be driving around in a convertible with some horny Joe, or checking into health farms. This shouldn't be allowed. It was all Will's fault. He left me high (but not dry).

'Well, if you don't help me with my advertising,' I said, 'you're in big trouble.'

I continued my journey inside his clothes. I felt my way over a landscape of zippers, and I unzipped his trousers slowly, reverentially.

'Someone will see,' he whispered with difficulty, between kisses. I was sucking hard on his middle finger.

'No, they won't.'

We were locked in a dark crevasse, secured against a wall. No one could see our hands, our tongues. The music throbbed in my ears, and then there he was: he was throbbing in my hand.

I have never engaged in the boxers versus Y-fronts debate. Once you get that far, who cares what style separates you from the Holy Grail? Will was strictly a boxer shorts man, but the boy was wearing tight, white Y-fronts, and they were bulging all over the place, moving around like a flamenco dancer. I stuck my hand in daringly. I couldn't wait any more; I had to pick up my prize. He gripped my hand by the wrist, and for a moment I thought he was going to deny me. Maybe for one moment shyness, or the public, had the better of him, but I wriggled my fingers out of his grip. Rising up like some Godzilla out of the sea was his hard dick. It had pushed its way through the gap in his Y-fronts.

His dick was an amazing sight, an architect's wet dream. It towered out at us. My fingers couldn't meet around it. For a moment, I could see what he meant: someone would be able to see. It was long, but it was the firmness, the hard within the soft, that was so breathtaking. I didn't care if we were seen or not. I was a lucky girl. The boy sighed his assent appreciatively. There were people around us, dancing and drunk, but I ignored them, blotted them out of my vision. I got into a rhythm, pushing the skin backwards and forwards. It was like a miniature elephant trunk (but the word 'miniature' seems misleading). I touched the ridge at the end and slid my hand over the top of the cock. I covered the tiny hole from where a small tear was suspended. Shameless. Shameless.

'Oh my God,' I whispered. The phrase 'four-and-a-half years!' reverberated in my ears. Will's disapproval would be a sight to see. I couldn't stop myself from tugging at the boy, from exploring the velvet casing, the hard silk rod.

'Oh God, oh God,' he groaned in my ear.

Suddenly, his prick sprouted forward and my trousers felt damp as though someone had rested a wet umbrella on me.

He bit his lip.

'I'm so sorry.'

Chapter Seven

We began to walk quickly out of the club. I was scared the feeling would wear off. My sexual excitement had recently been such a fragile flame.

The boy led me to an alley, a narrow path between the backs of tall buildings on either side. What was the matter with me? I wasn't like this even with Will! I knew my face must be raspberry coloured. He looked embarrassed too. He stumbled around awkwardly, looking around for somewhere to sit. I didn't know where to look, so instead I stared at him. I wished I were a talent scout. I had the perfect hero. His face was exquisite. The gap, the tender slope, between eyelid and eyebrow enthralled me. I wanted to press my fingers there, to kiss him there. The longing in his eyes was more beautiful than anything I had ever seen. I felt like I had won the lottery.

He took his coat off, and we sat down on a step at the back of a Chinese restaurant. There were a few dustbins further down the street, but where we sat was clean, and I didn't notice anything other than the juice flowing in my knickers. There was a faint smell of noodles and rice, and there was a hum of kitchen noises.

We got straight back into it, my tongue in his mouth, his tongue soldiering in mine. I pushed him back onto the ground.

It didn't take long, with kissing like that, for our hands to search around for something to grab hold of. This time, he was the first to move from the sanity of our backs to the delights of our fronts. Quite nervously, like a robber tiptoeing in, he put his hand to the front of my shirt, over my breast. I gave a little meow of pleasure. That emboldened him. He squeezed tighter. I could feel my vagina contracting, affected by the invisible lines connecting nipple with clit. He unbuttoned my shirt with nimble fingers, and met my bra. I could feel his thumb gliding on the lace, searching for an entrance, and I couldn't stop groaning my approval. All the while, he kissed me delicately, strongly. Our tongues met outside our mouths: sometimes, he grazed his teeth along my lip. He struggled his hand around my back, and I could hear the sigh of my bra as it was released.

The kissing was glorious, but it wasn't enough. He may have been young, but I wasn't. I needed more. He pulled the cups of my bra down, exposing for him (and for anyone else who happened down that road) my double Cs. They were outstanding. He stared hard and then traced his fingers around them. Seconds later, he had lowered his head and was stretching to reach the tips of them with his tongue as eagerly as they stretched up to him. I had never seen my nipples so engorged, so grateful, as they were then, and as I felt them enter the tunnel that was his mouth, I almost fainted with pleasure. I think, from the rapturous expression on his face, that he nearly did too. Perhaps he had never seen any so big. I remember thinking then, that there really was no going back.

He held my breasts tighter than I usually like, but it felt tremendous. I wanted to tell him how good I felt, but I didn't know the words. I didn't even know what to call him.

'What's your name?'

'Marcus.' Of course, it would be something exotic like that.

He looked up into my eyes with open amazement. We had all the time in the world, but I was too turned on to go slowly. His attachment to my nipples was making me lose control over all rational thought. Almost.

I pushed his head up, away from my breasts where he was nursing so beautifully.

'You didn't say how old you were.'

'What?' His fingers were drawn to my nipples like Icarus to the sun.

'How old are you?'

'Eighteen,' he whispered, drinking in my bosom. A train thundered overhead. Just one minute away, there were cars speeding people to work. In thirty seconds – we would have no warning – they could be on top of us: they would see everything, no tickets for the spectacle. I could see the traffic lights of the main road, indistinctly, and hear the squall of the distant cars.

'Have you ever made love before?'

'Yes,' he said. He blushed.

'Did you lie about the other questions too?'

How could he not have done it? The only eighteen-year-old virgins at school were spotty or gross.

I didn't want fumbling fingers or thumbs any more; I wanted the real thing in me now, and nothing else would do. I wanted him, that mountain that rose out of an expanse into nothingness. I didn't need any help with lubrication. I was gushing, and I wanted to feel his cock first, before anything. Sod the foreplay. Foreplay wasn't enough; forty-four play, maybe.

I manoeuvred myself over him. First I squatted, hovering over the top, almost enjoying the emptiness, the vacancy that was soon going to be filled. Then, sinking down, I felt his prick cling and slide down the sides of my cunt. It was a physical shock. I gasped with pleasure as his dick stuck to me like a metal object attracted to a magnet, and he slid it further into my welcoming pussy. I was full of him. My vagina clenched him tightly. He was locked up me, and he was kissing me: he was kissing that bone under my neck; he was kissing my ears, even breathing inside them. His hands were crushing my bosom. My nipples were swollen to three times their normal size. It was a grip that said it all: awe, amazement, gratitude. I felt like one of the wonders of the world. I don't know how he managed not to come straight away. I nearly did. I felt as though I was in a trance. It was spiritual in a way. Yet, at the same time, I couldn't help thinking that to be this excited was faintly obscene. He was still wearing his trainers.

'Is this OK?' he whispered. Bless him, he didn't know how OK it really was. I nodded dumbly. His cock went so far into me that I feared it would emerge out of my mouth. I didn't know I had that much space to fill. This was deep, so deep I was almost howling. I was riding on him, grazing my knees in my haste. If only life were always so sweet. I put his hands to me, to open me up at the front from where my curls were to lower, where the line opened out to a small valley filling with thick, creamy longing. The whole area was one rough sea, and we were riding through it smoothly.

He was breathing heavily, but he wanted to tell me something.

'You're so gorgeous,' he gasped in between his own groans of pleasure. 'You're so – so beautiful.'

He ducked down to my breasts so that he could take long, hard sucks. My nipples sprang out, flirting, dark-red cherries. His lips were so succulent around them. He squeezed them together persistently, making shapes with them; I had never seen my own breasts look so sexy. He bit around my neck, and I was scared he would stain me with his fuck-bites. He threw me up and caught me as I rebounded against his rod. I moved up and down, stepping up the pace. He was so hard, so firm even inside my slippery hole. I slammed down as hard as I could; he lifted me up, and then I was pressing down on him again. We were reaching closure. I really didn't care. I didn't give a damn what anyone thought of me. I was going to ride this bucking bronco and stay on. I wanted it now, now, now. More, more, show me how horny I am.

'Oh, oh, you're so lovely,' he whispered. It sounded like he was pleading with me not to be.

With one hand, he took hold of the spare skin on my flanks and with this handle he steered himself in and out of me. He was holding me up and then pulling me back down again. He sprang under me, thrusting up to meet me as I jerked down.

'You're so horny; you're so sexy; you're so –'

His face changed, and he looked shocked, frightened even with the force of his member.

'I can't stop: oh, oh, I can't –'

His dick expanded. I felt his throbbing growth, even where there was no space to grow. It was jammed against my swollen pleasure zone.

'Oh Wills, Wills,' I roared, interrupting him. I was orgasming, like a clucking chicken. I matched each thrust of his with a thrust of my own. I shook with waves of pleasure, and I gripped him as hard as I could, shocked at the golden pleasures my own body could excavate.

We stayed in the alley for a while. I was shivering, overwhelmed with the force of my orgasm. And I was so happy. The distress of the last few weeks seemed so trivial, so inconsequential, compared to this. Marcus thought I was cold, so he wrapped me in his coat, like a Christmas present. I wasn't cold.

When Will and I used to make love, Will always asked if I came, and I always said, 'kind of', because I did, kind of. Or because I thought that I did: I used to feel shaky and warm. Afterwards, however, after the strangled condom was draped forlornly into the bin, I used to wonder if that really was it. Had I come, or had I just gone? With Marcus all the uncertainty over the big 'O' was wiped out. I knew now for sure that I had just come, hard, violently even.

We did the things you do when you've just fucked, although he didn't look sleepy, and he didn't smoke. He held me close, and his long eyelashes did tickle my cheek. His hair fell into his eyes, but he didn't brush it away. He had his hand up my skirt on my thigh, and he kept pummelling my skin softly. It felt nice. If I had someone to do this to me every day, then I wouldn't have any cellulite.

'Was that better than the party?'

'Much,' he said. His hand felt so hot up there, as if I was being centrally heated.

I told him about my job and how important it was to me, especially since my relationship had finished. He asked what had happened, and I said that he met someone else.

'He must be crazy,' Marcus said, and I think he meant it. 'You're so beautiful,' he added. He clutched handfuls of my hair, letting the damp clumps slide through his fingers before holding it again.

'Do you like my hair?' I asked coyly. People always

complimented me on my glossy mane. Will loved it. (Or used to love it.)

'I like your hair, your face, your lips, your breasts . . .' Marcus began kissing me again. But thinking about Will had made me start to see reason. Will would go mad if he knew what I was up to.

'I have to go.' I yanked myself upwards. I had come to my senses abruptly, painfully. What was I doing here in some seedy alley with a kid? But Marcus pulled me down.

'I want you,' he said defiantly. I felt like I had created Frankenstein's monster. From awkward virgin to begging Casanova: how could he have transformed so quickly? His eyes looked half pleading, half certain that I wanted him. Who was I to disagree? His fingers pressed furtively into my flesh. I wanted them to go for a raise.

'No,' I said lamely. I had to go. But his eighteen-year-old fingers were marching under my skirt. His lips were sullen and mutinous. I leaned forwards to kiss them. It was just a kiss, a friendly kiss.

'What about your friends? The party?'

'I want to be with you.'

His trousers strained: I saw the emerging tent shape (it was a full-blown circus ring), and I decided I wouldn't, couldn't resist such flattery. If a man could get a hard-on for me three times in one evening, then who was I to cock a snook at it?

I couldn't stop myself from ducking down and licking his dick, taking long licky icky strokes – more delicious than ice cream and half the fat – enjoying the sight of my pink tongue loving the edges of his penis. There was none of that 'I'll do you if you do me' feeling: I wanted him in my mouth. I pushed him inside my cheeks, covering it in my saliva, and nicked it carefully with my teeth. My thighs were already damp and I couldn't bear the suspense of waiting for him to touch me.

He pulled down my knickers. He didn't pull them very far – they trapped my legs together – but they were far enough down for him to make a comfortable entry. I knew my pussy was bubbling and burning, like a fucking lava pool. I tried not to make any noise: I didn't want him to know that I was nearly coming, just by the nearness of his fingers to my clit. I had no choice but to stay, but a sound escaped from my mouth. It was a low-pitched groan, like the women on porno videos make. He caught his breath as his wet fingers told him everything he needed to know.

'It's OK, isn't it? You want me, don't you?'

I could barely speak. I nodded. I had to have him inside me now. Just one more time, one more touch: his penis was so right for me. It would make me feel better when he launched himself; everything would disappear, all the crap, all the rubbish of Will's rejection. Marcus was my aspirin, healing my aches. His finger landed in my hole, and with a gasp he started to caress my sex. He rubbed me with his hand, voyaging into my womanhood. I rubbed him back euphorically, all open-wide wetness, but at the same time I was appalled at my lack of inhibition.

This time, I sat flat back on the step, my legs flung over his shoulders. He was half crouching. His hands were supporting himself on the step, in the ready position of a runner. I showed him how I wanted him. I opened my legs and told him to look, really get a good look, and then, when I couldn't leave it empty any more, I reached out for him.

I fixed myself to him. We were like pieces of mechanical equipment that had to be attached together before they could work properly. Screws, hammer and tongs. He pumped into me. He humped me. His face was so far away that it was almost blurry. We stared at each other intently, but as my excitement mounted I grew too embarrassed at my own arousal and looked away. He was so gorgeous; his features were so fine. What must he think of me?

I could hear the cries of the Chinese chefs as they worked in the kitchen behind us. They were pummelling meat. I could hear flesh fall on a chopping board; eager hands were moving it around, preparing it for consumption.

Marcus pulled himself in and out. He moved my hips up and down. He was a fucking champion. He moved me up and down, standing now, while I flopped on the step. I felt like my whole body had disappeared, replaced by this giant, throbbing clitoris that had to be serviced.

'Come on,' I begged. I could feel my face burning. 'Do it to me hard. Oh, Jesus.'

The chefs were working on their food, shouting across to each other, 'noodles, table two', and 'ice cream', but their noise was almost obliterated by the sound of my vagina slapping against his dick and my arse flapping against his balls.

I was horizontal, suspended off the ground by the step at one end and by him at the other. Anyone who had walked into the alley at that moment would have come face to face with my mound of pubic hair, the skirt yanked down my legs. I was a dirty slut. I had gone mad. I got his hand and opened the front of me. With his dick, he continued moving roughly, shunting me up and down, but his hands were gentle and exploratory. He untangled my black pubes, sinking deeper into the path through the forest. I opened as wide as I could, to help him, to teach him, and I loved the way it looked. I really looked like a whore. I was spread there with my cunt wide open, gagging for stimulation.

'Play with me,' I ordered my student. 'There, there,'

I demanded, as his rude index finger spotted my clitoris. He learned quickly, and he took my barked commands well. I was almost too sensitive to touch: he had to dodge around me, and then he found his way, and his finger went up and down on its virgin quest.

'Oh, you're so gorgeous,' he murmured.

I could feel my face heat up even as he moved. His penis was the perfect fit. It was made for me. This couldn't be wrong. I could feel the hotness of his skin against the tightness of my cunt. The strokes, the control, everything was perfect. I wanted to tell him, but I couldn't.

The noises from the kitchen were getting louder; whoever was there was getting close. Dangerously close. I wanted them to see me. I wanted them to see my display. Surely no work could be better than working on this? His balls were tightly appreciative behind me.

Marcus must have heard the sounds from the kitchen too, because somehow his rhythm changed, and he was smashing into me, in time with the chefs. His face started contorting with pleasure. Thump, thump: someone was pounding inside, and Marcus was pounding inside me. I could hear them shouting about food. I could hear the sounds of a tap gushing water, the noodles flapping in a colander, the slicing of vegetables, the slap of meat on a work surface.

I was moaning, strange grunts. I was shocked at the sound: it was so earthy, so wild. Yet at the same time, it excited and aroused me. We could get caught. What a sight we must have made. I imagined Will was watching me too. Will was masturbating over me. Will sinking into me, a fountain of come all over me.

'Will, Will,' I begged. 'Yes, oh yes, don't stop.'

Marcus responded by picking up the pace. He was rock hard now, unbreakable iron, rigidly rubbing against me. I gripped his arse, and pulled it to me. It was so tight. I loved the shape of it, the putty in my hands. He really had won the golden globes. I felt my way around and under to the belly of his balls.

'Is there anybody out there?' someone shouted.

I was too far gone, past the point of no return. Even though I was half naked in the street, giving myself to a man I didn't know, I wouldn't stop. Even though I heard the click of a window opening, I couldn't hold back. I continued moving inexorably to my goal. I wanted them to watch me come.

'Is anybody out there?'

'Yes, oh yes, yes,' I screeched. I couldn't help myself. I battered myself against Marcus's hardness, throwing myself from the waist down into his massively fine cock. He accelerated into me, rubbing where I needed to be rubbed. My breath was coming fast, like a marathon runner's. Then I felt him explode inside me, and I was coming, coming back again. 'Fuck, fuck, Will, fuck,' I wailed desperately. Poor Marcus, terrified of discovery, put his hand over my mouth.

'Ssshhh.'

He splattered against me, three, four thick spurts; yet my body continued jerking out of control even when the gushing had stopped.

Marcus dragged his coat over me as we collapsed again on the step.

'My God, I don't believe we just did that,' I hissed. To quieten me, he slid his finger between my teeth. It tasted musty and milky. It smelled of me. I sank my teeth in gratefully.

'Is there someone out there?' I heard one of the cooks ask another.

'Just cats mating, I think.'

Chapter Eight

*A*t the next office meeting, Ms Feather made a point of categorically denying that there was anything untoward in her and Finnegan's relationship. Ms Feather had heard some rumours. Some of the staff blushed furiously; there had been a spate of e-mailing lurid speculations, and Ms Feather, nosy cow, had read them. She insisted she wanted to 'nip the gossip in the bud' before it got out of control. Finnegan sat back smugly in his chair, the smirk on his face seeming to mock everything she said.

'I am in a new relationship,' she added rather unnecessarily and beaming at us all, but me in particular, 'but with someone who has nothing to do with this company. Under no circumstances would I ever endanger our good name by doing something so unprofessional as "screwing the crew".' We laughed politely. But the general feeling, I believe, was that none of the crew would consider it either.

'Glad to hear it,' said Duncan mildly. 'You know, if there were anything of that nature in this office, I would be most disappointed.'

There was nothing sexual about Duncan at all. He

was a very good husband and a good father of five children. He didn't send out missiles of availability like some men (like Finnegan) did. And he was scrupulous about reputations. We all knew that he would be more than disappointed. Anything or anyone that threatened to put the name of our company in disrepute would be history.

Then we started to talk about our new direction, and what we had found when we talked directly to young people. I said that what we needed was tongue-in-cheek, information-based advertising. We would just give out the facts with a sprinkle of humour. Stress that the trainers weren't just for running in. Put the dogs in trainers and have them pee up trees. Simple, wasn't it? But deadly effective. Teenagers love dogs. We would try to chop up the CDs – I envisaged a Chinese chef using a carving knife – but fail because the CDs were unbreakable. I spoke clearly and slowly. Actually, for once, I felt very laid back about the whole thing. So what if it failed? Nothing ventured, nothing gained. I noticed Duncan made a few notes and so did Finnegan. His writing wasn't even joined up. Ms Feather just sat back in her chair, letting her long, blonde hair and glazed eyes speak for her.

After my presentation, I went downstairs to share a cigarette with the doorman. I liked the security staff: they were friendly and unpretentious, which provided a nice contrast to the advertising staff. I had also recently noticed that, at work, the more superior staff said 'Hi' when talking to an inferior, and the inferior staff said 'Hello' when talking upwards. It was as though everyone was making clear his or her status – 'high' or 'low' – and I wanted to test my theory. 'Hi,' I said to the doorman that day. He was dressed in a tight grey uniform, a bit like a pilot's, and a couple of buttons had failed to do up over his muscular chest.

'Good morning,' he responded, astutely. 'You look happier today.'

By the following week, everyone was running around, talking about me, talking about the new strategy. Our clients leaped on the suggestions, and more and more work was coming in. Even Ms Feather begrudgingly congratulated me.

'Hi!' she said, waving me to her desk. 'That was such a good idea you had.' She looked up at me curiously. 'You were so mousy before.'

Really, I thought. Maybe that's because no one ever listened.

'I didn't think you had it in you!'

I've had a lot more in me than you could imagine, I thought smugly.

'What happened to you?'

'Nothing.' Oh God, why could she always turn me into a snivelling first-former?

'My God, Sally, you are a fucking genius,' said Finnegan later that week, when the filming had been done, and we were sitting around waiting for the final cut.

'Thank you,' I said awkwardly, unused to praise. 'It wasn't just me: it was the kids, too.'

Finnegan looked at some of the designs I had done for another campaign that was due to start. Then he put them down casually on his desk.

'You don't like me, do you, Sally?'

'What makes you –'

'I know.' He smiled although his eyes looked solemn. 'But it doesn't matter as long as we work well together.'

* * *

A couple of days later, he came back with one of my designs that they were going to use. Finnegan looked pleased with himself. I had noticed that when he was in a good mood, he stroked his portly chin.

'Sally, if you play your cards right, things could go very well for you,' he said. He seemed to wait for me to say something profound.

'Thank you,' I stammered. He stared at me intently.

'Keep coming up with the goods, keep using that source: squeeze it dry, as it were.'

I smiled, thinking how strangely appropriate his imagery was.

Chapter Nine

Marcus and I were lying on his sofa mock fighting, as you do. Well, I suppose you shouldn't do with boys who are almost half your age, but I was. Marcus poured me a glass of lemonade – I don't think he drank tea or coffee yet – but I didn't bother drinking it. I set the glass down beside the sofa and stroked his face.

Marcus loved kissing. And he was great at it. I suspect he had far more practical experience of it than I did. As a normal teenager, he probably kissed for three hours every weekend and after school, whilst normal adults like me only kiss for those cursory two minutes before sex, as a kind of green light to the rest of the traffic. I had forgotten how good kissing was: it was achingly good.

When I used to kiss Wills, I used to worry that I wasn't doing it right. He often complained that his jaw was aching, or that my mouth was too wet, and sometimes he would simply jam his lips closed like a toddler refusing food, but Marcus was different. We were lying dreamily, and we kissed the way the French must have intended when they invented it.

Our tongues glided around into each other's hollows. In, out, pink, red, pressing, probing, and the deeper our tongues went the more turned on we were getting. He had such agile lips – thick, smooth and sensitive – and his mouth opened flexible and wide. I just couldn't help thinking that we were the perfect fit. Weren't there some statistics that showed that women reached their sexual peak in their thirties, and boys in their teens? I knew our bodies said that we were made for each other, even if society didn't agree.

For a second, Duncan's homely face was there hanging over me, saying, 'Sally, we are not amused,' but I blinked him away. I wouldn't tell, and Marcus certainly wouldn't.

I could feel Marcus was very turned on. He was big inside his black wool trousers, pressing against my thigh. I was already wet, but then I had been since I met him outside the college gate at 3.40 that afternoon.

I shouldn't have gone back. I promised myself I wouldn't. But somehow, the promises of self-denial made the act all the more tempting. I knew he would agree. I couldn't help feeling like I was fucking to the memory of Will. Although Will liked to think of himself as a bit of a lad, he had a conservative sexual appetite. He would say I was a pervert. I could see him saying it, his face pinched up like when he ate red chilli. 'An eighteen year old, that's disgusting. You're old enough to be his mother!'

'You made me this way,' I would retort. 'It's your fault. No man my age could satisfy me, after you.'

I had gone to St Matthew's. I stood, not so near the entrance that his friends could see me, nor so far that Marcus would miss me: I stood just so, in my jacket, with my clipboard and friendliest expression. When he found me, his serious expression turned into a great grin. He didn't conceal his pleasure the way older men do. He was happy and that was that.

'Hi,' I said with a queenly wave.

He dashed up, pushed his arm through mine and said, 'Hello. I knew you'd come back.'

I hoped the teachers thought we were long-lost cousins or something like that. I didn't really care. I actually said hello to some of the students as we walked away. I could barely believe my cheek. He said that we could go to his house, as his dad worked late every day. I was hesitant, but he explained that his parents were divorced, and he stayed with his father in the week. He always worked late. He added, a little sadly, that his Dad never came home for dinner; he always had microwave meals on his own, and I thought, poor lamb. It was my duty to comfort him, to make it up to him, in the interests of generating further ideas for advertising, of course.

I loved watching his arse when he walked ahead of me. His buttocks curved out, protruding attractively at 90 degrees to his slim legs. His back muscles were taut beneath his flimsy white shirt.

'Hurry,' he said, leading me to a crowded bus stop where groups of young men and women were standing around, studiously ignoring each other.

'No way,' I said, and extravagantly hailed us a taxi. 'This is quicker.'

I had the whole scenario planned out. As soon as we got upstairs, I wanted to hold each bottom cheek in my hands. I wanted to suck on his cock until he was huge, and then I wanted to insert him slowly inside me. I wanted to feel his balls banging against my arse. I was going to tie him up to the bedposts with his stripy St Matthew's College tie. I was going to blindfold him, edge down his trousers, and then get on him and ride away to the clouds. But when we arrived at his house, Marcus said that he didn't want us to go up to his bedroom. I guess he was embarrassed at what was in there. When I thought about it, I was glad: I didn't really want to make love amidst toy cars, posters of soccer players and smelly underpants.

Besides, the living room was made to fuck in. It was as if it had been designed to be the set of a porno movie. It was the opulent lighting, I think. The room was roasted in a sensual, opaque glow. The sofas were made of rich man's slippery leather. There were huge candelabras on the table and a commanding black piano against a wall. The carpet was thick too and white: they obviously had no worries about getting it cleaned. I should have guessed that Marcus came from a wealthy family. He had that quiet self-assurance that only money can buy. My parents would have been uncomfortable in a room like this. They would cover the sofa with plastic sheets and take their shoes off at the entrance. They would wonder why there was no TV.

'Do you play?' I asked, nodding at the piano after he had covered my face with bruising kisses. I was scared the afternoon would end. I didn't want it to be over too quickly; I wanted us to linger together in this room for ever, locked in our own magic spell. By way of answer, he sat down and started to play. He played beautifully, of course, although I didn't know what the music was. It felt light, sensual and entirely appropriate. I watched how his hands swept the keys, how his body swayed slightly to his own rhythm, and I thought, Marcus, you are going to be so wonderful when you are older. I wished he were older now. Oh God, please give this man fifteen more years. He would make the perfect husband. The husband you dream about when you still believe in Santa Claus and the tooth fairy. I watched lustfully as his fingers caressed the keys. Such dextrous fingers. I love a man who works with his hands.

I remember once hiring a local boy to dig up the concrete of my back garden. I watched him from the window. He was very young, and when he took off his shirt it seemed as if all the muscles in his body were fighting to display. I took him out teas every few minutes – he must have drunk the whole pack – and I watched the sweat, mingled with mud, drip off his forehead. Later that evening, I had snuggled up to Will pretending that he was the gardener. Will had not understood my sudden passion.

Marcus's piano playing affected me in the same way as the workman had. The blood rushed to my vagina; my sex was throbbing fast, and I wanted to get my knickers off as soon as possible. Musical foreplay. I started taking my clothes off bit by bit, dancing around the room to his music. I raised my arms over my head and wandered around. When Marcus turned around, his eyes were out on stalks, like those joke eyes that pop out, and the piano playing kind of petered out.

'Keep doing that,' he breathed.

'Doing what?' I asked, faking innocence. I started picking up my clothes off the floor, picking them up and putting them down again, flashing him a look at my arse and a peek at the slit of my pussy. Round and round the room I floated, my feet deep in the soft carpet. If you could have seen the look on his exquisite face, you would have done it too. I got down on all fours and pretended to tidy my file and bag away. I sat down on the sofa and, yawning, opened my legs as wide as I could and then shut them again.

We resumed kissing. We had been kissing deeply before, but we were kissing even deeper now. My teeth couldn't help but dig into the side of his mouth. I was wide open to him, and I was thinking if he could penetrate me this deep with his tongue, think how deep he could do it with his penis. Perhaps I should have been ashamed of myself, but no: when I touched him, I couldn't believe anything was wrong. However much I told myself that we shouldn't be doing this, it only served to delight me more. I felt like a hypocrite, because the fact that maybe it was wrong or that I was corrupting youth did excite me. The thought of it drove me on as it had done before. I was corrupting him; he was creamy and virginal, and I was the wicked witch. Marcus's skin was so smooth it was almost damp. His arms were thin and wiry. Sharon said she didn't like skinny men, because they made her feel fat, but I had no such hesitation. He made my body look womanly. He made me feel sexual. Wills never made me feel like that. I always felt slightly dirty if I expressed my pleasure too vehemently. Anyway, the point is, he didn't mind the age difference and neither did I. That, I think, was the point of it all. As for the point of his penis, that was already slimy and ready. I felt around in his pants, pulling off his jeans, but keeping his briefs on for a moment.

My only remaining fear was that it wouldn't be as good as last time. Maybe last time had been like a freak typhoon or something. But my nerves were already fleeing. I was already dripping at the prospect of touching him and having him touch me. There are two penises that make a woman wet. There is the one attached to the man you love (Oh Wills, I miss you), and then there is the large, silky kind that was attached to Marcus. It was with incredible good fortune that I had found this one. The stars must have been licking their lips at me.

His penis was cylindrical and hard. I couldn't help but think of NASA and space programmes: this was the perfect rocket design. It looked aerodynamic. It wasn't like the ones in porno movies, those awful ones that may be big but they just flop red around the room like alcoholics. This was firm, healthy and just so right. I couldn't help admiring the colour as well as the shape. It was not too purple, nor too red: it was golden-pink.

I caressed the shaft of him with my hands. It was that mixture of soft and hard that I loved. I dug in for a handful of his tight balls, and he groaned with pleasure. Already there was a little tear of eagerness at the end of his penis, a tribute to me. I dropped my face to it; I had to take it in there, to suck it, to make it grow harder in my mouth like toffee.

'Marcus, you are so good,' I crooned into him. He lay back on the sofa. I steered him, forcing his penis at different angles against his body, allowing it inside and out of my mouth, teasing him, tempting him.

'Please, put it in your mouth,' he begged. He was too gentlemanly to ask for a blow job. I was all too happy to comply.

The door opened. There was this little noise, like 'Oh'.

We turned around. Standing there, in the arch of the patio doors, was a tall, blonde girl. She was wearing a short, white T-shirt that just covered her breasts – buds, I should say – but exposed a flat stomach complete with obligatory teen belly ring. She had on blue shorts over long, slim, just-been-on-holiday brown legs. She was the kind of teen I never was but always wanted to be. She was the kind of girl in American high-school movies, not English ones.

But I could see immediately that she was all looks, but no trousers. She had that popular unthinking way about her. Was I that horrible when I was her age? I wondered. Girls today, I thought, and I felt like a Grandma. But where is their individuality; where are their balls?

For a second I was a little disappointed in Marcus's choice of girlfriend. He had taken the easy way out all right. He had simply scraped off the best-looking girl, without even caring if he liked her or not. But then he was the captain of this team and that team, and she looked as if she were president of the glee club. They were a good match. Other people probably liked them being together. Teachers and parents would encourage it. Successful teen dates turn into successful marriages, and successful families breed successful kids. Or so the theory goes.

Marcus squirmed up to sitting position. You could see the kid was in big trouble: there was me tugging at his dick, and there was her tugging at his heart-strings. I had to be big about this. I had to blag it out, or else I, or maybe we, were in big trouble. There was no room for coyness here. She could see what we were doing, unless they hadn't got up to the blow-job chapter yet in biology. Actually, there wasn't a blow-job chapter, was there? Not even a kissing one. The book went from cutesy baby to hair-under-the-arms, period-pained teenager, to happy, breast-feeding mum. Sexually frustrated career women don't get a look-in.

'Hello,' I said, bolshily.

'Hello,' she said, in a voice no bigger than a sparrow.

'Oh, I'm sorry. Is this your girlfriend?'

'No, she lives next door,' he said, as if that precluded any other form of relationship. What a sweetie.

'Do you go to St Matthew's too?'

'No,' she said, 'I left there. I'm a singer.'

Marcus said the names of one of those teen bands that burst onto the pop charts. Like rainbows, colourful and pretty, but vacant and ephemeral. Probably she and her band made videos in school uniforms, pouting and sucking lollipops, but it was all a lie.

This girl cavorted on a stage, but in private, she was as timorous as a hedgehog. Just for show. Then they came home and had beans on toast with their families: that is, unless they go to their neighbour's house by mistake.

'Do you want me to leave?' I offered.

Marcus shook his head, bless him.

'Do you want her to leave?' No answer. Of course not.

She stood still, her hand over her big O of a mouth. She made no move to escape, though, so I had to give her some credit. She just stood there, fascinated.

I didn't want her to think I was Marcus's girlfriend. I wasn't. I was just after his body, a thrill, and a hint about what young people think.

'Why don't you stay and watch?' I said, extending the hand of friendship. I was amazed at my balls really. She looked horrified, but she didn't move, which I guess we both interpreted as a yes. Marcus, who hadn't managed to speak again, dashed up chivalrously and fetched her the piano stool. She felt her way down onto the seat.

Marcus lay down, and I pulled off his pants again, right the way down this time. His penis sprung back up as if by magic. It was amazing she didn't look more impressed. I guess all pricks looked big to her. They do at that age. It's not until you've seen three or four, taken a good gander at them, that you can appreciate ones like this. It was a darling. My very own millennium dome. I curled up next to him and sank my face in his pubic hair. He moved his hands around my head; he had very tender hands. He had a very small mole on one side of the head. That sweet freckle fascinated me, and I licked it long and hard. Then I turned my attention to the vein that ran around the back of his penis, giving it as much as I could. He made these moaning noises, and I slipped my fingers down to the crack in my legs, and we were both enjoying ourselves. I kissed his balls and licked around them, rubbing them with my own slime. I was enjoying the power. Why shouldn't I? I thought. I have been powerless for so long. I played with his nipples too, teasing them and catching them with my tongue. As I did it, I thought, this is how teenage sex should be, free and lovely.

Marcus undid my trousers, and as he pinched down my knickers, he started groaning. That was even before he got his fingers in. When he felt how wet I was, he just lay back with this grateful look on his face, with me kneeling open to the side of him. I bent over him to swallow his cock. His fingers excited me: they were big like his dick (yes, there is a correlation!) and rough. He wiggled his thumb up and down. I led him with my hand to show him what I liked. Marcus slid his fingers up and down my cunt, and I could feel myself growing creamier by the second.

Occasionally he stopped and, with the fingers that had been inside me, he touched himself, wrapping my juices around his. He was so sweet. He worked on my clitoris, squeezing the knot of pleasure with his thumb and index finger. I wanted to get penetrated. I swung myself around ready to mount him on all fours, rodeo style, when I heard these whimpering noises from behind me. I had almost forgotten she was there. She whimpered on, telling us she didn't want to be forgotten. Covering her eyes, scrunched up on the chair. Paws over her face, her long hair bowed.

This is useless, I thought. We couldn't fuck with the weeping Madonna over there.

'What's the matter?'

She wasn't really crying. She was peeping through her fingers.

'Your dad will kill you,' she said.

'He won't mind,' said Marcus, which we all knew was a lie.

'Just who are you?' she said nastily to me: 'A prostitute?'

'You don't have to be a prostitute to have sex,' I retorted.

'Isn't he a little young for you?' she added coolly. That hurt.

'Why don't we go upstairs to your dad's room?' I suggested. Not only would it be more comfortable, more private, but, call me a pervert, I quite liked the idea of taking the son on his parents' bed. More things I hadn't done and should have when I was sixteen. Marcus looked shyly at her, and she looked back at us.

'Come on,' I said, and so she did. We set off upstairs. Me, the Pied Piper, and two of the children of Hamelin trailing behind.

They had a huge bed: white, all white and high, you had to climb up it to get on. It was fantastic. There was no way my parents would have known what to do with this! Marcus jumped on it, and she sat down next to him. They were holding hands, ever so cute.

'Are you staying then?' I asked.

They started whispering; there was fierce gesturing and nodding and shaking of heads.

'What's going on?' I asked sternly. Marcus rushed over to me and explained in a low voice.

'She likes me. Umm, but I don't like her.'

'What did you say then?'

'I said that maybe I would go out with her next week.'

We smiled, understanding each other. One problem solved.

'Well, take your clothes off then,' I said. I kept my

arms crossed, not only because my tits were honestly several times the size of hers, but also because I quite liked myself in the headmistress role. Sally, the head teacher: watch out, her bite is even worse than her bark.

He helped her take her clothes off, and to pull off her bra. But she wanted to keep her T-shirt on. I don't know why, you could see that she had nice breasts with pointy nipples underneath. He was very gentle with her. She was very apologetic. She edged down her shorts, embarrassed, and then folded them up and put them on the side of the bed. She had on white knickers with a tiny blue bow in the centre. She looked at him hesitantly; she didn't know whether to take them off or not. She was so timid. Then she pulled them down, and there she was, all golden mound and weenie T-shirt. She lay back, her hair smooth on the pillow and her eyes flicking all over the room. Marcus stroked her hair, while looking at those compelling fair tufts of pubes. I guess we both wanted to have a look at her from that angle. When I looked at her then, for the first time, I realised how beautiful a woman is. Actually, it wasn't her, it could have been any woman, but it was that crest, that triangle of hair stretching under her belly. The secrets it held. There was no way you could look at it without thinking that it was some kind of prize: some kind of gift mother nature had bestowed upon us all: women were blessed in having it and men in getting it. For a second I wanted to send up my prayers to some unknown spirit, then I decided I wanted to worship the thing that was real and in front of me instead.

Now I know how a man must feel when he sets out on his first crusade. Her legs locked together every time I tried to touch her. They sprung back straight, zap, shut scissors; she wasn't having any of it. And I did so want to touch her: I wanted to get my fingers in past those yellow curls and locate the damp stretch of pinky skin that I knew lay underneath. But I decided to leave her for a while, and I got to sucking Marcus again. He closed his eyes, and I closed mine; I paddled his hand between my legs, and he could just about reach. I licked his penis up and down, drawing it into my mouth, letting it out, taking pleasure in the long strokes and concentrating hard. His pubic hair was different to hers. His was straight and black like fur, and it brushed gently against my face. I put the penis as deep as I could into my mouth, locking it in my inside cheek, my fingers back operating on my own slit. Then I noticed that she was watching. She was so interested that her legs fell further and further apart.

I had to pretend I knew what I was doing, otherwise she would have stopped me. I just started stroking her up and down on her thighs, up and down and around and around. She had soft, creamy skin, and she let her legs move gradually apart, just an inch, no more, at the top. It was enough for me, though. I felt around the curls of her pubic hair. Her head was back, and her face passive. Her lips were open, and she had one finger trailing around slightly in her mouth. I noticed that she had started arching her back, just slightly, giving me what I wanted, poking her little titties forwards in their protective wrapping and widening her legs just imperceptibly. I wondered what she had studied at St Matthew's. Probably home economics, I thought scathingly.

Then, slowly, I edged my fingers in. Bull's-eye. It felt strange to be in another woman's pussy. It felt like mine, but also different somehow. Instinctively, I guessed what she would like. She didn't want some idiot storming in there like MI5; she wanted a tiptoed ballerina's entrance. I got my finger and started to rub her very lightly with it at the front opening, where her clitoris should be. Hey presto, she was moaning and pushing it up. And, like a mirror, I was soaking wet too. Marcus was massaging me, his face so sweet and dreamy. I thought we could come now, we all could, but it wasn't enough. I wanted to feel her in my mouth. I wanted to taste her pussy. I wanted to breathe her in and do her, make her come with my tongue. I wanted to rub her clit with my tongue and feel its presence in my mouth. I wanted to fuck a woman.

I've never felt like that before. I've never had the slightest interest in being intimate with a woman. I didn't mind the idea of lesbians, and I thought I could possibly tolerate a woman masturbating me – sure, yes, male or female could do the job – but I had never considered the idea of giving pleasure to a woman. They say that most women have a lesbian experience in their life, but I must have been one of the one percent who hadn't and had never contemplated it: as far as I knew, none of my friends had either.

But she was so excited, and Marcus was so excited, and I don't think any of us cared who was going to do what: we just wanted stimulation. And her pinky-red vagina was staring me in the face, like Oliver begging for more. It was so wet: the whole shell of her was covered with this moisture, like an invitation. Marcus was really turned on too; he was working on his penis, with no qualms. He was thrashing his wrists, pulling the foreskin up and down, looking at me with pleading eyes. He wanted me to tell him what to do. Take the initiative. What about me? I thought. There I was doing all the work, and no one was touching me. Something about their passivity fired me up. They were completely willing, completely defeated. My own Plasticine creatures to do with what I liked. It was how I used to be. I had to take control. She was going to allow anything to

83

happen, and I was going to take anything I could. He wanted to fuck, I could feel it, and I was going to take that too.

I spread her legs wide, split beaver on the bed, and I knew that I had to get my mouth in there over that hole. Marcus was watching me, encouraging me, my beautiful student lover. I wanted to show him how to do it. I wanted to teach him how to make a woman happy. It may have been a case of the blind leading the blind, but I didn't need eyes to slide my tongue thickly down the gaping pink crack. It was amazing: silky, wet and narrow. Streamlined pussy. I had to open her out like a flower, pulling the sides apart so that I could press into her. I breathed in her smell deeply and then worked all over her with my tongue. And then I realised what men have always known, that it's bloody hard to know if you are doing it right, it really is. I wished she would say something, but she wouldn't. Anyway, I felt it was OK. She was wriggling around. Her breathing was thick and heavy, and her hands had stopped dancing at her sides, but were flat, palm up, in defeat.

I positioned myself on the bed with my arse in the air, my face still buried in her cunt. I told Marcus to get behind me. I wanted him to fuck me from behind like a dog, while I got to grips with her slippery vadge. I told him to get inside me quick and give it to me hard. He gripped me around the hips tightly, and then I felt him searching for my hole with his hands and then edging forwards towards it. First the tip went in, and then, after what felt like ages, I felt him sink it all in, the whole eight inches or whatever of it. He was so huge that I almost lost my balance, but then he pulled me back into place and started working his way in and out of me. With his penis safely launched inside me, his hands dived straight for my clit like I had taught him before. He was playing with me like he played the piano, stroking my wetness as I licked hers. He slammed his balls right up me and jammed my arse down onto him. He was so rhythmic: he slid his dick further and further in, and then, just as my vaginal muscles clenched hungrily around his shaft, he was withdrawing out. This boy was amazing. I was pushing up and back into him. I didn't want to start losing control so early in the game, but I was. I couldn't stop myself from breathing hard into her welcoming muff.

'Yes, yes, Marcus, please, oh yes, Marcus, fuck, fuck, fuck.'

This got her going though, the little virgin: I felt how turned on she was. I really went wild with my mouth. I had no shame. It wasn't difficult: she had taken over and was bouncing up and down into me, doing her own work very nicely, thank you. She was making these rumbling noises that were driving Marcus and me wild. The oohing and aaahing, the expression of enjoyment, the sound of sex, there's nothing like it. Even when you are on your own in a hotel room, and you hear those sighs and groans from next door, and you curse and say the walls are too thin: still, it turns you on, right? I was almost coming; she was almost coming: we were both on the edge of it. It would only have taken a tiny movement, but then, just as I thought she was going over, I felt her hand abruptly push my head back away a little, just when she was nearly there. I knew this; I recognised what she was playing at. She was afraid to lose control. She was afraid to come. She didn't want to orgasm. She was the same as I used to be: I wasted twelve years being like that. I wasn't going to let her make the same mistake. I was going to make her come whether she liked it or not.

She had her hands over my tits, and she lifted me up. She wanted to suck them; she sucked them tight, tighter than any man had, and as she did that, I felt the blood rush to my pussy. It felt wonderful with her gnawing at my nipples. She had none of the fear that men have: she just pulled at them hard between her lips, extending them, but I wasn't going to let her finish like that. I knew what she was doing: she had decided she wouldn't go over the edge. I was going to have to push her.

I pulled back and got down again between her thighs. Marcus was breathing fast behind me. I wondered, absurdly, which of us was going to come first. I didn't want it to be me or him, I wanted it to be her, but I didn't think I was going to be able to delay it. I was helpless: already pleasurable shakes were coursing through me, but I wasn't going to give up. I sank my tongue into her as deep as I could. Again, she tried to push me away. She was so scared. But I wasn't going to give up. I whipped my tongue up and down the path of her secret sex, up and down hard, sucking her inside lips, and her hands fell off my hair. She was still mutely protesting that she didn't want to come, but she would, I knew she would. Her white stuff covered my nose and mouth, and now, confidently, I breathed the cream in, loving the smell of sex, the touch of throbbing skin. I forced back her legs pitilessly as she struggled slightly against me. She was gaping wide, a huge hole desperate for the filling, and I filled it as best I could with my lips, my tongue and my fingers. My nose joined in, burrowing into her. I was a woman with a mission. I was rubbing her in all the right places, and Marcus was getting faster behind me. I felt like we were all racing cars, but she was thundering fast to the finishing line.

I had never been to bed with a woman before; she was the perfect starter pack. The transformation was the exciting thing. Yes, it was definitely that. One minute, she was tight and cold as ice cream, and the next she was open and boiling hot. She still wasn't saying anything, but now there was no more protesting or pleading, just these whimpering noises, loud, louder now. Marcus was clutching me tight and digging it in: he really had learned well. He had got his fingers round and was dialling me. I was waiting for her: we were both waiting for her, but we couldn't wait for ever. Marcus was groaning, loud, rock-star groans. It wasn't just the touch and the sound, but the sight of her sprawled there, vulnerable in her pleasure, giving it up to me. And she did give it up. She didn't know how good the destination was going to be; she didn't even know where she was going any more, but she had stopped pulling on the emergency stop. She must have forgotten her prudery about the T-shirt. It was up, a scarf around her neck, and she was massaging her own tits. There was nothing left to hide. She was pushing her legs open as far as she could, little gymnast. She was on the edge of orgasm, and I'm sure Marcus must have been in heaven to see the backing singer of an all-girl band (on the edge of stardom) in such a state. With his penis jammed inside me, I certainly was.

She was wonderful, thrashing up at me, rubbing her cunt up in my face. She was abandoned; she really didn't give a fuck any more. Then, I don't know what made me do it – I've never wanted to do it before – but I sank my finger up the small pucker of her arsehole. It was totally glorious to invade another cavity; I wanted to get into all of her, everywhere. She yelped when I did it, and I watched her almost spitefully; her eyes were petrified, but then, when she opened them again, they were all glazed, as if she had taken a shot of heroin. She was totally lost; I'd never seen anything like it before. My finger was warm up there, my private occupation. My own little army searching for

Lebensraum. I had never let anyone do that to me, and never would want to, but I couldn't resist doing it to her. She was almost over the edge, and I felt sorry for men because they can never have that total abandonment that women have. It was different from the way Marcus lost his virginity. His pleasure fanned out from his penis, and it was a pleasure he no doubt kind of tasted almost every day. Hers, though, was all over her body and all the more rare, like an exotic species of bird. She was thrashing so hard at my mouth, I thought I was going to suffocate, and I didn't mind at all! With the fingers of one hand, I dug deep into her anus, the betrayal of her vulnerability; with my other hand, I was a masseur, caressing her clit, and with my tongue I wormed consolation into her vagina. She was loving it, loving my finger poking around her back passage, her fingers poking around joining mine, rubbing herself at the front and into my mouth and tongue. She was loving it.

And then she was coming. Her arse was going up and down on the bed. You would think there was a trampoline behind her, she was so young and springy, so desperate. And with each wriggle she made my finger was snaking its way up further into her, and my tongue was working, and my other fingers were working on her clitoris, and she was screaming, 'Oh, Jesus. Oh Jesus. Oh Mary, mother of God.'

That set Marcus and me off like a chain reaction. He got faster and faster, and then he seemed to triple in size against my nerve ends and volcanoed inside me, setting me off. I was railing hard against his penis, as hard as I could. I couldn't stand it: I was gagging for it, and I pushed back into him. I thought he was going to tear open my skin, and I impaled myself on his rod. One, two, three hard shunts. As he shot inside me, he hammered his pianist's fingers into my clitoris, and I gasped. My body wasn't mine any more. It was acting of its own accord and it was jerking, jolting, coming out of control. Marcus was shouting, and my voice joined him, only louder, more triumphantly, and I had no control over that either. I came, howling for more. Even when the shudders that ran through me, like the aftershock of an earthquake, had ceased, I couldn't stop myself from calling out (although, thankfully, the words were lost inside the soaking recesses of her fresher's cunt).

'Wills, I love you, I love you, Wi-ieeeeelllls.'

(It's a terrible habit of mine. If our split is permanent, I should get hypnosis.)

We collapsed there on his dad's bed. Pulling up the covers around us, I was in the middle of them, and they both put their arms around me, whispering how good I had made them feel, chuckling at the memory. I felt contented like a mother squirrel hibernating. I remembered the rhyme, 'there were three in the bed and the little one said, roll over,' and felt like giggling. We dozed off for a while.

When I woke up, Marcus was licking my breasts, nibbling at my nipples. I stroked his thick, dark hair. He smiled up at me, and I thought with a half-nice, half-scary feeling that I could easily fall in love with that smile. There was something so wholesome, although not wholesome in a conservative way, about him. He was honest, I suppose, and I didn't know many men who were. I scolded myself again; he was only a boy. It had to finish here. My research was over; I had overstretched my assignment. I touched his face. He didn't even have stubble on his chin. It was as smooth (possibly smoother!) than mine. I wanted more pleasure, more of him, but I really had to get back to the office. It was already early evening, the twilight time, when people start to anticipate the pleasures of the night ahead. And I had already had

89

my fill of pleasures. They would have to last me for the year ahead, or at least until Wills came back to me. I wondered what Duncan would say if he knew how I was getting my insight into young people. But I did love Wills, I was sure of it: why else would I bellow out his name so?

The girl started waking up too, and I didn't even know her name. But I knew I didn't like her much. Marcus deserved better than that: someone like me.

'Why don't you two little ones have a fuck now?' I suggested liberally. Silly cow.

'No,' she said and cuddled up to me. Obviously the feeling wasn't mutual. She was trying to prize open my legs with her little hands.

'I want you, please.' She seemed suddenly to realise that she didn't know what to call me. She didn't know my name. 'Miss, you are wonderful; thank you. I want to make you happy.'

'No, come on, why don't you two do it? Go on.'

They looked shyly at each other.

I felt my way around Marcus's family bathroom. I brushed my hair and put some make-up on. I was humming to myself, talking to myself, incredulously. I am Sally; I have just made love to a woman and a man. They think I am incredible; I think I am incredible. I am incredible! I wished Wills could have seen me. He wouldn't say that I was unadventurous then. He couldn't say that. He would eat his words. I would serve them up to him on a plate, and then I would jump down and undo his trousers, and we would live happily ever after. I had a body clock to worry about; I had to think about having kids myself. Wills would make such a good father. I wondered, idly, what Marcus's father was like.

When I came back in the room, the girl's long, skinny legs were twisted around Marcus's shoulders, and he was pumping up and down into her like a good boy. She was screaming out her prayers like a good girl. Marcus was unstoppable. He charged like a beautiful bullet train. I knew well how he would be rushing up and down her tunnel, taking her to a destination. No wonder they called him Marcus, Mark arse: he was bobbing around her now like a buoy on a stormy sea, his beautiful arse as white as a firefly. Kids have so much energy. At least someone had shown her how to have fun. I deserved a medal for that at least.

They didn't hear me leave.

Chapter Ten

'Will you be my baby's godmother?' asked Sharon. I had just got to work, and the phone was already ringing. My first reaction, as always, was disappointment that it wasn't Will.

Oh God. I started screaming with pleasure, and I bombarded her with all the right questions, but as soon as I had put the phone down, I sank guiltily into my desk. What I had done, with Marcus and the girl, was what Sharon would call a stupid thing. I had taken Marcus's virginity, but in a way he had taken mine too. He had made me come; he had made me share my coming with him. I tried to stop thinking about it. It was absolute madness, what I had done. I couldn't help fearing that it would come back and haunt me. I wished I could talk it over with someone.

'Bad news, Sal?' said Finnegan, peering over me, a hangover evident. He rubbed his eyes, and I felt a spray of gritty sleep.

'No, it's good news,' I said. 'I'm going to be a godmother.'

'My, my,' he said quizically. 'I didn't think you were the sort.'

The next few days I kept busy, throwing myself into my job. I wasn't alone in feeling a rekindled motivation about work. My colleagues worked hard too, and we chatted much more than before. We discussed campaigns; people who hadn't spoken for years had now started speaking again. Someone said that they actually felt enthusiastic about coming into the office. A new Thursday-afternoon head replaced the Monday-morning feeling that we had carried over all week. Our work was gradually getting noticed, and the more we were noticed, the better the work we produced.

Working late had other advantages. The one who works most in the office is not the most ambitious, or even the most conscientious: the one who works latest has the most fear of being at home. (Maybe that was Will in his previous incarnation as boyfriend of yours truly.) That way, I didn't have to worry about whiling away the pre-bedtime hours with nothing to do except think about my sexual misadventures.

Ms Feather, however, left the office earlier than usual these days. Sometimes she went to the gym for a workout; other times she made herself up in the ladies' and emerged with her face stung with lipstick like a child ballerina. She always strutted into the lift with a throwaway cliché like, 'Keep up the good work, guys,' (she insisted on calling us 'guys'), or, 'Hey, you can sleep when you are dead.'

One evening, at about seven o'clock, Finnegan and I were preparing for a big photo shoot the following day, when I got a message that there was someone to see me. Janice, that week's temp, giggled maniacally, (I preferred the woman who came last week, but she left to go to an ashram in India. All the temps left after Ms Feather got hold of them.)

'It's your boyfriend,' Janice squealed; she had even put down her nailfile.

Finnegan looked at my shocked face, and said coolly, 'Well, you had better go then: don't keep a gentleman caller waiting.'

'Thank you so much; I won't forget it,' I blurted out. Oh my God! I dashed downstairs impatiently and looked around expectantly for Will. Will had come for me! Perhaps he had sensed what a success I was at work; perhaps he just missed me.

Marcus was standing in the entrance, only yards away from the doorman, who gave me a conspiratorial wink. My heart flipped. So did my temper. I wanted to smack Marcus, punch him and then pull off his clothes. His hands were stuffed nonchalantly in his pockets.

'What the hell are you doing here? Are you mad?' I snarled. It was fun, occasionally, being a Rottweiler.

'No one knows,' he said, simply.

'But they will find out. I have my job to consider.' And even then, it wasn't only my job: there was Will too. I didn't really want him to find out. And Sharon: she would kill me – torture me, then kill me. I felt like I was in a spy movie, and on no account must I get caught.

'I can't believe you would jeopardise me like this. How dare you call yourself my boyfriend?'

But he wouldn't let go. I was scared he would drag me down an alley and rape me. Or was it the other way around? His lashes were too long and too dark. I had to do something.

We went to the coffee bar where Will and I had sat only a few weeks before. But instead of sitting face to face, Marcus and I sat side by side on the rubbery wall bench, our sticky thighs sticking together. I remembered how brutally Will had finished with me here. Now it was my turn.

The waiter looked surprised to see me. He raised his eyebrows questioningly. Then he loped over and curtly handed me a menu. He sighed, as if to say he would be over if and when he felt like it. I felt embarrassed when he caught me checking out his arse.

I turned to Marcus. I had to get rid of him somehow. Was this how Will had felt when he came here?

'How was your date with the girl?'

'Terrible,' he growled. 'I'm not seeing her again. It's you I love.'

'Look, this is ridiculous. I'm the same age as your mother.'

'No, you aren't.'

'What would she say if she found out?'

'I only see her at weekends,' he said. He started playing with the sugar bowl. The granules went round and round. He pushed the spoon in deeper.

'What about your dad, then?' I asked.

'He doesn't care about that kind of thing.'

'Oh, Marcus, you are just a kid.' I was quite enjoying this. I felt like a distraught tragic figure turning love away.

'But I'm not young, personality-wise, or physically.'

No, I knew that. I remembered the way he moved his fingers inside me, the way he looked. Was my gulping that loud? I had to control the situation.

'You are only eighteen. Do you know how old I am?'

'No: I don't care.'

'I'm older than my breast size.'

His eyes lit up.

'Really? Double C?'

'Very cute,' I said sarcastically. He was cute though. He leaned close to me and whispered warmly into my ear.

'You've got perfect tits.'

He was putting up a better fight than I had. Marcus acted how I should have done.

'What about your little friend?' I said bitchily. 'The singer, has she got perfect tits too?'

He turned bubble-gum pink. I noticed he had new stubble on his chin. I guess he was trying to look older than his tender years. He put his arm around me. I couldn't bring myself to shrug it off. He was so beautiful. I wondered if this was how Will felt when he was dumping me, if one move I made would have swayed him back to me. I should have tried.

'I dream about you.'

I nodded.

'I save you.'

'What from?' I interrupted.

'It's not important what from,' he retorted, faintly aggrieved, 'but I save you. And then you want to make love to me, and I say no, but you insist, and what else can I do? You make my cock so hard, and I try to be a good boy, and I try to resist, but you take off your bra, and your tits are so beautiful that I can't. And you are begging for me, and I can't say no, and you say that you have to have me and that you love me.'

I smiled back at him, my face flushing. He had saved me, I supposed.

'Well, there's nothing wrong with fantasising about it.'

Then – and still today, I don't know how he did it – ever so quickly, in one swift dextrous manoeuvre, his hand was fishing up my skirt. Within seconds, his thumb was shoving at my knickers, at the outline of my vagina, like someone knocking insistently at the door. I still can't help but wonder at the audacity of him. He was so cavalier.

The waiter arrived and, as he stood over us, I felt Marcus's finger fiddle its way inside my underwear, loosening the meet between knicker and thigh.

'What would you like?' the waiter asked, peering

at me intently. Over his lips were strands of dark hairs in danger of turning into a moustache.

'Just a, just a little tea,' I mumbled. Under the table, the eagle had landed. I felt Marcus's finger slide in, probing the path through my tangle of hairs, taking the road much travelled towards my slippery clit.

'Milk or lemon?'

'Huh,' I hissed back. The waiter stared at me, mystified. Marcus wound me around his little finger.

'Umm, milk, please.' He was going to try and make me come, there and then, with his finger. Well, he wasn't going to get away with it. The waiter looked at Marcus. I guess from his angle it looked like Marcus was trying to get something awkward out of his bag.

'Umm, something hot and wet,' he said vaguely, the little wanker.

'Tea?' said the waiter. I watched the wetness of his lips as he spoke.

'Oh yes, that's lovely,' said Marcus.

I'm not sure if he said it to me or the waiter, but the waiter eventually moved off. He continued to look at me with his hooded eyes from behind the counter as he filled the teapot. He had thick red lips, swollen like my lower lips probably were. Marcus's finger was making its own party rhythm. There was no stopping the motion as he drummed insistently on my clit.

'You're so wet,' he whispered, dazzled.

'So?' I said defiantly. 'Stop it.'

'Why?' His face was mutinous. Captain Fletcher on my *Bounty*. The waiter brought the tea, eyes still hooded.

'You're too young for me; stop.' I was going to be a godmother, for God's sake. They didn't go around behaving like this. I should be baking cakes for bring-and-buy sales.

'OK. I will.'

For one second, he pulled out his dancing fingers from my hotness. Then the next moment, he ducked down under the table. I couldn't believe what he did.

He fixed his mouth on me. I could feel his breath hot, and then the insistence of the wet tongue. He rubbed his face into me, and then his tongue was at work, licking me, doing overtime, licking me. I heard a slurping noise, so I started to drink my tea loudly, but my hands were trembling too much to lift cup to mouth.

The waiter was watching me. As I felt the irresistible pressure of Marcus's tongue, I knew that the waiter knew: he knew exactly where Marcus's tongue was voyaging. I wanted him to know how wet I was. I wanted him to admire me too. I wished Will could know that I was admired. Marcus was worshipping my clit. I wasn't just a reject or a dumpee: I was fancied and adored.

When Marcus wasn't tonguing me, he was whispering, deep down into me, so his words reverberated around me.

'Oh, you're so beautiful; you're so wet and delicious. I wish you could see how horny you look. Your pussy is soaking. It's so red and hot and open.'

When I peeped down under the tablecloth, I noticed that his feet were crushed under him. He was wriggling around under the table. But, although he was having difficulty getting comfortable with his body, his face was comfortable in mine. He even put his nose inside me and rubbed around my inner lips. Eskimo kissing. He was only eighteen, but he was a more devoted lover than any I had ever had. My pussy was contracting around him. It was drawing tighter and tighter and holding him in like a shell. I was attached to him. I felt waves of pleasure course through me. Maybe the heart pumps the blood around the body most of the time, but the vagina does a damn good job at tea time.

Marcus reached out. His hand fumbled around on the table, looking for something. He found it. I felt the cold metal at the front of me: the spoon's head was pressed against my hot clit. The contrast between the hotness of my body and the coldness of the external force was exquisite.

And all the time he was doing this to me, I had to maintain this unperturbed exterior, like Lady Muck. I had to pretend that I was just enjoying an after-work drink, and that my companion was a family friend. Perhaps Marcus was a wayward nephew searching for advice, or the company protégé. I had to pretend that there was no moistening, no tidal waves in my knickers, no earthquake in my vagina.

Across the restaurant, I saw the waiter leisurely undo a bottle of wine. I watched the corkscrew work in and out of the bottle, just as Marcus's tongue and fingers were screwing inside me. The waiter looked over at me intently; his tongue slid wetly over his swollen lips. He poured the wine into the glass, and I felt my milky secretion flow inside me. My body tensed up tight, tighter: I was desperate for a release, desperate for an ending.

Marcus emerged tousle-headed and reached out across the table. He applied thick blobs of cream between his thumb and index fingers. Then he went back down again. I had to sit back and let it happen. Sod it, it was easier to succumb than protest. I covered my mouth with a napkin, closed my eyes, lay back and thought of England. A thousand English men serving their country, serving me, on the floor, licking me, licking my hole, warm and moist. His breath was hot on my loins. His fingers continued exercising me.

I felt like the cat that had got the cream. I gave a low-pitched groan to show my appreciation. The waiter was staring openly at me now. His eyes bulged, and he was licking his fat lips. Maybe it was in admiration, or perhaps even envy. I took in his light-brown hair and unusually wide, blue eyes. I knew that he knew. I wanted him to know. My arms were spread out, almost as wide as my hidden legs were. I gripped the white tablecloth. The pressure against my burning cunt continued. Marcus's fingers were on my buttocks, pleasuring me there. The burden of keeping quiet was killing me. I wondered if I was going to black out: the excitement was too much for me. This was a nice café; I didn't want to be banned from here for exhibitionism or public indecency.

Marcus jerked my body into his tongue. I felt like my pussy was eating him up rather than the other way round. I wondered what he could see down there in the darkness. As his little finger united with his tongue, tickling me, I gave way to my body. I let the waves of pleasure soak over me. I was quivering with orgasm. My body erupted in waves of pleasure. The volcano was awake.

I knew I couldn't, mustn't, pierce the genteel hum of the restaurant. I managed not to shout my orgasm. I came hard and fast, but I achieved almost dictatorial control over my vocal chords. But, although my mouth didn't betray me, my body did. My legs quivered helplessly, and my hands tightened uncontrollably. I pulled the tablecloth up to me. Marcus's tea, the plate of scones, the jug of cream, and my bottle of water all tumbled over.

The waiter dashed over with a cloth just as Marcus was returning like a hero from his triumphant crusade. His hair was ruffled, and his face was moisturised with my come.

'Thank you,' I said faintly to the waiter.

'You're welcome,' said Marcus euphorically. He

thought he had won, but it was over between Marcus and me. Although he had given me this wonderful present, I wasn't going to back down. It, we, should never have started. We were absurd.

'Let's go,' I said. I felt energised, ready to jump around the café, the street. I had come alive. Will used to think I turned mad after sex; I felt like someone had changed my batteries.

'I can't.'

'Why not?'

He gestured into his lap. His penis was up and outstanding. An Eiffel Tower amongst us. I would once have felt sorry for a man with a hard-on. I would have dropped to my knees to pray. Not any more; he could peel his own cucumber.

'Don't ever do that again,' I warned.

'But you like me,' he said. 'I know you do.'

'Let's just say, I like all young men and not you in particular.'

I was surprised to see the look of hurt fly across his eyes.

'How do you think I feel about that? I'm not just anyone,' he declared bravely. 'I'm myself; I'm different.'

I had to be cruel to get through to him.

We stood at the door. I felt the waiter's smouldering glance. I wondered how Marcus and I looked together. It was madness.

'I'm not interested in you as a boyfriend,' I insisted (perhaps protesting too much). 'You are just a chance to have fun, get to know young men. You are just – just a young prick to me. It could be attached to anyone. I happen to like, um, virgins.'

I didn't get to where I am today without managing to lie stylishly. I didn't want to be another freaky story in a magazine that you find in the dentist's surgery. I didn't want to be in love with him.

101

His expression was how I always wanted a man to look at me.

'I won't give up, I promise you. I won't come here again, but you know where I am. Every day I'll be waiting for you.'

It took a lot of strength to walk away. If he had come after me then, I think I would have given in to him, but I suppose even he knew when he was beaten.

I don't know why I was so determined to finish with him. It wasn't just his age, although that was a big factor. Perhaps one reason was fear. If I carried on seeing him, then eventually Marcus would hurt me. He would let me down or betray me, as Will had done. Another factor was that maybe, cruelly, I wanted to do to Marcus what Will had done to me. I wanted to be the dumper, the one in control. Perhaps the biggest reason, though, was the reason I could never admit even to myself. I still believed there was hope. There was still a chance that Will and I would get back together, and I wasn't going to do anything to jeopardise that. I suppose the thing Sharon said about meeting someone else had come true. But I wasn't over Will yet.

That night, I went to bed early. I lay on the mattress, and I dreamed.

Marcus and Will are together in a glass cube, like a prison. It's my fault they are locked in there. They don't talk to each other; each has secured one side of the cell, which he guards jealously. They sit or lie on their beds and think; maybe they think of me. I can watch them day and night. I sit on the roof of the cell begging them to notice me, but they don't. I slide on the glass devastated, rattling and tapping to attract their attention, but they don't seem able to hear. They certainly can't seem to see me, and my efforts are wasted.

Eventually someone, a new guard maybe, feels sorry for me, and I am allowed in with them, my two hungry lovers. Will sees me first, and he is ready as soon as the glass door closes. I fly at him, like a homing pigeon. I grab his penis out of his pants and massage it awake. I love the colour of his dick, paler than the skin on his chest, but not white, more beige–brown. His pubic hair twists and curls in my fingers. I kneel on the floor and place his cock between my breasts; he catches my breasts possessively in his hands, pushes them around. He feels the nipples and groans.

'Oh Sally, it's been so long,' he says. 'Oh, God, I want to get out of here.'

It's impossible. I have to make their imprisonment better for them. I owe them that. They deserve so much.

He holds my head, encouraging me to suck him. He grips me into the place he likes best.

'Oh, yes, Sally,' he whispers. 'Suck me hard. Make all this disappear.'

I suck him until I think I can't suck anymore. I suck him like liquorice, and he gets stiffer, like whipped egg whites. The insides of my cheeks are aching, and my pussy wants touching. I want to have him inside my cunt, not my mouth. I see Marcus is waiting his turn patiently, his face scarlet with arousal. I pull him closer, so that I am sucking Will, and my hands are on Marcus's prick. His penis dances in my hands, long and heavy. I am going to make them come. My hands and my mouth work in unison. I work hard and fast. They make different kinds of noises, but I recognise their pleasure. Will rubs his hands in my hair, and Marcus's hands are on mine, helping me do to him what he likes best. Their cocks are fully erect and pulsating. Will rams his at my throat, and Marcus's moves faster in between my fingers. They are going to come.

103

Suddenly, a guard grabs me under my arms, and I am ripped away from them. I see Will tries to continue by himself, but he cannot. The guards have had enough entertainment. They are jealous, so they treat me cruelly. They fling me back onto the glass roof. I hammer and hammer, but soon Will and Marcus don't even look up. I writhe naked on the glass; I show them my glistening slit, my breasts pressed against the pane, but still they don't look up. They don't seem to see or hear me any more. They go to different sides of the cell, reverting to enemies.

Then I see Marcus is crying. Wet globules slide down his Pre-Raphaelite cheeks. He is curled up like a small boy on the bed. Then I see Will can't sleep either. Kind Will goes next to Marcus, lies close to him. They must comfort each other. I am happy to see them together, so friendly. I see Will's hand is making a distinctly unfriendly movement. His hand soldiers over the crest of Marcus's round buttocks. It marches onwards, and then I see him suck his finger so that it is rimmed with wetness. Then he places it in Marcus's bum. I see how Marcus hisses like a balloon with the gas let out. Will tries to force a further finger into Marcus's arse, but Marcus shakes his head hard from side to side. Will opens the hole, and the thumb climbs in there. Marcus howls in response.

Will makes him stand up. Marcus stands wearily against the glass walls, his hands outstretched. Will body searches him, savagely slicing apart his buttocks with his hands, twisting his fist inside that private place. Will undoes his pants, and his inflated prick rises up ready to attack. Marcus doesn't yet know what's coming to him. Will slides his sex deep into Marcus's behind. He charges with no mercy, his stick digging into those soft cheeks. His shunting gets faster, as though he is pushing a car, only Marcus has nowhere to go but the glass wall. There is no way out. Marcus howls. The tears continue. His face is raw with frustration. As I watch, I see how Marcus loves it. He wails, but I know that he loves it. He loves it. His penis is rigid, pressed; he fucks the glass.

My fingers were right up inside me. My hands were like spiders freed from their cage. Given full rein, they took over my body. My body barely managed to keep up with my fevered thoughts. With one hand, I alternately battered and caressed my creased sex, feeling the small nodule of global pleasure, and with the other hand, I stormed and dived my pubic hole. My legs jerked around me, and I cried out Will's name.

At last, I had learned how to come by myself, and now I just wanted to go. I lay on the bed exhausted. I hadn't known I could do that. I had had no idea of the power of one.

Chapter Eleven

*E*very night, coming home from the station, I tried to conjure up the call from Will that would change my life. To ensure this happened, I employed various subterfuges. I always walked between the cracks. I made a ritual of brushing my hair for thirty strokes before I left work, and I read both my horoscope and Will's religiously. If his predicted romance and mine didn't, then I was in despair, and if mine did and his did too, then I was in heaven.

One evening, although neither of our horoscopes predicted romance, my dreams came true. I had already kicked off my shoes, changed into casual trousers, and put a potato in the microwave before I realised that the red light of my answering machine was flashing.

It was Will. It suddenly seemed so logical: I had said goodbye to Marcus so Will had come back to me. I called back immediately.

'How are you doing, Sally?'

He sounded as concerned as if he were my doctor, and I had been diagnosed with a disease. Ironic really, when he was the one who had made me sick. I pictured him in home-from-work mode. The briefcase flung on the floor, beer in the fridge, shoes under the table. Irresistible, even if I were in the mood for resisting, which I wasn't.

'Not bad,' I said. Euphoric, actually. 'How about you?'

'Sally,' he said; his voice was huskier than I remembered it. 'I'm sorry about . . . everything.'

'It's OK,' I said breezily. 'Is life wonderful with your new friend?' I wasn't going to bestow the title of girlfriend on her.

There was only one correct answer to that, but Will said something almost acceptable.

'Yes, great, but she's working late all this week.'

'Oh.'

The 'working late' flew above me, the great white hope. Have you ever made something happen by wanting it? For a few moments, then, I believed I could create anything. I could do anything in the world; I just had to want it hard enough.

'I hope we can still be friends.'

I felt myself grow damp between my legs. He wanted me! Will still wanted me! I would show him the new things I had learned. I would let him look at me, let him feel me. I would come for him. My nipples were alive to the sweet sound of his voice.

I got round to Will's fast as a bullet (after I had washed and dried my hair, changed my underwear, and put on a top that I knew he liked and volumes of make-up and deodorant).

'Hiya.' He tried to look surprised to see me.

'Hello,' I whispered. This time, though, he said how nice I looked. He asked if I had lost weight. Men, they have no idea.

'Do you want to watch a video?' he asked, as I had expected he would. He brought some crisps and wine from the kitchen. He was barefoot as usual. I wondered if he had made any changes to the bedroom. Will had been threatening to paint the ceiling ever since he moved in.

Will's lounge was lovely. The walls were burgundy red, and there was a leopard-print rug on the floor. I remembered the first time we made love on it. I couldn't help wondering if he made love on it with her. I still knew nothing about her: Sharon had embargoed all information, and I could barely feed off the images I had.

We sat there on the sofa, like two fishing gnomes. My legs were crossed in front of him. I don't have the best legs in the world, but they are shapely. I discreetly stuck out my tits. Marcus had said they were beautiful. Marcus may not have been the most discerning partner, but he was an ego booster.

We drank gallons of red wine, and I giggled at Will's funny stories about the people at work. I couldn't follow the characters, but I enjoyed the anecdotes about the larks that they all got up to. I thought they sounded immature, but I didn't say so.

Will asked me about my job. He didn't usually.

'How's that woman, Penny someone?'

He had a better memory than I did. I couldn't remember any of the people who filled his every day.

'She's a bitch.' I laughed crudely: I always tried to show off when I was with him. 'You remembered her name!'

'What about the bloke, Fingers?'

'Finnegan. He's OK. I think they were shagging for a while.'

Will sipped his wine thoughtfully.

'Why?'

'Oh, she had this new guy, and I just sensed something weird. Huh. And they go well together.'

Although recently I had realised that maybe he wasn't as bad as she was.

The film could have been in Croatian for all I cared. I didn't watch the screen. I wanted him, but I couldn't make the first move. The anticipation was worth it. I felt like a child in the run-up to Christmas. Had Santa got me what I wanted? The things I had bought him – photo frames and candlesticks, books and a vase for flowers, empty – were still dotted around the room. Did his new friend know they were from me? Did she hate me as much as I hated her?

The film finally ended, and Will changed channels to the football. If I were staying over, I used to go to bed at this stage in the evening, and Will would come in later. He always said it was only ten minutes later, but I know he lied. Sometimes he stayed up until 2 a.m. watching crap programmes.

'More wine?' he offered.

'I won't be able to get home,' I said wide-eyed, giving him the opportunity to invite me to stay the night.

'I'll call you a taxi,' he offered. His lips were stained enticingly red. The first time I was kissed was by a boy who had just drunk Cherryade.

Once, I would have leaned forwards, unthinkingly, to kiss Will.

'No, erh, yeah, I'll have some, please.'

Finally, when the wine had done its task demolishing all my inhibitions, I did lean over and kiss him. First with just my lips, and then I got my tongue to scissor open his lips. He lay back, his head heavy against the sofa; I couldn't tell if there was surprise in his response or pleasure. His lips felt heavy, and unfastening them was like undoing an attic trap door. But I knew I had to get in. I had some tricks up my sleeves. I had learned a thing or two since we had been apart. I wanted to show him.

He put his hands on my shoulders and pushed me away from him gently. All the while, he studied my face closely. Will had the most amazing face, more beautiful than handsome. His blue-grey eyes were fringed with the brown lashes. I felt my vagina twist and contract with something like nostalgia. A sexual heat engulfed my body. I wondered if he could smell it. He looked in my eyes; I felt ashamed to meet his. On the screen, one of the midfielders made a break for the ball and was slipping away from the opposition. The commentator started gibbering wildly with anticipation. I reached for the remote control and zapped the sound down.

'It's all right,' I consoled him, and leaned forward again. Whatever his words, his lips were calling me. I had to rest mine on his. I felt a sudden understanding of that old-fashioned word 'intercourse'. I wanted to exchange with him. To get inter-him, of course.

'Don't get the wrong idea, Sally: I just want us to be friends,' he murmured to my shoulder as I hugged him tight.

Friends who fuck. I knew he wanted to. You learn to read the runes after five years. The hairs on my back were prickling. If I had had a metal detector, it would have been glowing: I had just struck gold. My hand felt its way to his chest. I hadn't touched his nipples for two months. Surely they missed me?

'Just friends,' I agreed. I leaned over to kiss him again. It was a very English kiss. His lips remained stiff. He didn't really kiss me back, although my lips bounced off his roundness naturally.

'Oh Wills,' I whispered. I was already soaking through my knickers. I knew his lips so well. The pinky redness of them, the fuller curve of the lower lip and the thinness of the upper were engraved on my memory. I loved the space between nose and mouth, and then the nose, proud and erect. A mirror to what was happening in his trousers.

'Oh, Wills,' I begged.

He didn't do anything. He looked defeated.

I let my fingers do the talking. I pulled his T-shirt away from his trousers and slid my fingers underneath. His nipples were like firm erasers rubbing at me. Does each one have an individual print? I wondered. Perhaps that was something the police could explore? I wanted to explore them. I got the small pink swell between my teeth and sucked on it.

I felt a strange power run through me. There was to be no mistake, no denial: this had to happen. Finally we could be together again. No one makes love like a woman scorned. No one has so much to prove or so much to conquer. I had waited so long for this. Not two weeks this time, but months of despair, months of thinking of him, scraping myself with dreams of him.

He was wearing button-front trousers. I fumbled my way into them, enjoying the time it took. Softly softly catchy monkey. He was wearing boxer shorts that were a Christmas present from my mother. I wondered if he wore them on purpose. Was it a symbol of his return to me?

He didn't touch me. His eyes were closed. I wished he would open his eyes, but at the same time it wouldn't matter how I looked. I pulled at my silk scarf and tied it around his eyes. He couldn't see me any more. He might even forget which one of us he was with, but by touch, by feeling, and by listening, he would remember. How I felt under him was more important than anything else was.

Wills sat back docilely. His hands were by his sides: he had decided not to touch me. He would let me know he was willing by other means. His genitalia uncurled like a pig's tail, and stood straight and

111

ready. Firm as Cleopatra's Needle. I needed a stiff prick. An adult's one. Will's penis was not the longest, nor the widest, but like life itself, it is not the length but the quality that counts.

'No strings,' he whispered.

'Yes strings.' I tied his wrists behind his back. I pulled my top over my head and flung it on to the floor. I reached back to unclasp my bra, and threw that too. I liked the way my scorned clothes looked on the floor, a pile of passion. My tits were glowing. My nipples were stuck out like buttons on the remote control. They should come free with every cereal packet. With his eyes blindfolded and his hands tied, Wills was all mine. He had no escape. He was in my power. I could do what I liked with him, so I did what I loved. I climbed on top of him and straddled him with my thighs. I wanted to go down, to feel him poke his prick into me. I slid myself on to the cock I loved. On to the man I loved. He was going to love me: how could he not? No other woman was going to feel this wet for him. I was the fucking Mariana trench, a great soaking, gaping cavern.

'Wills, Wills,' I whispered.

He still didn't move. My knees tried to gain control of the settee. The seats were soft, but I held my grip. I lowered myself on to him, slow and mechanical, like a crane going down. Down, down I sank. He grew stiff inside me, my iron man. It was true: I could create my own destiny. All I needed was Will power. Will in my power. I had my darling back. We couldn't be any closer than this. We were doing what came naturally. He filled me up. I fucked him like that. I felt him twitch and flicker inside me. It drove me on; I was up and down, faster, faster. Watching his lips, watching his honey mouth, only I could make his face look like that. I kissed him full on the mouth, submerging him in me.

On the TV, a fierce tackle led to possession of the ball. A goal was imminent; I could see the crowd was roaring. I pretended they were bellowing for me: yes, yes, they wanted me to score, they wanted it.

'Oh, Will, yes, yes.'

I was almost there. I shoved up the blindfold so he could see me. So my breasts would flash before his eyes, so he would know what I felt. He would see the love in my eyes, in my lips, even in my nipples, swollen up and red like raspberries. I bounced on his lap, feeling the shaft ascend me, and the balls tightened, wanting to have some too. Wills thrust deeper and deeper as I wriggled ecstatically, feeling the rising storm.

Will turned me over so that he could have a clear run. I pushed back on to him as far as I could. I was arched on the floor. Down on my hands and knees. His hands held me steady. He stood like a Roman soldier driving his chariot. He gripped my flanks, banging himself in and out of me. You might call it doggy style, but why waste it on dogs? I call it 'the way-to-get-deep-penetration style', the way to go so you can jerk back, back, back, deeper on to it, and not have him see your face. My knees gnawed at the rug. He picked up speed like a racing driver, accelerating to the finishing line.

'Don't stop, don't stop, don't – oh.' My body sustained a violent series of jerks as I rammed myself back against him. I reversed into his prick, like a car smashing into a wall. I felt his carnal explosion inside me, felt myself explode around him. My sex felt heaven-bound. I felt every part of my body howling with ecstasy. I had my orgasm. I had my man. I had him back again.

'Wills, Wills,' I screamed, as I felt his come rip through me like rage. Like sunlight bursting through the clouds.

'Oh God,' he choked. 'Oh my fucking God.'

Chapter Twelve

*A*fter the successful showing of our new series of 'factual' adverts, our company was invited on to TV to join a panel discussion about the ethics of advertising. Ms Feather, naturally, took it upon herself to represent us, and to attend, with Duncan, the black-tie do afterwards.

We gathered around the TV to watch the preview. Even I had to admit that she looked excellent. If TV puts five pounds on you, then they were welcome on Ms Feather's skinny frame. (I would have looked like a great woolly mammoth.) Her skin on the screen was flawless. Her lips looked fuller than in real life, and her nose was patrician like on a coin. I stared at her with enmity and star-crossed envy. We all leaned forward to listen.

The presenter said that our company had created controversial and memorable adverts. She wanted to know how we had thought of the idea.

'We went to the street,' said Ms Feather triumphantly. 'At first my colleagues were sceptical about this idea, but I convinced them that we, in the ad industry, take ourselves far too seriously,' she continued. 'Big egos had got in the way of what we should be doing. We seek only to inform humorously. I think, essentially, our adverts are a little tongue in cheek.'

'All right,' whooped one of the farts, fist in the air. He was another one of those who had originally dished my ideas.

I felt tears pricking my eyes. Was I the only one to know those were my words? Ms Feather was voicing my ideas as though they belonged to her. I bet she rehearsed them in front of the mirror. They were my lines: I wrote them. I did all the work for the company, and this was my thanks.

No, I wasn't the only one to know. Mr Finnegan looked at me with an expression which on anyone else might be read as sympathetic.

'She's all style and no substance, Sally,' he said. He went back to his writing. He was sitting with his feet up on the desk away from the rabble, but I know he had been listening to everything. Why was he always trying to cheer me up? I didn't need his cheap words. He looked like an ageing pop star. And why did he always wear that colour shirt? It didn't suit him at all.

Then Duncan and Ms Feather came in, and the office was alight with hugged congratulations and cigars.

'Champagne anyone?' I heard Duncan say, as I ran out of the building. I wasn't going to cry in front of them, no way.

Outside, it was a scorching hot day. Summer had arrived prematurely, and I was still in heavy clothes. I shot past the waving doorman and felt the torrent of tears unleashed. After we had finished fucking, Will had undone his bonds and said, 'There's Coke in the fridge, if you want it.' Fucking made Will thirsty, and his big fear in life was dehydration. I was still high as a kite. 'There,' I had said smugly, 'you always

115

used to say that I was good in bed.' He looked at me and, when I saw that look in his eyes, I realised my mistake. For him, I was just as good at breakfast, or a TV dinner.

He didn't need to say it. He didn't need to spell it out for me, but he did. He called me a taxi.

'You had better go now, Sally.' That was it.

I staggered over to St Matthew's. I went to find Marcus. My man, the one who had promised to be there for me, had sworn to wait for ever. I didn't care what they thought about me any more. So what if he was eighteen? At least he liked me! At least no one could steal him from me.

I waited one hour, two hours, two and a half. The crowds filed out of the college door, but Marcus didn't materialise. I sat, depressed, on a college wall, feeling my face burn in the humidity. The sky was a thick, muggy grey; a storm was coming. I waited until there was no one left and the caretakers were locking up. Marcus wasn't there. Even Marcus had screwed me over. My little lover, my lapdog lover had let me down. I felt like the shutters had gone down on my emotions. I'll never allow myself to get hurt again. Never. I had let someone touch me. Not just on my legs, my breasts, but my heart. It wasn't true what he had said, and it wasn't true what Sharon had said either. How was I going to get over Will?

I noticed two guys looking at me. One of them had a briefcase. They might have been teachers. They jostled with each other, looking like they had something to say, and then one pushed the other up to my feet.

'Can I help you?' I asked.

They both went bright red, and then one stammered, 'You are from the agency, aren't you?'

The one who was speaking was tall, broad and

blond, but with dark eyebrows. The other one was dark, long haired and skinny. They looked like a typical surfer and his surfboard.

'Uh huh.'

'Do you want to ask us anything?'

'Why should I?'

They shrugged. The dark one kicked a can, and we listened to it clatter away.

I wondered how much they knew. Little bastard: you can't trust anyone. They said something to each other, and then looked back at me uncertainly. I felt impatient. I felt my pussy twist and curl. My body seemed to feel restless and angry. I was sweating, and it wasn't just the heat.

Oh Will, look what you are doing to me.

'What are your names?' I asked, after I had studied them for long enough. No one was going to dump on me again.

They didn't have Marcus's exceptional looks, but they both had something.

'Andrew.'

'William,' said the other one, to my consternation. Was the whole world full of Wills, coming back to haunt me? I have three Sharons and two Traceys in my life. Sally, I'm on my own, but was there a colony of handsome fellows named William?

'I used to know a William,' I said. It was the first time I had referred to him in the past tense. I felt the anger catch in my throat at the dirty memory. There I was, thrown down the pit again. The bastard. When I looked at them, I felt such strange, mechanical emotions. I wanted to degrade them. I wanted to hurt them. On behalf of women everywhere. What right did they have to treat us in this way?

'Do you want to help make advertising more honest, more interesting?'

Both of them smiled brightly.

117

'Marcus said you were really ... nice,' William added.

'You can come to my house tonight,' I said quietly. The words seemed to speak themselves, from the pit of my consciousness.

'Can't I come on my own?' said William, the more eager one.

'No, you have to come together.'

'Is Marcus coming too?' he asked.

'No, definitely not.'

Wills used to love cooking, which was just as well, because I hated it. He used every plate in the kitchen, every saucepan in the cupboards, and frying pans I didn't even know I had. The sweat congregated in drops on his forehead. He worked hard at cooking, like he worked hard at everything. He carefully nursed dishes of duck, or pork with ginger. He wickedly submerged strands of pasta in boiling water. He fried meat until the juices bubbled over, a lick of hot flame.

At least with this date (could I call it that? It would probably end up more like a raisin), there were none of the usual worries about what to cook. Instead, I concentrated on worrying about what I was going to wear. I considered wearing a red basque, red stockings and suspenders. Sharon and I had bought them to wear for the *Rocky Horror Show*. We sat in the cinema, throwing rice in the wedding scene, bleating and booing, and I got popcorn in the laces. I finally elected a black lace bra, mini knickers, stockings and suspenders. I was a walking cliché, but then sometimes clichés are the things that make you happiest. Flowers, meals out, stockings and suspenders seem to constitute the best kind of passion scaffolding. I wanted them to think I was a vamp. I wanted them to shiver with that lethal concoction of desire and fear. But it was I who felt fear. I threw my shabby gown on top.

(Will's eyes had been so cold. I had shown him how much I wanted to have him. I had let him see how turned on I was. I had humiliated myself.)

It was raining heavily. The heat of the day had finally erupted into a storm. I couldn't help thinking they would have to be mad to go out in this weather.

When eventually the bell rang, I sprang to the door and positioned myself as seductively as I could against the wall. I heard myself say something like, 'Hello, boys.'

Two half-drowned sailors had washed up on my doorstep. Andrew's longer hair was stuck in clumps over his skinny cheeks. William's hair had developed an unhealthy kink.

'You didn't bring an umbrella?' I said, stating the obvious. It didn't bode well for their powers of protection.

They shuffled apologetically around into my living room, and then William sneezed, so I invited them to take their wet clothes off. It was the perfect excuse.

'How about you?' William said daringly, gesturing at my robe.

'I'm not wet,' I lied. My knickers, at least, were damp.

They took off their shirts. Andrew revealed a dark, surpisingly muscular chest. William, evidently a sportsman, was more bulky. His skin was baby pink-white, and his pectorals were so toned that they almost resembled breasts.

For my birthday, a few months ago, a couple of guys at work had given me a bag of grass. I had never smoked it. Will wasn't interested, and I was afraid I would get melancholy by myself. I asked them if they wanted to smoke.

Andrew pulled the bag to him and rolled up. His

119

hands softly worked the fragile paper. I watched how his tapering fingers rubbed the weed together, then arranged it in the sheet, and how he licked gently down the length of his creation, with his eyes half shut. He put it in between his thick lips and inhaled deeply before passing it to me. I did the same and then passed it to William.

The room swam pleasantly. Life seemed somehow friendlier than before. And my position, sprawled on the floor in my best underwear, seemed better than ever. I giggled, and they giggled too. They were both incredibly handsome. I wondered if all teenagers were, or if I had just got lucky. I felt like the organiser of a Mr World competition. I watched their beautiful male bodies as they lounged around on my floor. At the peak of their physical prowess, yet not knowing it, their minds were still full of complexes and contradictions, their bodies full of yearnings. I remembered being sixteen, and couldn't help thinking (as all of us are tempted to do), if only I had known then what I know now.

It felt nice, yet I was somehow unspeakably furious with them. I put on some salsa music, and Andrew leaped up. I jumped gladly into his open arms. I was surprised that he had offered: I had thought he would just waste away in the corner.

William was jealous. I loved that. He was languishing on the floor, watching us. I saw the sullen turn of his lips and took in the precious dark hollow under his nose. His body was so sturdy and well honed. Andrew swung me around the room confidently. He twirled me around and around and, every so often, my gown flashed open, just over where William was sitting. He seemed to perk up at this.

'It's my turn now,' William said determinedly when the song ended. He manhandled me, sliding close to me, and I felt the atmosphere change: my body grew charged with tension. I still couldn't stop giggling, though. Wasn't this the funniest thing: little old me with two handsome and willing boys? Two boys, Will! It's simple maths. One and one make two. Two is better than one: divide my legs, subtract my self-restraint, add the cocks and feel the pleasure multiply.

William positioned his knee between my legs and whirled me around the room. Again, we were both treated to occasional glimpses of thigh, but this time the man on the ground, Andrew, didn't notice. We twirled together faster and faster. With my eyes closed, I felt as though we were on a merry-go-round. I could hear Andrew applauding in the background.

The next song was a slow one. I felt nervous for a moment; William made my breathing tight. He pulled me closer, squeezing me manfully against his chest. I could feel the rise and fall of his breath. He stroked my hair. When I opened my eyes, I saw that Andrew was staring at us from across the room. His face was wistful yet distant, like someone watching the Sunday movie. I knew Andrew wasn't interested in me. I had worked that out in the street. He had only gone along with this for William. I think I may even have known it before he did, but Andrew only wanted to touch his friend.

Suddenly William's face was closer. His eyes were large, his nose was strong, and his lips were on mine. He still moved me around, but I was frozen, gripping onto his head. He put his hand straight on my butt. Hole in one. He scored ten out of ten for enthusiasm.

The music stopped. The rain slashed hard against the windows. We all looked at the glass and saw the raindrops slither and slide down. There was a crack of thunder.

'Put some more music on,' ordered William.

Andrew picked up the CDs gently and held them delicately between his thumb and third finger. He was so sensitive. I just wanted to hold him, console him. He seemed to possess a deep-down sadness.

William pulled me closer: he wanted to kiss me again. There was a clap of thunder, and I pushed him away, laughing.

'All good things come to those who wait,' I said. He looked aggrieved. 'Let's tell each other stories,' I added.

'What kind of stories?' he asked reluctantly. He wanted to get on with it right away. I wasn't having any of that. There were three of us; I wasn't going to leave anyone out.

'Rude stories.'

He looked more interested.

'OK, you first.'

But I didn't want to tell them. I wanted to hear theirs, to get into their minds as well as their bodies. I had unlimited access to my own fantasies: it was other people's that were mysterious for me.

'No, you first, because this is my fantasy, to bring two boys here to my house.'

'OK,' he said. He really was very willing. 'You come to give a talk to the school. You are wearing a short skirt, and you sit at the desk. Your legs are open, and we can see the gusset of your panties.'

Gusset! There was no word in the English language that I hated more.

'You are really strict with us but, as you tell us more about advertising, you grow more and more animated, and your legs widen. We watch as only a small stretch of cotton protects your fanny from us all. You realise that we aren't listening to you, we are just watching, and you get angry. You ask who the ringleader is and find out that it's me.'

He definitely wasn't a virgin.

While William was talking, Andrew had rolled us another joint, and we inhaled luxuriously.

'You call me to the front and say you have to punish me. You pull down my trousers but, when you see me, you don't know how to react.'

I loosened my gown, pulled down my knickers just to my thighs and put my index finger along my pubic bed. They both stared at me. William began to stroke himself, and then Andrew did too. William seemed to forget that he was mid-story, so I reminded him.

'Go on.'

'You bend me over your knee and spank me, in front of everyone, but I love it. That makes you furious: you are shaking with anger. You say that I humiliated you, in front of everyone. And that I'm not to look at you again. I say that I'm too big for you, and I would make you come straight away. You say that I'm wrong, so wrong, and that I'm just a young boy and I don't know anything. You challenge me to prove it; you do what I wanted all along, and you sit on top of me, in front of everyone. Then you start sighing about how enormous I am and begging me never to stop. You scream that you are going to come, and then you start bouncing around on my groin, and I make you come.'

I smiled. I like a story with a happy ending.

'Please let me touch your tits,' he begged, when he had finished his tale. I brushed off his hand, but he jumped down to his knees, like a priest about to take the sacrament. There were no figures of eight with his tongue for me. There was no hesitation. He was hungry. For eighteen years, he had been waiting for this. He pulled at my tender nipples. Both boys were hard. Andrew looked away from me, embarrassed.

I had two penises to chose from. Two erect penises! I moved the boys closer together, and they shuffled side by side. I felt like a snake charmer. I ran my tongue up one and my fingers up the other, taking it in turns. I was in a prick emporium. (I wonder what

123

the collective word for penis is: a cacophony, a symphony or an orchestra?) Two cocks to suck. I felt my sex canal flood with excitement. I had two dicks in my mouth! I rubbed them together and pulled them closer. William's cock was curved like a banana, and Andrew's prick was more bulbous at the end, like a pear. I couldn't wait to feel him inside me. I knew the effect its massive proportions would have. He was a stringy, wiry boy, but his dong was an enormous aberration of nature, some throwback to Neanderthal man. William's face was glowing with satisfaction, but Andrew wouldn't look up. He fidgeted with his hands and swallowed nervously.

'Do you want to fuck me?' I asked.

'Oh God, yes,' groaned William. Andrew didn't speak. I felt sorry for him. He wants to screw you, William, I thought to myself maliciously.

I had an idea. I clicked on the answering machine; the first message from Will rang out from the tapes.

I was hot and excited. I led the two of them into the kitchen and pressed myself against the washing machine. I jammed the washing machine buttons, and it started vibrating hard. I was back against the tumble dryer, which was spinning like a top. The vibrations pulsated up my bottom, they whipped up my entire body, even causing my teeth to clatter together pleasantly.

William moved first; he grabbed me by the shoulders and prepared to slide himself in between my legs. Andrew stood still and uncertain. Will struggled against me: we were linked like two awkward ballroom dancers. I felt his balls push against me, and then his dick was submerged into my hot space. His dick fitted tighter than a glove on a hand, more like a ring on a finger. I felt myself clenching around it. William drove into me. His bottom slammed up and down, tossing pancakes. I was a whore and angel in the kitchen, because I was fucking and washing clothes at the same time. One day he was going to look back at this as the day he realised his talent. At the same time he was tearing at my breasts with his tongue. I thought he was going to kill me with his anxiety to have them both in his mouth.

Andrew was writhing against the fridge, playing contentedly with himself. I watched him; I knew instinctively that he was jealous of me. It made me show off. He wanted William, William wanted me, but I wanted him. We were lost.

'You're so hot, so horny,' William was telling me, but he couldn't have known how simultaneously erotic but painful that was to Andrew.

'Come here,' I said, gesturing to Andrew. William looked over, puzzled at his friend's reticence. Andrew reluctantly stepped forwards. But he was breathless, and his cock was still huge. It looked even bigger than ever in his little hands.

'Come on, Andrew,' said William generously. 'You can go next, yeah?'

Andrew shook the hair out of his eyes. When he was next to me, I put my hand on his prick and started to move the foreskin back and forth. He took a sharp intake of breath, and then leaned in towards us. He had his arm around me, and then, to balance himself, he had to put his arm around William. It must have been painful for him. He closed his eyes, and I worked him harder. I knew he was imagining that it was William's hand that played with him; I knew he was imagining that it was William he had against the machine. It made me laugh. I don't know who I was laughing at, but it made me laugh.

I was shagged up against the machine. I put my arms around my big boys, my lovely big boys, listening to the voice of my other big boy on the telephone. I couldn't stop myself: the vibrations shook me to the core of my body, rocking my clit up and down, and he shook me too. I felt like I was being torn in half by illicit pleasure.

I heard Will's voice on the machine. I knew it by heart. Message no. 4.

'Hello honey, I'm on the train now. Just to say that I'm late, that bastard made us do some overtime. Anyway, I'm on my way now. I'm coming.'

I was coming too. I gripped Andrew's hair. I had almost forgotten who I was with: I could have been with William, Andrew, or Will, any of them. All I could feel were the amazing sensations that spiralled out from my body.

'Oh Will, Will,' I whispered, shuddering, into William's ear. The music played on in the living room. William looked thrilled. He pulled out of my hole and came gratefully in my face. Andrew came last. He was still hanging on to William, hanging on for dear life, as his face distorted and his body convulsed. The come burst out of him, and I noted with glee that it landed on William's well-exercised buttock cheek.

'It's your turn now, Andrew,' proposed William.

'You don't have to do anything,' I consoled him. 'Why don't you just tell us a story?'

'Don't you fancy her, Andy?' he asked incredulously and bustled up protectively to my breasts.

'I, you are my, er –'

Poor soul. I had no doubts that I wasn't in his fantasy.

He sat cross-legged across from us, like a guru. He looked incredibly beautiful in his isolation. William kissed my nipples alternately.

'I'm naked, and I'm strung up high on a wooden cross. Everyone hates me; they throw things at me and call me names. There are all these people, and they think I'm dead, but I'm not. At night, the kinder people come back and try to revive me. They kneel in front of me, but the only way to give me life is to touch me there. You give me the kiss of life. And you kiss me back to life.'

I sipped my drink pensively. Andrew certainly had an unusual imagination. They both did: they were St Matthew's finest. William stroked my legs and tried to sneak his hand upwards.

'Tell us more,' I encouraged him. I had a feeling there was more to this than we had heard.

'And then sometimes it's you: you're up there on the cross, William, and you look so exquisite. Your body is covered with bruises, and your skin is white. We can see your knees, the spread of your muscular thighs, your groin, covered with those golden curls, and your cock is incredible, and they all try, but only I can do it.'

William looked up. His hair was stuck up from our lovemaking, but now it looked as though it had gone up with shock. He shrugged wordlessly.

'I think he wants to suck you,' I hinted diplomatically.

'No, no way,' said William. He shook his head as Andrew bowed his with such a look of shame that I wanted to get up and run away with him. Instead, William and I kissed lingeringly. His tongue sought my mouth and squiggled around and round. I leaned back, Oh, God, this was such luxury. Sod Will, sod Marcus, sod everyone else. I moved my hands and fondled William's flat stomach. And beneath it, his penis began to grow, long as a fucking beanstalk.

Andrew still looked hangdog, but his hard-as-rock erection was tremendous. I met his eyes, and I nodded at him. He knew what I meant, what I was condoning, but at first he didn't, couldn't, do what he wanted.

I pulled my mouth away from William's and whispered, 'Go on, then, you know you want to.'

While William was kissing me (I mean really deep-throat kissing, French, Spanish, or wherever it's from), Andrew tentatively moved his fingers over to William's penis. I locked myself on William's lips so he couldn't complain. William made this noise that was half pleasure, half revulsion. Andrew sensibly didn't give him time to change his mind. He started giving him vigorous strokes; he had none of the clumsiness of girls. Men really do play a different ball game. I kept my tongue firm in William's mouth. He had no escape from self-discovery. Andrew lowered himself to get a closer look at his friend's delicious rib of beef.

'He wants to kiss you there,' I murmured to William. I felt I owed him that. William said that he didn't want him to, but he was looking at me, looking like he would suffer anything for me. He leaned over and plucked my nipple as if it were a berry and stayed under me. We kissed, and I watched how his penis twitched as though desperate to be manipulated.

'Touch me,' he said to me.

'No, let him: he wants to,' I said. Machiavelli should read my textbook. We resumed licking and drowning in each other's mouths. His penis was like a flagpole that wouldn't be run down. He gripped my hand roughly, put it on his cock, and started to beat my wrists up and down, but I pulled away. Andrew was waiting, patiently, pleading. He looked so long-lashed and faithful, like a dog waiting for some encouragement from his master. I could never treat a small animal cruelly.

'Shall I let him?' William asked finally. He looked like a cherub suckling in my bosoms. The devil in me itched.

'Why not? If it feels good.'

Before William could speak again, Andrew had already leaped eagerly at his chance. He lay down with his face square in William's lap. William's cock surged in his mouth. William sighed, perhaps with the shock of it, and I saw that the skin on his arms was full of goose pimples. As if to distract himself from the things that were going on below, he continued to grope me further. I let him, of course: I loved it. He squiggled his little finger up to my moist fanny. He tapped against my vagina, slid around the front, the back. I was throbbing; my pussy was beating like a drum. I loved the sight of them together, the two boys together at my behest. Breathing heavily, I lit up a joint for that extra bit of freedom, and William and I shared it. William was servicing me digitally, and Andrew was servicing him orally.

The smoke was hot in my mouth. I felt it travel to my chest, and I knew my eyes were red. William and I kissed. I gripped the back of his neck, so he had no escape, and he told me again how horny I was. I told him how horny I felt. He knew it though: my cunt was a reservoir of pleasure. We didn't let Andrew have any of the joint. I felt powerful, as if Andrew were our slave; we could do anything we liked. We passed the joint back and forth. Andrew was making snuffling noises, whinnies of pleasure, as he sucked and sucked at his friend's cock.

When he looked down at his fellating friend, William's expression was torn between revulsion and pleasure, but his hands were square on Andrew's sloping shoulders. Physically, at least, it was clear Andrew had won. William eased him on and off his member. Andrew continued industriously, while William fingered me. I felt pleasure fanning out from my core; it felt like my body was unravelling. Just let go, let go. William and I resumed kissing, and I secreted my tongue in his mouth.

Then, with an unexpected roar, William pushed Andrew off. Andrew jumped up and staggered to unsteady, guilty feet. He looked frightened. Then William grabbed Andrew tightly by his taut buttocks and pulled him close. Andrew's penis seemed to surge forwards dashing into William's open mouth. William swallowed him. He knelt at Andrew's legs, and Andrew could only watch wide-eyed, his hands coming around to clasp William by the back of the neck.

It was my turn to feel neglected, but not for long. William straddled me on the floor and, his huge prick covered with Andrew's juices, pumped up me. William masterfully fucked us both simultaneously, the effeminate gay boy, and the domineering straight girl. His lips were locked onto Andrew's todge, and his cock was ramming up me like a juggernaut.

'Oh yes, yes.' We were humming beautifully together, like a church choir in unison. Andrew's eyes were rolled back, his breathing shallow, and his lips puckered into a heart shape. I had never seen anyone so lost, so absorbed in passion as he was then.

I didn't want to, but I came first. I screamed Will's name again. My body felt loose and liberated. As I quivered in ecstasy, I remember thinking, if only I had a camera to preserve this moment for ever, for posterity.

'Are you in the same class as Marcus?'

God, I sounded like a woman in love; Marcus this, Marcus that.

'No,' said Andrew. He looked uncomfortable. 'We aren't.'

'Are you driving back?' I asked. I was sat on the settee with my feet up, the silk dressing gown on. Still time to catch the last five minutes of my favourite TV show.

'Yes.'

'What about Marcus: does he have a car?' For God's

sake, I was inserting his name into every conversation. Prying, trying to find out more.

William said simply, 'No, of course, Marcus can't drive yet.' Andrew looked at him awkwardly, as if to say, shut up, William.

'Why doesn't he learn?' I remember this moment well, because one minute I was smiling, reorganising all the things that had tipped onto the floor. Seconds later, I had lost the smile.

'Marcus? He's much younger than us: he's only just turned seventeen.'

Chapter Thirteen

*T*he train was packed the following morning. There was no space to read the newspaper, so I read the woman's next to me, until she stared at me angrily. As the train thundered along the tracks, my body jiggled uncontrollably. I lost my balance. I tried to grip a pole but fell forwards on to a seated man, my boobs into his face. It was Finnegan.

'Sally, please take my seat,' he said, standing up graciously.

'No, I'm fine,' I lied. I didn't want to owe him anything. The woman with the newspaper huffily pushed herself into the space.

'Where did you disappear to yesterday?' asked Finnegan politely. 'Duncan wanted to congratulate you.'

'Yes, me and all the minions.' I couldn't help the sarcasm.

'Sally, your work is good. We all like it. Ms Feather may be trying to take the credit for it, but you don't have to let her walk all over you.'

It was a funny idea. I saw her in her stilettos,

treading and puncturing my skin. I pleaded for help, but no one listened.

He scratched his chest. He was wearing a good quality shirt and, as he rested his hand over his heart, it seemed that he was trying to tell me that he was trustworthy or something. I wondered fleetingly what it would be like to touch him there. What would his nipples feel like? There is something so sensual about feeling a man's heart beat. His eyes were watery blue under storming Heathcliff brows. It felt as though he wanted to say something, but he just started gabbing about work again. We had some big accounts at work now. Chocolate advertising and one, less exciting, for a huge law firm. I noticed the woman who had taken the seat was now looking up at Finnegan with glistening eyes, as though she found him attractive. I really didn't know that women responded to him in that way.

I was going to pretend to have to make a phone call so that we didn't have to walk from the station together, but he offered to wait, so we set off silently. I wondered what Will was doing. Just how long could I hold out hope that he was going to come back for me? How long was he going to take to get fed up with her?

'Your wife is on the phone,' said Leanne to Finnegan as soon as we arrived. 'Hello, Sally,' she added nervously to me. She hadn't known how to treat me since I had moved up the office hierarchy.

'My ex-wife,' Finnegan corrected her, although it wasn't clear whether the remark was addressed to the air or to Leanne. I shrugged carelessly. 'She's always interfering: my son is off school, and she blames me.'

'What's the matter with him?' I asked, trying and failing to be polite. Who cared?

He stretched back.

'He's at that age.' He looked at me, as if I too deserved his condescension.

Why couldn't I get on with Finnegan the way the others could? I found him repulsive: he brought me out in goose bumps, and yet, and yet. Somehow I hated it when he wasn't in the office. His dark hair was receding, and his forehead looked disproportionately long.

He clipped the receiver under his ear and, at the same time, switched on his computer. The screen lit up. I could hear his ex-wife's voice, distant squawking, and his replies were curt. He stretched back in his chair like a dirty great orang-utan. He did two things at once. Three things: he was still looking at me.

I wouldn't be able to control him.

I watched his index finger work the mouse. His middle finger pointed upwards, and I looked away, feeling suddenly lonely.

My underwear was still crumpled on the living-room floor when I arrived home that night. I stepped over it imperviously. Finally, a letter from Will had arrived. I ripped it open eagerly. Maybe he wrote it the morning after we slept together, spent a couple of days thinking about whether to post it or not, then, in an emotional flash, sent it. He would have got the stamps from the newsagent's that we used to go to together for our lottery tickets. I could almost see the expression on his face as he composed it.

    Dear Sally,
    What can I say? Which words can I use; how best can I arrange my mixed emotions? (Will fancied himself as a poet.) It was great to see you again.

(That sentence was embroidered by three question marks.)

I have decided not to tell my girlfriend about what happened, and I trust you will be discreet.

(I mean, who would I tell?)

I just wanted to make this clear to you again. I am flattered by your strong feelings towards me, but we have both moved apart, and IT'S OVER.

(As if to sweeten the blow, he added the following parting shot.)

Hope your mum is well; stay in touch.

You cock-sucker! I slammed the pillow down and punched it, wishing it were his head. What did it matter, success at work, success at play, when your heart aches? What about the rest of my life? What about me? I felt so sick, I couldn't even finish my cornflakes. There was nothing I could do. Then I remembered. As Sharon would say, there is only one thing for a woman to do when she feels like this. Get your hair done.

Chapter Fourteen

I wriggled nervously in the black leather chair, then leaned back against the edge of the sink. The hairdresser pulled back my hair. The water wet my hair and trickled down the back of my neck. The hairdresser smoothed it back into the basin. The warm spray from the shower made my head tingle.

When I arrived at Medusa's Hair Salon, without an appointment, the hairdresser/manager was just sitting with her feet up leafing through a 'Red Satin' book. She said she could fit me in, no problem, and she had asked a few questions about the style I wanted.

'I feel like a big change,' I had told her, unconfidently. I have always regarded hair salons with the same trepidation as dentists', which is probably why I have always had long hair. Will used to love my hair, draped over my shoulders, nestling to the bottom of my breasts. When we first started going out, Will sometimes curled it around his fingers; when we kissed he used to tug it, just short, sharp shocks to my scalp, or he would wind it round and round until it became tangled.

The hairdresser had grinned back knowledgeably, saying she knew exactly what I needed. I guessed she was about fifteen years older than me, warm and sunny in a way that suggested she was covering up a troubled past. If she had been famous – a singer, or an actress – she would have been the kind of dignified yet brassy sort who has a huge gay following.

She massaged my head with shampoo. I felt the tips of her fingers rub my scalp, healing and soothing me. She laboured over me with devotion. There was none of that summer holidays/boyfriend business. At one point, when the massage grew more vigorous and I almost felt as though I was losing consciousness, I let out a short grunt.

'Enjoying it?' she asked.

'Mmmm, yes.' I had to bite my lip to stop from crying out.

Then, telling me to close my eyes, she applied the warm spray. It felt so thorough, I thought she was washing out my scalp. She shielded my eyes from the shampoo. I thought that was considerate of her.

She dried my hair, led me over to sit in front of a mirror, and started cutting. She kept having to hold my head up. Each time a tendril fell away, I felt freer. I was letting go of part of him. I was losing the old life, and it seemed to me that even my face changed shape.

Tentatively, I told her what had happened with Will. How he had hurt me, how he had used me.

'I just feel so angry all the time.' I felt so agitated, so disappointed. I told her how I had tried to win him back. I told her about the letter. I didn't tell her about Marcus, or the singer, or the two lost boys. I had a feeling that she wouldn't mind. But you never know. Pieces of my hair lay on the shop floor, circled around us.

'I have really strange dreams,' I proceeded awk-

137

wardly. 'Not just about my ex, but others too. They trouble me.'

'Why?' she asked. 'Everyone has weird dreams.'

'Not like me, they don't,' I said, making faces in the mirror. 'Do you?'

'Sure. I have this recurring fantasy that some regular customers of mine come to the shop late at night and make me have my hair cut. I don't want them to, but they pin me down. They tie me up on the chair, and then they shave my hair off. They make me look like one of those women, the traitors, who had affairs with the enemy during the war.

'Wow,' I said admiringly. No, my dreams weren't so weird as that, yet.

'That's not all,' she said. She stopped cutting for a moment and seemed to be measuring my face. She combed my hair.

'They play with my breasts, all three of them. They are very orderly about it, each waiting his turn. And then they make me pull up my dress, and I'm not wearing knickers, and they are shocked, appalled really. They get some hot water and a sponge, and one of them soaps me there while the others watch, and one holds me down. Then they get a razor and, very slowly, very delicately, they take turns to shave my pubic hair. I watch as the hair disappears, one, two, three stripes, and it is gone. Then they tilt me back so they can catch out the stray hairs around my hole. I watch the curls hit the floor. When I look down at myself, I am amazed at how I look. I look so innocent somehow; I have this woman's body, but this gaping, pink, vulnerable pussy. Somehow, I think it looks quite animal, or even alien. And they get the mirrors so we can have a closer look, and I see in the mirror that my slit is soaking. For the first time, I see how that really looks. White discharge sticks to the naked lips, and they open me up wider so that they can get a closer look.'

She stopped abruptly.

'Funny, aren't they, dreams?'

I looked down at my nipples. They were as hard as two peanuts. You're in a hair salon, I told the unruly pair. Stop it. But they remained upright. If I had been a man, I know my erection would have been right up to the reception desk.

'Yes,' I said. 'Very funny.'

She held the mirror behind me. I could see the back of my head, and hundreds and thousands of images of her reflecting back at me. I looked gamine, pixie-featured. Was it me? Or was it someone else? My face seemed daring, up for anything. I had cut off my past.

She invited me into the back area of the salon. It was a small room equipped with fridge, a kettle, a wardrobe and a large bed. As she stretched to put away the towels, I noticed her breasts were enormous. And the nipples too were like round, raised saucers staring at me. Why? We weren't cold.

'So?' she said, with her eyebrows raised. I felt her appraise me. I was too scared to look down to see what tension had done to my breasts. I felt at a loss as to what I was doing there. I was also a little scared that she was going to try and convert me. We had a load of religious evangelists in my area, and they always gave me the spooks.

'Your hair looks good like that,' she said casually. 'It suits you.'

'Thanks.'

'What's wrong, then?'

I didn't know. All I could feel was pain. Her eyes were nonjudgemental. Now, I was worried she was a witch. I didn't say anything yet.

There was a stillness about the place, like a library on a Sunday. She drew the curtains, shutting out the world and the craziness of the day. She lit a stick of incense, and the room was filled with the smell of coconuts. She lit a couple of candles. It reminded me of how I had burned Will's letter over the cooker; the cruel paper turned black and slowly withered. There were ethnic objects in the room too: a Tibetan prayer bell, Indian shawls and Japanese fans.

I couldn't find my voice. I was like a child again, afraid to tell the teacher the answer.

'Do you want to lie down?' she asked quietly.

'I don't want to mess up my hair,' I said: a poor excuse, but under the circumstances ... She came up behind me and touched my cheek gently.

'It really looks lovely.' Then her hands moved ever so lightly on to my flanks. I dodged out of their way.

'What do you want to do?'

'I don't know,' I said honestly. I hated to admit it, but without the help of either alcohol, smoke, or extreme passion to liberate me, I really had no idea what my desires were. They were unused to being at the forefront of my concerns.

She walked around the room carefully, looking at me from different angles.

'Do you like my room?'

I could only nod in reply. The cat had stolen my tongue.

'I want to make you feel better,' she added softly. She sat down plumply on one side of the bed. She pulled off her shoes, and I saw her stockinged feet were tiny.

I found my voice.

'How can you make me feel better?' I asked. I sounded different to usual, low and throaty.

She stood up, and I saw she had left a heavy indentation on the mattress. She undid her shirt. It was white silk, and she shrugged it to the floor. I liked the way she didn't worry about folding it up. It

140

suggested she only cared about the important things in life. Her bra was big, white and lacy. One nipple stuck out rudely through a gap. She undid the bra expertly and threw it on the floor. There was a red line under her bosom, where the underwire must have dug in too deeply. I stared at her nipples. They really were enormous, far bigger even than mine. Her breasts were oak-brown like the rest of her. They hung low, but full and fruity.

She unzipped her skirt. It was a long, dark, flowery piece, not the kind of thing I would wear. She was wearing black stockings. If I were being nice, I would say she was voluptuous. If not, that she had 'let herself go'. She had probably been a cola-bottle shape in her youth, but in middle age she had spread into a Guinness can. She was, as Ms Feather would say, a prime candidate for the gym. Her legs were stocky and strong, but above her thighs she was less firm.

She looked up at me hesitantly and then started playing with her suspenders. I liked the pattern the belt made on her stomach and on her legs. Their impracticality excited me. There was no reason to wear stockings nowadays; the only possible reasons were aesthetic. What was she thinking of, stripping in front of a stranger, another woman?

'Leave them on,' I whispered hoarsely.

She waited. She had a slight moustache of fair hair over her lip but, in this light, her face was more beautiful. Her nose was long and sharp. It felt like a long time passed, but I suppose it was only a few minutes. Although at the time I was only thinking of what on earth to say next, I suppose I was really dwelling on more fundamental questions: whether or not I was ready to allow my sexual desires (yearnings that, until then, I hadn't even realised that I had) to become reality.

'Take off your knickers,' I said finally. She was

wearing big knickers like huge, white cotton flags. By comparison, my G-strings were like tampon cords.

She moved them down slowly. She wasn't embarrassed of me, not even a bit. She wasn't afraid to watch me and I was bold enough to watch her back. The area above the stockings was amazing; the black lines of suspender caught between the folds of flesh. The knickers parachuted to the floor.

'Open your legs and show me your –' I didn't know what word to use '– hole.'

She sat down again, and I moved towards her. She tried to put her hand on her shoulder, but I wanted to look first. It was a red and pink gash. I wasn't ready to touch her yet. I was licking my lips with anticipation. There was so much of her body that I wanted to see.

'Turn around.'

She lay on her stomach. She put her arms out either side and submitted to me. She looked so peaceful and comfortable that I was afraid she would fall asleep like that, so I told her to kneel with her hands flat on the floor. I wanted to have a look at everything. I didn't want to touch her, not yet. I walked around her, like I was admiring an object in an art museum. One of those sculptures where you can't understand exactly which bit is what. I didn't know what to do, but I wasn't worried about it. I knew that it would come to me. I had to trust myself like she was trusting me.

I took in the look of her arse. It was huge, creamy white. Two huge circles; I couldn't resist. I touched them, pressed my fingers into her flesh, and she whimpered, 'Yes'. She was thick-skinned.

She was a vision of obscenity. A dirty woman. I was still fully dressed, and she was bare, giving it up to me.

'You look obscene,' I said. Pornographic. I felt my

fanny whistle into life, like the stirrings of a furry animal after hibernation. Ob-scene. I loved the way the word sounded, the shape my mouth formed when I said it.

I slapped her buttock cheek hard. Her body shook. Her tummy was loose, looser than mine was. I wanted to slap her again. I did. Her frame swayed, but she stayed upright. The cheek went red with the force of the blow. She was so big and unlovely, but yet so desirable. Obscene. I felt around the suspender belt.

I slapped her again. The left cheek. Then I pulled at her buttocks roughly and got a good look at her arse-hole. In comparison with the wealth of backside, the anus was a tiny, sacred thing.

I smacked her again. I was still angry.

'Why don't you take off your clothes?' she turned around and asked me. She was still on all fours, like an animal preparing for the mount.

I didn't want her suggesting things to me.

'Maybe,' I said airily. I might as well; I was proud of my body. Next to her, I was compact like a small, reliable car. At least I wouldn't have to hold my stomach in.

'What's your name?' I asked as I struggled out of my clothes.

'Mrs Robinson,' she said. We both laughed at the appropriateness of it. 'In the wardrobe, I have some things,' she added.

'What kind of things?' I asked suspiciously.

'Have a look,' she invited. She maintained her doggy-style position, her arms locked. She must have been used to it.

I still didn't know what I wanted, but I was curious. I opened the door and found a whip. I had never used one before, and at first I wasn't sure it was one. The base was long and thin like a black cucumber, and the rope stretched out like a snake on top of a pile of clothes. I thought of Will. What I would have done to him. I mentally superimposed his face onto her cheeks and whipped as hard as I could. It was all I could do to stop myself crying out with vicious pleasure. She made no attempt to restrain me. Each time the whip fell on her massive buttocks, she cried out. Her body shook, and she readjusted herself.

'Please touch me,' she begged. Her voice was urgent.

'Roll on your back.'

She rolled over. She was so pliant, my very own play-dough. She lay with her legs up, and her breasts rolled either side her underarms. I felt sorry for men who chose wholesome over whoresome. This was far more interesting. Her bigness didn't intimidate me. It was exotic to me. I wasn't used to it. In advertising, we didn't see women like this. The only women I knew were skinny, scrawny girls, gaunt like greyhounds: girls like Marcus's neighbour. Mrs Robinson was so different from all of those. She was the opposite of the girl; her body was older. It was looser, yes, but just as exciting. Her zones of pleasure were more plentiful, more substantial. I was overcome with a passion for seizing hold of her thick, wanton flesh and rubbing it.

I kneeled over her. I hadn't kissed her yet, and I didn't much want to. She was a slut, and sluts don't kiss. Instead, I wanted to touch her formidable breasts. They overwhelmed me. I fell on them, sucking them like a man, fumbling between her legs. I didn't want to go at it gently: I wanted to do it to her clumsily, like a man. She was so big and lovely. There was so much of her, acres and acres of fuckable material. I squeezed inside her, gripping hard. I squelched over onto her body so I was lying on top of her, my hand deep in the dangerous waters of her cunt, and she squeezed me down into her. Her hands were wandering over my back. This is how a man feels, I told myself. If I were a man, I would have put it in her then, before she could catch her breath. I loved feeling her cunt. With the triangle of hair, I thought it was like the Bermuda triangle. It invited and yet repelled me. I would never navigate out. But, like a sailor stung by a mermaid's cry, I was lost.

I started kissing her lips, kisses like hundreds and thousands on a fairy cake. I was scared: I thought a woman would be more discerning, harder to please, but she seemed to like what I was doing. I tried to kiss her like Marcus had kissed me.

She slowly opened her mouth. Then, before I even realised it, my tongue was poking inside, delicately at first, quivering in between her lips, meeting her tongue, then more confidently, exploring the reaches of her teeth, her gums. It was such an intimate thing; I had never felt such a physical entanglement. I had to close my eyes, because our eyes were so close. I was afraid our noses would clang, or she would think my face was ugly. Entering her mouth was somehow more personal than anything else we had done so far.

We kissed some more, lingeringly. She was doing the same back to me, tonguing me, entering me, caressing me. I realised that we had started making love. Perhaps whenever women get together they can't help but make love. They fuck, they screw, but they end up making love. They may be as good soldiers as the men, excellent as warriors, but our most wonderful skill is our lovemaking. One woman loves well, but two?

I struggled up and pushed my bra off. She gasped, almost wincing at the sight of my breasts. I suppose they did look good – they were still young and supple – but breasts are breasts, and hers weren't bad either.

I moved down her body, and her fingers fluttered at her sides. I could feel my wetness seeping through,

I was so turned on. Not by her looks, but by the way she looked. She was luscious and rich, and I wanted to explore everywhere.

She said that she wanted me to use a dildo. I found that in the wardrobe too: a pink cylinder and a fine, curly wire, attached to a small rectangular box for the batteries. I played with the switch, feeling the dildo vibrate in my hand.

She sat on the bed, her tubby legs hanging over the side, her skin reddening, and I loved her for her lack of inhibition, her lack of self-consciousness. She was bold and, because she was bold, she was beautiful. I opened her muff. Her entire body was a giant pleasure dome, a funfair with water slides, rides, and a haunted house.

I drove the thing inside her. I held her wet inner lips apart and saw how the vibrator shook against her coin-shaped clitoris. I had never seen anything like it. She didn't take her eyes off me as I salivated at the openness of her. And I didn't take my eyes off her. I wanted to go into it myself. I dug the thing inside her. It was wringing with her lotion. I got on top of her again: I couldn't hold back. I was pushing myself up and down her body, massaging my tits against hers, my tongue against hers, as I held on to the vibrator, making sure it gave her what she wanted. Like a man. And she held me tight, her hands now holding my arse, the line between arse and leg that she had long lost but still appreciated. She was sucking my face off me and, although my cunt was bare and she was the one who was full, I contrived to rub my clit against her as she shook. The vibrator up inside her made me move fast against her. My fingers were stroking her, certain now, and as her body jittered, mine jittered too. I managed to keep quiet about Wills by clamping my mouth to her cheek. I

146

don't know how long the little tooth marks engraved on her excess flesh stayed there.

I had come with no penetration! Look, Ma, no hands, I wanted to say.

Mrs Robinson was giggling quietly. She reached out one hand and left it heavy on my breast. I didn't like the possessive way she did it.

'Have you done that before? With a customer, a woman?' I asked. I felt the edge of contempt creep into my voice. Surely she felt humiliated by what we had done? How effortlessly she had succumbed, had allowed herself to be taken.

'Yes,' she said simply.

I noticed the hand on my breast had a gold band on it.

'Are you married?'

'Yes, why?'

'It doesn't count as infidelity, does it? It's just like friends,' I said feebly.

(You may have seen the advert. It's not one of my better ones, I'm afraid. We were back to that old chestnut, sex, again. The two women are sitting in a bed and, while picking a chocolate, one says to the other, 'It doesn't count as infidelity, does it?'

'Hmm, it's pretty close.')

She smiled up at me. She was so pretty when she smiled. She was voluptuous. No other word was good enough for her. I also felt sick and shaky. What was going on with me? I said I would never sleep with a married man! Didn't a married woman count? She looked sleepy. She put her arm around me, and I leaned back into her uneasily. She had folds of flesh in her stomach, and she exuded warmth.

'You remind me of how I was at your age. Don't waste your life feeling angry.'

'I'm not.'

'Whoever he is, he's not worth it.' I didn't like it, her way of talking about me, revealing me.

'What about you?' I asked crudely, turning the tables. 'Why don't you leave him?'

'Because I still love him.'

'Hmm,' I said moodily. I didn't get this love thing any more. I had loved Wills, and he had left. I could have loved Marcus, only it was ridiculous, and yet I had just made love very adequately to her. I couldn't say we just fucked, there was too much tenderness there. Although we were strangers, we knew each other.

'A few years ago, I left my job. But after I left it, everything felt strange, and you know, the thing I missed most were the holidays. They had lost their power for me: every day was a holiday, so the very thing was meaningless. Now that I'm married, it's the same thing: girls like you are my holiday.'

I lay on the bed and thought about it. She touched me, trailing a long finger up my forearm.

'Why don't you let me do something for you?'

'No, no, I don't think so.' I shut my legs and added girlishly, 'But I had a lovely time.' I almost said, 'Thank you for having me.'

'What's the matter?' she asked, ignoring my excuses.

'I don't want to.'

'There's nothing wrong in enjoying yourself.'

'No, thank you.'

'You don't want me to take control, do you? Why is that, honey?'

She had put her finger on it. I didn't want her to.

'I've worked so hard to try and be strong,' I said limply.

I had taken control of Marcus, the girl, and the two boys. I had dominated them all, taken from them what I wanted. I wouldn't let anyone do that to me. I had learned not to be weak ever again. I wasn't going to rely on anyone. I was just going to use them like he had used me. I wanted to make him love me, and I couldn't do that.

'I don't want to be weak ever again.'

'Hey, it's not a sign of weakness: submission is a sign of strength. Look, it has nothing to do with the you outside the bedroom. You can be the president of a company, and you can still like being tickled. In fact, the more powerful you are, the more you probably would want to be dominated – have someone else take the power.'

'I'm not a lesbian,' I said, although, after the things I had done to her, I was admittedly skating on thin ice.

'Labels,' she said. (For a moment I thought she had said 'labia'.)

'What?'

'Lesbian, gay, feminine, masculine. They are just words to put people in pigeonholes. Why shouldn't we enjoy ourselves?' she said. 'After all, we are both consenting adults.'

Consenting adults. The words rang uncomfortably. We were, but was Marcus? And the others? I wondered about the truth of what she said, and I could feel her looking at me patiently.

'You just made me feel fantastic. Let me do that for you.'

It was tempting to let her take the strain. I had been so active, so out of character, but I didn't want to revert back to my old passivity. On the other hand . . .

'You are so stressed, aren't you, baby?'

I nodded.

'Just lie down on your front.'

I did as I was told. Make them go away; make it all right. She had lotion on her hands. They smelled of vanilla.

'Think about what I'm doing to you.'

149

I did.

'No.' I tried to get up. She pushed me down. Rough yet loving. She hovered over me. Suddenly a blob of cold moisture landed on my back, and then another. She smoothed the wetness into me. She went up and down my back. Her hands slipped wetly, and I inhaled. I could feel each bone. She zigzagged along my spine, rubbing it hard. I could hear my stomach letting out a gurgle of digestion. I wriggled with embarrassment.

'You are so stressed. Let me take care of you, just like you did for me.'

She treated each muscle, each bone with the same intimate attention. I suppose part of my fear was comparison. We had the same kind of body: surely one of us would be superior. Maybe someone the same age as me would make me feel like that. But she was different. She was much older for a start.

Her hands played music on me, roaming my back, looking for tension to heal. I became more aroused. I wanted her hands to wander off the beaten track into somewhere more exotic.

'Do you like it?'

'Yes.'

Even if I wasn't, my arse was sticking up, pleading for it. Didn't she know that was why it was protruding there? The stroke of her arm went up and down my back, and then she worked on my shoulders. I neighed and moaned.

'Think about a beach, a tropical island: you are lying in the sand.'

I remembered my fantasy. I imagined how good the sun felt. The string bikini snapped up, sand in my knickers. The sun lotion was a puddle in our hands, in the pits of our arched backs.

I wanted her to go lower. I wanted her to reach my

arse. Marcus said my arse was beautiful. I wanted her to vote her confidence in me.

'Do I look beautiful?' I asked, little-girlishly.

'Do you feel beautiful?'

'Yes.'

'Well, that's the important thing, isn't it?'

The answer was unsatisfying but, in another way, it was enough. I did feel beautiful. I felt horny, ready. I wanted to get explicit.

Will was enthralled with the firmness of my arse. He liked me to wear tight clothes. Whenever I thought about going on a diet, he would pinch a cheek and say, 'Don't lose weight from here.' At night, we slept in spoons, and he would bury his penis in my arse.

Stop thinking about Wills.

Her hands were everywhere. She massaged the ticklish bit along my sides firmly. She had nurse's hands. They kneaded me confidently and unstoppably.

I wondered what Wills would say when I told him. (I mean, if I told him, if he found out). Like every man, he had a big fantasy about seeing two women together. And she was all woman. There was nothing hermaphrodite about her. All that sucking and sopping, all that wetness. Perhaps I should have done it once, to keep him happy. He wouldn't like to see me with her though, too messy, too abandoned I suppose.

Forget him.

I felt my body unwind, the tensions fading. I felt like a little girl again, when I could hand everything over to my mum. There was nothing to worry about. The adults could sort it all out. I was innocent in the tree house.

I felt her fingers move lower. She must know I wanted it there. Slowly her fingers moved round to the front. The room was silent, and I could hear her breathing and mine. I was louder than she was.

Her fingers were inside me. Rolling my hole, like a chef shaping sushi. I gasped as I felt their trajectory. Did I feel right to her? Was I the right shape? Men didn't know what was what and what was supposed to go where, but women did.

'Am I OK?' I whispered uncertainly.

She was kissing my back, small circular kisses, bites, tongues. A trail of saliva chilled my back. I could smell vanilla. She was using two hands inside me now. I felt faint. I wanted to put the pillow over my head.

She pulled open a curtain, revealing a full-length mirror with a gorgeous ornate frame. But it was what I saw in the mirror that was the most mind-boggling. I saw the sticky hole, my muff, like a flaming red planet.

She was kissing my bottom cheeks. I wondered how they looked to her. Her fingers knew exactly what they wanted: one was getting to know the size of my vagina, and the other was en route for my clitoris. She was climbing the stairway to heaven. I could feel the rest of me vanishing as my cunt began to take over my whole body, to colonise my sensations. Wills was in there. Wills had been there.

I was losing any sense of where I was or who I was with. All I could feel was the glory of being fondled. I opened my legs wider, and she spread my buttocks wide. I could feel that she was watching me, appreciating me. She played with my G-spot. As she teased it, I felt my clitoris flicker alive and ready. The puckered hole responded by sending out signals to the rest of me. I was nearly coming.

She had her lips here, her tongue peeping in there.

She pulled me over onto my back. She wanted greater access. I lay on my back, my arm over my pink face, my breasts exposed. My whole body was vulnerable to her, aching for her. Every orifice was open for her to pleasure. I started massaging myself. Stroking my breasts, at first tentatively, and then gripping them as my vagina was gripping around her tongue.

Her head was in my legs: the ostrich and the sand. Oh God, if only I could carry her around with me all day long. She was adorable, gorgeous. If I had resisted before, I had changed, broken through the pain barrier. Now I was going for it. She was far away inside me. All I could see of her was the crown of her head, the hair mingling with my hair. I was scared I was going to suffocate her, but she seemed to love it. I felt my breasts. I pummelled them. I lifted up my legs: they were bent at the knees, and my thighs had started trembling. I was open to anything.

'Look, Sally.'

She made me watch as she slid the dildo in.

She was rubbing the tops of my legs, where the tops of my legs turn into my pussy. Finding that small line of sensual separation. She was locked in there. I wouldn't let her go until she let me go. Then I heard the noise. A small electric contraption was humming towards me. It was the size of a chocolate bar, family size. It was black.

It hit the spot. Oh God.

'Oh God, Mrs Robinson,' I whispered.

I was massaging my clit against her fingers, wriggling up and down, responding. She was going faster. I could hear the sounds of wetness. She didn't even raise her head to take a breath; she was a deep-sea diver, a nonstop lover. I was wailing: the fingers, her whole hand was up inside me, and I felt my body spin into her. I was going to come like a firecracker, between her lips, her tongue, and her fingers. She was everywhere. Snuffling in me, pressing me, taking me:

I was stuffed like a Christmas turkey. Everything else was blotted out. Even the sight in the mirror took second place, a back seat. The whole world could have stopped turning; I had only one thought on my mind: my cunt, my clitoris, my feeling, me, me, me.

Then I felt myself relax.

She brushed the new tangles out of my hair. I watched myself in the mirror. I was shaky with embarrassment, pleasure, even rebellion.

She made green tea and served it in tiny porcelain glasses. I sipped at the unfamiliar taste. She said that it was good for me, but I wasn't sure. She said that her husband was a businessman, and that he travelled all over the world. She sometimes went with him, but she preferred staying at home and working. She loved her job, because people came to her with their problems.

I came back to the old question. I guess I just couldn't get my head around her answer.

'But how can you stay with him? If you don't love him?'

'He's not a bad guy, but he's just fifteen – no, maybe twenty per cent of my life. I have other things going on.'

'I can't think like that, not about my partner.'

'Perhaps if you had other things going on in your life, then whatever happened to you wouldn't have hurt so much. Perhaps you wouldn't have been so angry.'

I wanted to confide in her. Not just about Wills, but about everything. But how could I? I thought she would be disgusted. She was so refined, so aromatic: wouldn't she be disgusted if she found out?

She came to the front door to see me out.

'This is for you,' she said as I was leaving, handing me the dildo. She must have rushed off to wash it

154

while I was lacing up my shoes. We kissed each other on both cheeks. Now for the first time she seemed shy, vulnerable in a way she hadn't even seemed when I was whipping her like a horse.

'Occasionally, when you use it, think of me,' she said quietly.

I promised I would, but even then I knew I had moved on. She had helped me move on. The anger dissipated. I was left with a hum of contentment, self-awareness, and although it started to disperse the next morning, and had almost disappeared by the end of the week, I would always remember that moment.

Chapter Fifteen

I woke up suddenly out of a hot, foglike sleep. Someone was in my bed. It was about a week after my meeting with the hairdresser, and I was naked, sprawled over the covers. I hadn't heard anyone arrive.

'How the hell did you get in?'

'Through the window around the back.'

'How long have you been here?'

'Most of the night,' Marcus said and rolled towards me. 'I was watching you sleep. You looked so beautiful.'

I couldn't believe his cheek. He had taken his shoes off, but other than that he was fully dressed in jeans and a T-shirt.

My bed was a double; I bought it with Will in mind, about five months after we met. I got the bed to convince him to stay with me sometimes. It worked. Compared with his aesthetic futon, my bed was luxury. It wasn't a four-poster, but it was pretty close. I must have spent most of my wages on it. You should have seen my mother's face when she saw it!

I snuggled down under the duvet, feeling relieved

and cheerful; it was nice to have someone in there with me again. I noticed that the bed already smelled different.

It was 6 a.m. I had an hour and a half until the alarm would send me off to work.

Marcus kissed me. I held the back of his head, fingered his hair, and kissed him warmly back.

I shouldn't have. It was exploitative and cruel, but I couldn't stop.

Sometimes I woke up in the morning expecting Will to be there, sometimes I forgot. I still met people and had to explain to them that it was over. They asked me what I had done at the weekend, and I had to lie to everyone. I was living a lie. I still had pictures in my mind of him and some woman, some woman who he had transferred everything to. Mostly I had been thinking of Marcus, his fine muscles, his dark skin, the shadows under his eyes, but sometimes those thoughts led me to Finnegan. I tried not to let them, but it was as if I was doing a puzzle, and all the routes led nowhere, except one that was leading to him.

I touched Marcus's velvet skin, his soft, downy cheek. He was so sensuous and feline.

'Where were you?' I asked.

'When?' he asked, puzzled.

'I came to look for you, outside the college, but you weren't there.'

'I was sick,' he said, 'for a week. I couldn't stop thinking about you.'

He moved closer; he buried his face in my breasts, and I felt his cock twitch against my thigh

'We mustn't have sex,' I whispered, biting his ear. The lobe trembled between my teeth. I breathed out into his provocative little ear hole and licked my way around the edge. What fun it was to make the rules and then find a way around them.

We were fumbling, but that was because we were so desperate. It was somehow sweet and holy. I liked that he was fully dressed. I rubbed my nudity around him. It made me feel like an animal, or Lady Chatterley. Here was I gagging for it, and he was still fully dressed.

'Your tits are so wonderful,' he whispered, stroking them.

He was obsessed with my breasts, but then other men have worse hobbies. He didn't mind that I had swollen to a size twelve; he loved it. I cradled him in my arms, and he sucked and sucked at me gratefully. It felt tremendous. I pulled his T-shirt up his back, and he rose to take it off. It got stuck over his head, and we laughed. When he finally removed it, I felt as though I had missed him. I pulled him tighter to me. I clawed his smooth back; I scratched him till he shivered. I was never going to let him go. I was drifting off into another world, but it wasn't sleep, although it was a kind of unconsciousness. I was sleep fucking.

'Oh, yes, yes.'

'You're so . . .' he murmured, but he didn't continue.

I stopped kissing his nipple and said, 'So?'

'So incredible,' he sighed. I went back to my task of chewing his pink buds. He had such a beautiful abdomen, flat as a playing field. I tongued down his stomach, pushing lower and lower, then felt a shock.

'What the hell have you done?' I squealed, as I met his hip with my mouth.

Marcus had had a tattoo. It was a dirty great letter, a black gothic S, surrounded by the inevitable red, ravaged skin of the newly tortured.

'I did it yesterday,' he said proudly.

'What's it for?' I asked. Sex, socializing, swinging, sucking?

'S. It's for you. Sally.'

Fortunately he hadn't gone the whole hog or I think he would have regretted it big time. Chances were that he would date another S one day. Sharon most definitely wouldn't fancy him, but there was a whole world of Samanthas, Sabrinas, Sues and Saffrons to contemplate. (I thought it was fortunate that my name was not Zelda or Zoë.) The idea that he had done that for me was lyrical, poetic. I kissed him over and over again, soft dandelion-fluff kisses. He sighed and stroked my newly cropped hair, saying my name repeatedly. He loved my new look; he said, he loved everything about me.

Will could go fuck his romantic pretensions. Marcus made all Will's gestures seem lily-livered and contrived. I drew down his jeans and thumbed down his pants. I pored over Marcus's rigid penis and examined it with treacherous intent. His arse was smooth and peachy-rounded. His thighs were huge, solid cylinders. Then I sank back into the mattress, pulling him on top of me. I was floating in a world between sleep and wakefulness, lust and love, boy and man. I wanted our last fuck, our last time together, to be a chunk of him for all his life. I wanted us to make a good memory for ever. I didn't want his overriding image of me to be as the woman he jerked off in a café. It was my duty as a woman, as an older woman, to send him off with the right impression.

What am I saying? I didn't think; I couldn't calculate. It was a morning fuck. There was no analysis, no sense, only the wonderful continuation of a dream. Sex has different qualities at different times of day. And in the morning it requires so little effort, and the rewards are so much pleasure.

We were lovely together. You can keep your Mongolian circus acrobats; you can keep your Salvador Dali imaginations. In bed, in lovemaking, there is only

159

one quality that makes the difference: sensitivity. I had thought it was a crime to be sensitive. I was told it was wrong to feel deeply what other people feel. But now I knew where it counted to be sensitive. Whatever the adverts tell us, neither cars, nor aftershave, nor glossy hair make a difference in bed. Neither body nor mind is important. The place sex belongs is in the heart. Marcus had the perfect heart, and I felt it work its magic on me. I felt the gentle roughness of his thrust and the responsive swell of my sex. He was a bloody hypnotist, only his pendulum didn't send me to sleep.

His lips were cascading all over me. Our gentle fumbling grew more and more frantic. We smiled knowingly at each other as we gave each other pleasure with our hands. I wasn't afraid to meet his eyes.

'Do it to me,' I ordered him. He responded by filling me up deeper and harder; he worked his way in and out quickly.

'I love you,' he murmured in my ear. The tip of his shaft blessed me simultaneously. My legs were behind his back; each thrust pushed them wide and pulled my sex wide open.

'More, fuck me, more,' I replied,

'I love you so much.' He said it over and over again as he drew in and out of the tightness of my sweet love nest.

'Harder, harder,' I insisted, clutching him tight.

'I love you.'

'Now, deeper, now.' I didn't know what I was saying. I felt like we really had become one. My body should not ever be alone again. It should always be like this, should always be linked up, mating, copulating, fucking. That's what I was made for. He pressed his body against me, gliding across me, surfing over me. I could feel a roar of enjoyment rising inside me, of pleasure, of love or passion. We held each other tighter. I was back with Will. Every moment of my life was with me, massing and imploding. My body felt like a great ball of pleasure. I was losing my memories, my mind. I looked at Marcus's face; his eyes were so tender, there for me. I felt like I had on the hotel balcony. When I looked at his face again, I saw that he was weeping too.

'I love you,' he murmured. He speeded up his strokes, and I felt my snatch clench around him, triggering helplessly around his dick.

'Willcus.'

His kisses blocked out my words and, as his lips squeezed against mine, I felt his penis swell and explode, his come mingling with mine for ever. He shuddered, his shoulders contracting and his arse tight in my hand.

'I'm sorry, Marcus,' I said resolutely. We curled up in each other like Gemini twins. 'We really and truly mustn't see each other again.'

The alarm went, and it was time for work.

Chapter Sixteen

'You look different,' Ms Feather said, as though I had arrived to work now resembling the Elephant woman. 'You've changed something.'

'She's cut off all her hair,' offered Mr Finnegan brightly.

'Oh, what a shame,' Ms Feather intoned. 'Your hair made you look pretty somehow.' She was a mistress of the double-edged compliment.

'We can see your face now,' Finnegan added ambivalently. I didn't know if that was good or bad.

I walked over to my desk, seething. Since Sharon had stopped working, I had no one to send my e-mails full of complaints to. I had no one to tell what a hideous company I worked at. I sat down and said a cool 'Hi' to my colleagues, who were all busily e-mailing their friends.

'Are you going to tell her, or shall I?' said Ms Feather loudly.

I felt myself pale. Maybe they had found out? One year more of this, no, maybe just six months, and I could get a good job, but if I had to go now I wouldn't get anything. I needed this experience under my belt, on my CV. I needed to collect an impressive portfolio. Temping just wasn't very tempting.

'You don't want to use the chocolate campaign?' I asked nervously.

'No, we are using yours, of course,' she said. 'It wiped the floor: all the others are rubbish.'

I waited.

'No, we have just got loads of new stuff to work on: shoe polish, candles and the solicitors, of course, and Duncan has insisted that you are the one who decides on the strategy.'

Ms Feather walked off, composed as ever. She was a good communicator, a good media figure, but – if the rumours were to be believed – Duncan despised her methods and manner. I hoped he hadn't turned this into a fight between us, because there was absolutely no way I would take her on as an opponent. She scared me.

Finnegan civilly shook my hand. It was the first time he had done that, and I was surprised he didn't hold on for too long. I had him down as a sweaty gripper. I wondered if he was aggrieved.

'Well done, Sally,' he said quietly. 'You've worked very hard.'

Finnegan was one of the most well-respected fig-ures in the advertising world. He could have moved on from our company: he could have gone on to greater things. We all wondered why he stayed, but it appeared that he was fiercely loyal to Duncan. Finnegan had rejected the advances of head-hunters on more than one occasion because he was faithful to the old man. I knew my promotion was no threat to him, but I was concerned that he wasn't happy with it. I saw him looking at me all day long. He smoothed back his hair and loosened his collar.

* * *

As I left that evening, Finnegan said something very strange.

'Sally, I hope you don't mind me saying this, but, by what means did you obtain those fantastic ideas?'

'What do you mean?'

I felt him stare at me long and hard. I knew he knew something. I felt an icy tremor of fear come across me. I couldn't trust anyone. Consenting fucking adults. They all were, but only just. And anyway, once the first rumour bitched out the office, who was going to believe me then?

For the next few days, I felt as though a black cloud was hanging over me. Despite my company's expression of confidence in me, I was scared to believe it. I had a strong feeling that the cards were all going to come down soon. When Will finished with me, it was totally unexpected. When, years ago, there was a fire at the railway station, I had no idea that something was going to happen, although everyone afterwards had said they had felt something was brewing. It was as if there was electricity in the air, a crackling kind of intuition. For the first time in my life, I knew with absolute certainty that I was heading for a terrible storm.

I thought with shame of those boys. How could I have done that? What would my mother do if she found out? I wondered about Marcus. Would he ever forgive me for leaving him?

A couple of evenings later, Ms Feather, little rucksack bag swinging on her shoulder, went down to the gym. I suppose she was what Will would have called 'a finely cut piece of lean beef'. When she caught me eyeing her trim frame, she looked back at me, smirking.

'Maybe you should work out a little bit, Sally. You

know you won't be able to find another boyfriend if you don't look after yourself.'

Finnegan, on the way over with a pile of papers, interrupted, 'I'm sure Sally doesn't have any such problem.'

He dropped the papers on my desk and smiled at me. I couldn't meet his eyes. I had a terrible intuition then that he knew. Why else would he say such a thing?

The dormant Catholic in me was clamouring to be voiced. I had behaved terribly. I deserved to get in big trouble. Something was wrong and pendulous in the air, a storm brewing. I don't know exactly what it was, but I knew I had to be punished in some way. I felt that I had been rude, I had gone too far, and what goes around comes around. Of course, I know now that there is no such thing as luck. Scrape the surface of a so-called lucky person, and you find the same woes and travails as the rest of us. Perhaps the only lucky thing is to be born with a sunny disposition that deceives everyone into thinking you are lucky. After that, all luck is self-made, a question of how we respond to the shit as it is chucked down the well.

I missed Marcus too. I thought about his enthusiasm, his beauty. I never saw anyone sleep like that. He slept so peacefully, I almost thought he was dead. I knew I slept fretfully.

I dream that I am getting married. I wear the wedding gown of little girls' fantasies. It has white bustles and creamy fluffs. I have a cleavage like an old-fashioned orange seller, and the skirt cascades out wide from my waist. As I walk up the aisle, not only do my guests all stand, but my male guests all stand to attention. Oh, I see that they try to hide it: it's not right to be erect at a mate's wedding, at the bride-to-be, but they can't help it all the same. One hundred penises salute me.

When I arrive at the altar, even the vicar blanches at my ivory bosom. My husband-to-be innocently holds out his hand. There is a peculiar rustling inside my gown. Marcus is in there, secreted in my wedding dress. He kisses my ankle chain (something borrowed), he pulls at my garter (something old) and lets it bounce against my leg. Then he broaches something new – my knickers – and eases them down. He proceeds to do something very blue: he opens my about-to-be married sex and starts to lick me. We solemnly make our vows but, as my husband says my name, I feel my clitoris swell, and I find it hard to speak.

'Take thee, yes, oh, yes, to be my lawful, mmm, wedded husband.'

I see that the vicar has his hands down his trousers. I know that his religious testicles are tightening. Marcus soaks my fanny; he makes long strokes as the church organ plays on. I am wearing a white veil, and my face is hidden from view.

'I do, I do, I do.'

'You may kiss the bride,' sighs the vicar enviously. My groom leans towards me; his tongue quivers in my mouth, and Marcus's tongue bristles in my inner lips.

'Oh yes.' Suddenly I am coming. I surge forwards into my groom's arms, and he holds me tight as I buck against him, completely unaware of the source, or even the force of my passion.

But I can't make out who the groom is any more, only I don't think it was Will. It was just as Sharon predicted. There were other men. I would eventually banish Will from my head. So that just left the big one, number three; everyone gets what's coming to them. I was frightened of what my punishment would be. I knew I had penance coming to me, I knew it. My just fucking desserts. I just didn't know what, how, or when.

Chapter Seventeen

*I*t was just Finnegan and me in the office, eight o'clock on a Wednesday evening, two weeks later. The others had disappeared. We were supposed to be working on the shoe-polish campaign, when he had asked me to come over to his desk. I had assumed he had a proposal or diagrams to show me but, when I got there, instead of asking for my ideas, he had pushed me against the wall. My head was against the surface, and my arm pressed behind my back. For a moment, I was too stunned to respond, waiting for what was going to happen.

'Don't or I'll scream,' I warned him.

Then I felt it: his other hand landed plump on my butt and roamed around, feeling its way along the elastic of my knickers.

'I'll scream,' I repeated. The wall was cold against my cheek, and there was a slight crack down it, in the shape of an X. Subsidence, I thought, and almost giggled. How could I be thinking about subsidence at a time like this? The hand on my bottom pinched me and bruised me. My trousers were much too tight.

'Sally, baby, don't you like it with real men?'

I froze. My punishment, the storm, had come. He had found out. Somehow, he had found out about the boys. This wasn't funny. This was serious. Visions of me on the dole in unflattering blue floated across my mind. My mother visiting me with food parcels.

Mr Finnegan carried on uninvited; one hand held my arm in place so I couldn't struggle, while the other one went walkabout, gliding up and down the back of my trousers and then under. I wondered if, through them, he could tell how wet I was. Surely not? They may have been too tight, but these trousers cost eighty quid.

'What the hell are you doing?' I hissed. The scream threats didn't seem to be working. It was time to engage in a good old-fashioned row.

There was no mistaking what he was doing. He pulled the hand that was holding me away: he had obviously decided I wasn't going to resist too much. Then he leaned against me, pushing me up the wall with all his weight. I could feel something pressing against me: it felt like a goddamn elephant's trunk, and it was hard and insistent, trying to get in. One of his fingers was tracing the line between my cheeks. Another was trying very effectively to finger me through my trousers. The material was disappearing up me. My trousers would be ruined. I was almost orgasmic. No one had touched me there since that morning with Marcus.

'You've got quite an appetite, I heard, Sally, but is it only for defenceless teenagers?'

'What the hell are you talking about?' I said and forced my way round towards him. He was much taller than I was, and I was left facing his white neck, replete with bulging Adam's apple. The trunk in his trousers was now gnawing at my zipper at the front. It felt good. I wondered how it would be to kiss his neck, to bite his apple really hard; I would probably get thrown out of the garden of Eden. He had his face close to mine. He was repulsive, but nevertheless I wanted him to keep going. I wanted him to screw his fingers into me and let me come without moving, without consenting, in his arms. I wanted to orgasm blamelessly, free from responsibility. Let someone else take over.

He looked down at me and tried to kiss me; I dodged my head to the side. He was good-looking but ugly at the same time, disgusting yet alluring. But I didn't want to give him the satisfaction of knowing that I found him horny.

'Sally, I want to fuck you now.'

His fingers had pushed their way up into my pussy. Despite the protection of my straining trousers, he was spreading my inner lips wide. I remember thinking that I hadn't shaved my bikini line or my legs that weekend. And there was no way that I was going to remove my trousers.

'This is rape,' I hissed.

'Is it?' He smiled, so arrogant, so sure of himself. So sure that I liked it.

I wanted to spit at him. I didn't want him, the arrogant sod. I opened my mouth and began to scream as loud as I could. He clamped his hand over my mouth and then dropped me. He left me there, dangling from the wall like a rag doll.

'There's a big difference, little girl!'

He picked up a bit of pizza that someone had left over and ate a bite. Then he spat it back into the box. He stalked out of the office, and I was still standing there like an idiot, trying to unmuss my hair.

Sharon proposed that we went out shopping for her baby clothes. She said I had been subdued recently. And she said that I wasn't to worry: there was plenty of time to meet someone.

'I'm not looking, really,' I said in the restaurant and, for the first time, I felt it was true. 'You know, being single, I'm finding out more and more about myself.'

Sharon studied me, then said, 'You're thinking about Wills again, aren't you?'

'Well . . .' I started.

'Forget him,' she said, sitting back, tired. 'You said yourself he was a lousy lay.'

I smiled lamely. It was true: all those times I had complained about Wills. 'Wills doesn't fancy me,' 'Wills was too drunk, stoned, tired, pissed off (delete as appropriate) to make love to me.' She had to listen to all that. But that's what friends are for. It was in her job description, and anyway, I had to listen to her: I even had to listen to her baby, holding my head against her stomach. Her child. Oh God, I had to forget about Marcus. My friends were becoming parents, and I had fallen for a seventeen year old. Something was definitely very wrong there.

'Haven't you met anyone else even remotely tolerable?' she said. Sharon keeps her standards nice and low. All she asks for is someone who doesn't make her nauseous, although, in her current state, I think there isn't a man alive who wouldn't make her sick. This is pregnancy before the bloom. Still, Hugh likes her pregnant. Takes all sorts.

I couldn't stop thinking about him. When I replayed my memory, though, I had Mr Finnegan slamming me up against the wall, removing my trousers, but this time it was Marcus who came forwards, who explored my arse and pussy, who rubbed himself against me. Mr Finnegan was just a voice, a face in the background, telling us what we had to do.

I told her about Mr Finnegan but, as soon as I had spilled the words, I wished I hadn't.

171

'He pinned you against the wall!' she repeated incredulously, chewing into her fish.

'Yes, but, you know . . .' My voice trailed off weakly. Sharon wouldn't drink, so I was getting drunk on my own, which was about as much fun as masturbating at an orgy.

Sharon said that if any man treated her like that she would castrate them. We agreed he was disgusting and as low as you can go.

It wasn't until dessert that she dared to refer to him again.

'You are not going to sleep with him, are you Sally?' I guess she knew me quite well. I tucked into my chocolate-coated calories: I was having cravings in sympathy with her.

'Of course not,' I said, as convincingly as I could. It was all right for her, she had a bun in the oven, and her sexual career was on hold for the next couple of years. What about me? What if someone found out I had been sucking the blood of young men?

'He's your boss, and he's married,' she said, the voice of wisdom. But I think she would prefer that I was screwing him than St Matthew's lads. What would she say if she found out? Water is thicker than blood when it comes to Sharon, but even so, some crimes are thicker than water. I knew she could be tremendously moral. I could imagine her snatching her baby, my godson or daughter, away from me, pretending I was some great monster, a danger to children, when it was clearly nothing like that. The thought made me sick.

'I don't think he is any more,' I protested lamely. 'He said he was separated.' But then Finnegan was secretive. Even his first name was highly classified information.

'They all say that,' she said wearily, and I wondered

172

if she was thinking of her baker, from long ago. 'And he's got children!'

'A child,' I said stubbornly. 'Almost grown up.'

'So that makes everything all right?' I was surprised at her prissy tone.

'There are other factors,' I insisted. 'I might have to.'

'Have to!' she spluttered. 'Why on earth would you have to sleep with your boss?'

Deep down I think I knew that, although Mr Finnegan was a complete bastard, he wouldn't snitch on me to the firm. Still, people do surprising things. I should know that by now. The thing was, I didn't know if I was being blackmailed or not. In fact, I quite liked the idea of being blackmailed. It meant I wasn't willing, it wasn't my fault: I just had to do it. And to tell myself the truth, which I wasn't going to do, just yet, I was thrilled about it. I wanted to fuck him, be fucked by him. I hated him so much that I had no doubt that it would be exciting.

The next day, I decided to e-mail him. I didn't know what to write. How could I say, 'I give up', without saying yes, without giving him permission? What if he had changed his mind? How could I ask him, without looking as if I was interested? I didn't have to.

There was a message from him that said, 'Tonight?' I typed back 'Maybe.'

A few minutes later, I got one that said simply, 'Seven o'clock?' and I decided I wouldn't return anything to that. It was more mysterious. He couldn't be sure whether I would turn up. I wasn't sure either.

I felt that the cloud was lifting. I was sure that my punishment was coming, but I suspected it was going to be far more enjoyable than I had anticipated.

It was hell in the office that morning. It was warm outside, and our air conditioning wasn't working. We

173

all hated each other. Ms Penny Feather hadn't arrived yet and, for some reason, everyone seemed to be waiting for her return in terror.

Whenever I glanced over at his desk, Mr Finnegan was frowning into his computer screen or at his papers. Maybe he was worrying about candles or shoe polish. We had so many people coming to us asking us to advertise their products that it was difficult to keep everything under control. When he ate, stuffing sandwiches into his mouth, I noticed his lips were gross and greasy. I had to resist the urge to punch him in the mouth, the arrogant pig. He was talking to the rest of the staff, giving them memos, chatting too, close by the filing cabinets, but he didn't say anything to me except one time when he caught me staring.

'Beavering away, are you, Sally?'

I gave him a sarcastic look. I desperately wanted a response to my nonresponse, something more solid than that. I imagined him slamming me up against the wall again. This time going all the way, fucking me from behind or maybe against the window, so I could stare at the people below and give them a wave. Or maybe up against the window in front of the window cleaner, and he could get out his dick and slam it against the glass.

When I had got back from Sharon's last night, I had shaved my legs and lain in the bath listening to Will's voice again, but this time it was a blur of images. Pure nostalgia or comfort, that was all. I lay in the bath and tried to focus. I thought about Will's voice caressing me, Mr Finnegan's hands moulding my arse and Marcus's penis poking inside me, but the bath water went cold, and I felt uncomfortable. I went to my living room in my dressing gown and tried to masturbate in front of the TV. But nothing was working: the TV was fuzzy, and I couldn't bring myself off.

Now I was soaking through my knickers. I was just crying out to be left on my own. It must have been my horny time of the month. I had to masturbate. I had to orgasm, and I had to do it before tonight. Otherwise I was going to be a walkover; I was going to come as soon as he touched me. I didn't want to give him the satisfaction. He was going to have to work to please me. I had a big lunch, because I figured that there would be lots of energy burned up in the evening, and then, as soon as I ate, I felt fat. He couldn't really want to do it with me, could he?

I got my chance later. Half the office was taking a cigarette break, and the other half was preparing the schedule for filming my fabulous idea.

I dived underground. I slipped my fingers down the front of my skirt. Of course, I was wearing a skirt: after yesterday's debacle, I wasn't going to wear trousers to the office ever again. I was barelegged; I've never got on with suspenders. My finger roamed around, opening my knickers. My finger was always a delight, always a friend, always my best friend. It did whatever it wanted. Each time it felt familiar, but delicious, exciting, especially in semipublic. If only Will knew the things I could get up to. He would never have left me.

I remembered the first time I let a boy put his hand up there, on the green at the back of the youth centre. I was quite late for fingering: most of the other girls in my group had allowed that holy temple to be penetrated in the second year, and I was desperate to get it over with. Passion didn't come into it. If, as I had heard happened quite often, some spaceships had landed on my back lawn, and little green men had emerged and chosen to fiddle with my genitalia, then I would have been quite happy. I wouldn't go any further than that, though. Not until someone else did. I remember the boy was quite surprised, maybe horrified, that his way wasn't blocked by the usual series of road works, but he clearly had even less of an idea about what to do than I did. (To give him some credit, he was a nice kisser; he was no Marcus, but a nice one.) Once his finger was enclosed in my pants, like a trapped gerbil, he took it upon himself to simulate a penis, a particularly vicious one at that, and I remember feeling nothing but awkwardness and relief that I had finally got that one out of the way. Been there, done that, been fingered. For him it must have been like playing that game where you put your hand in a box and have to have a good feel around and guess what it is. Baked beans? Or spaghetti? Or Sally's vadge?

Back in the office, I wriggled into my fingers, and my fingers wriggled back into me. No one knew better than I did how my pussy liked it. The weeks since Will had left me had seen me practising the art of self-abuse like nobody's business. By rights, I should have gone blind. I buried my head into a book so no one could see my pinkening face. My hand was up, pushing apart the curly hairs, slipping inside my own welcoming wetness. I got my body right under the desk; they had those low backs. I had never dared to do it before, but now I closed my eyes and pictured Marcus on top of me. In my mind he was driving hard into me, crying with relief, 'Sally, I thought you had left me. I love you, I love you, and actually I'm 36.'

And then I saw Wills was trying to touch me. He was hungry at my tits, and I said, 'No, Wills, I don't love you any more.' My insides contracted around my fingers, and I could feel my creamy wetness gush freely, making the way for my fingers to stroke away.

I was building up to a nice seesawing motion when someone tapped me on the shoulder. Leanne was standing over me. I was hot, hot by then: I didn't know if I could stop it. I fantasised that she was cupping my breasts, licking them, squeezing them. I imagined her jumping down in front of me so that I could nuzzle her pussy.

'Oh, I'm sorry to disturb you,' she said; she blushed a pretty rose colour and backed away. I tried to pretend I was doing my vaginal clench exercises – you know, to stop you peeing when you sneeze or skip – but I think she may have seen. I would have to wait until the evening, and Mr Finnegan would do it for me.

'Ms Feather has called an urgent meeting. We have to go over there now, well, when you are ready.'

She had eyes like a frightened deer. Leanne was engaged to Wayne, who she met when she was sixteen. Poor dear, she was worse than I was with Will. I looked over to the other side of the room; they were all there, all twenty or so members of staff, and they were all staring back at me sat around this big round table like guests at a feast. That's the big trouble with open-plan offices. What happened to the days when you could get some peace and quiet? I wondered how many of them had guessed what I was doing.

I pulled down my skirt, grabbed a notebook and walked over. They were all waiting for me. They were tapping their desks with chewed pens, smoothing their hair, flossing their teeth with their fingernails.

'So sorry to disturb your nap, Sally,' said Finnegan, smirking.

'That's quite all right,' I said, trying to regain some professionalism. 'I was meditating.'

I wished there were some kind of make up you could wear to make your face disappear.

'It isn't all right,' screamed Ms Penny Feather, the headless chicken striding around in front of us. 'Just what is going on with you all?' she shouted. 'This company is near collapse, she is sleeping, and the rest of you are sitting around like morons.'

All her good manners and self-control had disappeared. She was raw hysteria in front of us. Usually she and Mr Finnegan alternated: when she was angry, he would be saccharine, and when he was angry, she would be the calming tonic. Today was her turn. I wondered what the hell it was about. We all had work to do.

Mr Finnegan intercepted.

'What is it, Ms Feather? Perhaps if you explained the problem?'

'I have never ever been so humiliated in my life,' she continued. The legendary temper showed no sign of abating. In a way, I was jealous of her. I had never been allowed to have temper tantrums like that. My parents wouldn't have known what to do with me. All excess emotion was frowned upon and tidied away into the bread bin. All demands and hysterics were inconsiderate and impolite. Especially as the oldest child, I had to learn very quickly how to share. I had no doubts at all that Ms Feather was the youngest child and was used to getting people to listen to her. We were all agog.

'When I went to one of the schools on a "yoof mission" –' she was shaking with rage '– three boys attacked me. I managed to get them off me but –'

We all went very quiet. My brain felt like it had just been scrambled.

'That wasn't the worst thing. The worst thing was that they said, and I quote, "We thought that was why the advertising agency came here, to teach us all how to fuck".'

There was a heavy silence. I don't know how much time passed, but when the phone rang on her desk and she stormed over there, it was a huge relief. I felt sorry for the person on the other end of the line. The rest of the staff were in uproar. I sat as still as I could, believing that if I didn't look at anyone, then no one would look at me.

I could feel something rubbing me on my leg. It was Mr Finnegan's leg. I put my coat over me so no one could see. I couldn't believe it, not now, not with all the trouble I was in. The foot stayed.

Everyone was buzzing about it, trying to work it out.

'Which college was it?'

'St Matthew's,' someone said.

Finnegan's foot reached up higher to rest on my thighs. I still couldn't believe it. Then he wrote something on his notebook, and I thought he was going to contribute something to the debate, but he didn't. He just flashed it at me, Open your legs. I shook my head. No. He scribbled something again. I wondered what it would be, something like, Or I'll go to the police, I expected. He flipped it towards me, and it just said Wide, with lots of exclamation marks. I couldn't help it. I opened my legs wider, moved my knickers to the side, and felt with utter shock how cleanly he plunged forwards. He must have had extraordinary leg muscles, because it was perfect. He positioned himself over my clit and very gently began to stir me. Without doubt, he must have done it before. I put my finger down there to join him. I looked into my book; I could hear the meeting going on around me. I couldn't help thinking, this is me, Sally, the office mouse, and now the boss is rubbing my clitoris in front of all the staff. I would never have dreamed this could happen, even one week ago.

'Well, who here went to St Matthew's?'

'Don't be silly: none of us.'

'What did the girl look like?'

'Just a normal woman apparently,' another said.

'Quite pretty, midthirties, big knockers, big arse, apparently.'

'Oh, that helps narrow down the field,' one of them said facetiously.

'Lucky boys,' said Mr Finnegan, his sole contribution to the debate so far.

I started to lose control, with my other hand on the side of the chair; I let go, with my hand, my breathing a little fast, shuddering inside me. Ms Feather came back. I don't know what had happened on the phone, but she looked even angrier. Her eyes were narrow slits, and her fists were clenched. I don't know why, but, for once, I wasn't frightened to see her like that. It was actually quite horny. I imagined pushing her down on the desk in front of all these people, and pulling up her skirt, spanking her stupid well-exercised arse, and entering her, first with my hands and then with my mouth. I imagined throwing Mr Finnegan down and then sitting on his face, squashing him with my cunt, silencing him with my flood, shaking up the office. I imagined her screaming, and everyone cheering at me to poke her as hard as I could. I imagined her face shaking with orgasm and anger and shame. And Mr Finnegan shaking underneath me, working for his life, for his job, at my wetness. I stared unseeingly into my book; my fingers were working me efficiently. I was going to come in the middle of a meeting. I could lose my job.

He was speaking.

'I know the headmaster of St Matthew's very well,' he said smoothly, 'and I'm sure, Ms Feather, that you are worrying unduly. This is a storm in a teacup.'

There was a storm inside my teacup. His toes were attached to my clit, trembling there, and my fingers were sliding up and down, reinforcing him, making sure he did his duty. He had started it; he could bloody well finish it. I was at the point of no return.

No going back. One of my fingers went right up inside. He was massaging me with the soft sole of his foot; my fucking boss was fucking me with his toes! I came quickly and quietly, but the chair started to shudder, thumping its rubber paws on the floor. I jolted two or three times more, but I recovered fast. It's amazing the energy an orgasm brings. My mind felt focused and my body awake. I could feel my skin was hot, and I wanted to cool down. He withdrew his foot and slipped it back into his shoe. I felt a shudder of revulsion, but then, I told myself, maybe I had no choice.

'Is there anything we can do? Has anyone said the name of the agency?' I enquired innocently.

'I just want you all to know that I'm very angry,' she said, ignoring me as usual and making me feel like the office pipsqueak. She turned on her heels and went back over to her desk. She sat on her twirling chair, the lady of the manor, and put lipstick on in the mirror that covered the entire wall behind her. I think there was a collective sigh of 'bitch' when she left.

Mr Finnegan finished the meeting smoothly.

'OK, everyone, get back to what you were doing. Not you, Sally, you've had enough, erm, relaxation for one morning,' he said, having a good joke at my expense.

What a jerk, I thought. I wondered fearfully whether that meant tonight was off.

As I worked through the afternoon, I alternated between fury and lust. How dare he put me at such risk? How dare I put myself at such a risk?

I left the building at six and went to get a drink in the café. I took a seat and noticed there was a man at a table by a window. He was sitting with a pretty, blonde girl, but I felt he was looking at me strangely, or at least curiously. When I went to the bathroom to stare in the mirror, I could see why: I looked a sight. My nipples were sticking out like bullets – ah, the power of the imagination – and my cheeks were flushed like I had been drinking. My lips, usually rather thin and mean, were blown up and bright red. I was turned on. I tried to calm down drinking my cappuccino, but I couldn't. I was looking forward to the evening but only as a rather perfunctory exercise. I wanted to get it over with as soon as possible. I wanted to relieve the tension in my body again; I wanted to have the mother of orgasms, but I didn't want to mess around getting it. I really did want to come and go. I didn't have any interest in Mr Finnegan. I didn't fancy him like I did my sweet Marcus. The evening looked to be only marginally more entertaining than a self-indulgent bubble bath listening to Wills.

I picked up a newspaper and saw that there was another article about us, along with the obligatory photo of the glamorous Ms Feather. We were applauded both for our subtlety and for our universal appeal. One executive said that we managed to appeal to everyone without alienating anyone. 'From teenage boys to middle-aged women, is there no stopping them?' I put the paper down. One area we hadn't yet pursued was middle-aged men.

The handsome guy who had been staring winked at me, while his girlfriend wound her way up to the bar. She was six feet tall and skinny, like a supermodel. I shrugged back, and he smiled. It was that knowing, duplicitous smile that strangers share when they are attracted to each other. It shocked me, though. Once upon a time there would be no way I would make eyes at a guy with a girlfriend like that. Now I knew better. Looks, height, skinniness had nothing to do with it. He would have slept with me if he could have. He knew I could fuck. He had this supermodel with him that he could sleep with, and yet he still wanted to try out little old me! Something had changed. Something inside me had grown, and that was all thanks to Marcus and the St Matthew's kids, although what the little bastards were saying now could lose me my job and my reputation. Well my job, anyway; I didn't have much of a reputation to lose.

The doorman looked at me curiously when I tried to rush past him through the rotating doors.

'Hello again,' he said. He smiled, fiddling with his pen. He had long, black hands, and he wore a small, gold signet ring.

'I seem to have forgotten something,' I gushed. I didn't really need to make excuses, but the guilty always do. It was a corny reason, I know, but I couldn't very well say, 'I'm going back for a shag,' could I? I was already throbbing with anticipation. I may have talked down Mr Finnegan, but that was all defence against being disappointed. I wanted him to blackmail me. I wanted him to make me sleep with him.

Mr Finnegan was at his desk. He didn't look up when I came in.

'Well?' I said, standing at the doorway, 'It's seven.'

He looked at his watch, embarrassing me. I had been sitting in the café watching the little hand move around, and here he was, and he didn't even know what time it was.

'Hello, seven,' he said and stretched out in his chair languidly. Then he put his arms behind his head, the image of overbearing high self-esteem.

I hated the silence. I had to fill it with words, with marks of myself.

'You said I had to come.'

'You didn't have to come, Sally; you chose to come.'

The way he said my name made my pussy flip. I

183

was glad I wasn't a man. I would have had erections all over the place.

'Whatever,' I said, shrugging. I looked as sullen and unwilling as I could. I had my hands on my hips, and I pretended to be chewing gum.

He took my hand and walked us over to Ms Feather's desk where she did her preening and pouting. Great minds think alike, I thought. We weren't going to be messing around, just wham bam, thank you Sally. He didn't look the type to go for lots of kissing.

He swept everything off her desk, all of it: all the files with customers' names in, all the glossy brochures and the plain charts, all the little bottles of make-up and jars of creams to stop you wrinkling, and then he said, 'Whoops'. Raising one eyebrow at me, like some hero out of a Jane Austen book. I guessed it wasn't the only thing he had raised.

I was just standing there trying to look nonchalant, trying to hide the fact that I was wetter than a melting marshmallow.

He ordered me to turn around and face the desk. I stood shaking, my hands on the sides; I didn't know what he was going to do. First he lifted my skirt up, and then, changing his mind, he found the zip. He pulled it down, and I stepped out of it, trying and no doubt failing to be graceful.

'Bend over, Sally,' he said when it was off, and I bent in half. The desk was the perfect size. My bottom was up in the air. I stretched my arms out, but he caught them up and said, 'I've got you now, baby.'

I liked being called baby. It was the second best thing to being called Sally. (The worst thing is hearing someone else's name.) He hadn't touched me properly yet. I was growing anxious. He got some rope, and he tied up my arms; then he tied my legs, one against

184

each desk leg. I was imprisoned, yet I felt freer than I ever had in my life.

'Well, nice to meet you too,' I said, trying to make light of the situation. 'Do you want to play footsie?'

He didn't speak yet. It wasn't fair: I was totally wet, and he hadn't touched me yet. And he had better take my knickers off soon.

Then he started feeling me. He glided his hands over my legs, my fat calves and my dimpled thighs. Then he got down and started kissing them, kissing my legs, my calves, and the backs of my knees and my thighs. Then he started touching my arse with his hands. He massaged circles on my buttocks.

I was wearing a white G-string, and he pulled the string up and down. I could feel it dig into my pussy, and I was afraid it would get lost in there. I wanted him to pull tighter, and he did without me asking. It brushed against my clitoris at the front and all along my arse at the back. I started sighing. I couldn't stop myself. In my head, I kept repeating the words, 'Mr Finnegan is going to fuck me,' and it really excited me, the sound, the meaning of the sentence. 'I am going to get fucked by Mr Finnegan on Ms Penny Feather's desk.' I couldn't stop emitting little snorts of pleasure. He liked that.

'Oh yes, you love it, don't you, Sally? What a lovely arse,' he whispered. 'Does it feel good?'

He put his fingers inside the G-string line and wandered up and down like a piano player fingering the scales.

'No,' I lied. I hated the idea of anything in there. It was my bottom, no matter what I did with those kids, I didn't want him playing around with that. I felt a bit guilty about what I had done to those kids, but no matter. They had liked it. I remembered my arse was quite white compared to the rest of my body. Will didn't like me wearing G-strings. On our last holiday together, he said they looked cheap. What a hypocrite. I tried to block him out of my mind. I didn't want to come to the sound of Will's voice any more. I was finished with him.

'You've got the most fantastic arse I've ever seen. I want to live in there. They are the fattest, bounciest cheeks in this office. The best. You could win prizes with this arse. You should be on TV showing off your appetising arse.'

I liked the idea that my fatty cheeks were bouncier than Ms Feather's lean ones were.

He continued, 'I watch them twitch up and down this office all day long, and I think, what must it be like to have my face in there? That would be the best way to die.'

Who would have thought it? The normally reticent Mr Finnegan was quite verbose in bed, or on the desk, wherever we were.

'Oh yes, look at them.' He slapped. They stung. I bet they went all red. Still, they'd probably match my face: I was a beacon, a lighthouse guiding all ships to me.

'And what's this?' He was tickling me, winding his hands underneath. 'What do you hide under here?'

'That's my pussy,' I giggled girlishly.

'That's your pussy, is it? No, that's your soaking wet cunt.' He was right enough. It just came off the table at a lovely angle. Easy access was assured. He dug his finger in, and I would have put fires out with that spray.

'Jesus,' he said admiringly. 'I chose the right girl.'

I felt drastically underdressed. He was still in his suit; I craned my head around. He had taken off his jacket and rolled up his sleeve. He looked like he was going to work hard at something. I concentrated on not coming too soon. If his toe had been persuasive on my clitoris, then his fingers were three times more so.

'How many boys did this to you, Sally?' he said, and I felt a surge of creamy excitement. The inquisition was beginning. I could feel the wetness flow gratefully, but I ignored him. He would have to fight harder for his information. All that was classified stuff.

He slapped my arse hard with his other hand. Yet his fingers remained up me, like a screwdriver, I thought, screwing me up. He forced them in further, and I could feel my pussy twitch, rewarding him.

'How many boys did you fuck, Baby? Tell Daddy.'

'Three,' I said. I couldn't help but let a glow of pride slip into my voice. 'I had three boys.'

'Oh, yes, yes.' I think his whole hand was up me, loading into me. 'Did you love it?'

'Oh, yes, yes, I loved it.' I had visions of the boys pumping me: Marcus against the wall, the others on the ground, scraping my knees, the orgasm, their gasps.

'Oh, don't stop!'

That really excited him. But he withdrew the fist, and left me with just his finger, plump and searching. It wandered around inside me, slowly, going up my vagina and then round to find my clitoris, squeezing softly. He told me to spread my legs wider, please. And to show off my arse a bit, wriggle it around. Why am I doing this for you? I was thinking. The way I was positioned, I felt like I was at a shop being fitted for the most enormous dick in stock. Even so, the thumb was perfect. He was gouging me with his thumb. If he wasn't going to fuck me with his penis, I didn't care. The thumb was enough.

'Where did you fuck them, honey?'

I loved the idea that he was the general and I was

the mere foot (ha) soldier. His thumb wheedled its way in and out, and each time I felt myself soar.

'In the street, at the boy's house and on my washing machine.'

'You look so horny,' he said, 'I'm tempted to leave you like that till morning, and let all the staff take a look at you.'

'Don't you dare,' I giggled. I was in high spirits. Then he took out his fingers, and dismay shot through me. Things had changed a lot since I was a schoolgirl.

He just watched me for a while. I was desperate to have his finger back inside me. I felt lonely, exposed, without him. I felt naked and vulnerable, like the trees in the winter when all the leaves have fallen off. I wished I could untie my arms to feel myself, to show him that I could do it by myself if I had to.

'Well, well.' The questioning began again. 'You fucked them all. You are a little cradle snatcher, aren't you?'

'Yes.' I giggled. 'Not just boys, though!'

So now I was showing off a bit. I wanted his fingers to explore me again, but he didn't. He slapped me hard. I liked that too.

'What happened?'

'Please touch me, then I'll tell you.'

'No, tell me, then I'll touch you.'

'There was this girl, Marcus's friend, and we invited her to join us, and then –'

'Did you come, Sally?' he interrupted.

'Oh yes,' I purred. 'I didn't stop; I couldn't stop.'

'Did the boy make you come, the first time? The first boy you fucked, Marcus, did he make you come?'

Suddenly, I didn't want to talk about it. It was private. I didn't want to betray Marcus. He was sweet and kind, not like this stupid fingerless Finnegan. Maybe Mr Finnegan was just looking for a confession so he could get me locked away in some psychiatric hospital. I wanted him to touch me, have his pleasure and then sod off. I was throbbing for him.

'What – Sally, what was it like?'

'Umm, it was really good,' I said, biting my lip.

'What was the first boy like? Was he a virgin?'

For a second, I thought that maybe Mr Finnegan was gay. But then I realised that was hardly likely. I might as well tell the truth; I wanted to tell the truth. I hadn't told anyone yet.

It came out choked, like a sob.

'He was the first person to make me come. I never felt like that before. I really liked him.'

Mr Finnegan didn't say anything after that. I wanted him to go away; I felt embarrassed and humiliated. Was it Elizabeth Taylor who once said that no one can make you feel insecure except yourself? Well that was all very well, but Liz had obviously never been tied up with a boss she hated who knew everything about her little peccadillos and had made her come in an afternoon meeting with his big toe.

Just when I thought nothing else was going to happen, Mr Finnegan went off. I thought for a moment it was all over, he was gay, and a soft wipe of disappointment ran through me. Then he came back and dropped his swivel chair behind me. Then he sat down nice and cosy, with my pussy in front of his eyes.

'What a fantastic view,' he said, and I thought of a book that I have at home, *Great views in England and Wales*. I bet I wasn't listed, although maybe I should have been.

Then he opened me out and started eating me. That's the only word I can find to describe what he did. It was just like he hadn't eaten for a while, and here I was, this magnificent meal set out in front of him; he couldn't help himself, he just had to tuck in. He was insatiable, an absolute glutton. If you com-

189

pared it to the way I had worked at that girl, I was anorexic compared to this. His tongue trailed everywhere: he started at the front and then, to my embarrassment, he was trailing it in and out of my arse. He was licking around, and he was making gargling, enjoying noises. Little pleasure noises. I like that: I like a man who makes a noise. I love it when a man does that, because – even though I'd blown that girl, and I loved it – you never know if men truly enjoy it or not. I know the only time Will condescended to do it, he hated it. He said he didn't like the smell.

But Mr Finnegan was moaning, groaning and guzzling my pussy, or, as he said, my dripping cunt. With his other hand, I could hear that he had loosened his trousers.

'You don't mind if I touch myself?' he said, but I did. I needed the commitment of his fingers: I couldn't stand them to go away.

'Please,' I whispered. 'Please, please.' I wanted something more substantial.

He had big thumbs and one of them slipped inside me, inside the front crack, and began roaming around, looking for buttons to press. I could relax with him sucking at me and touching me. I could relax: I was going to come soon. I was seconds away. His hand was so insistent, so rhythmic, and his tongue was so perfect, that I started moaning, and we were both moaning, you should have heard us. I guess we sounded like cats mating. His noises made me bolder, even louder. I wanted everyone to hear. Everyone should know what ecstasy sounds like.

'Oh yes.'

'Umm, yes.'

'Yes, don't stop,' I screamed.

'I'm not going to stop.'

'Don't stop.'

'I won't ever stop, oh baby, yes, yes.'

190

I was rocking up and down and parting my legs as wide as I could: I wanted him to have as much access as possible. I also liked it when he stopped and looked closely, examining me, exclaiming with awe how wet and horny I was. Forget becoming a doctor for men, I think I should marry a gynaecologist. The joy of being examined every day.

Then I realised that he had stopped. He wasn't even looking. For a millisecond I was angry. How dare he spoil my pleasure like that; he hadn't come, had he? So many times with Wills we had got to that point, and then he came, and I was left like a baby whose candy has been snatched away.

'What is it?' I said, dismayed. He hadn't come, surely? Not yet? We had only just started. I hated when that happened.

'Look who's watching,' he said. I looked up into the mirror; there was a figure at the back of the room, staring right at me.

'No, no.'

I struggled. I could see the doorman. He had taken off his peaked cap and was watching us. He was wearing the uniform: beige shirt, tight trousers. He was tall and sturdy in the reflection. He was good-looking: stiff, not my sort, but definitely good-looking.

I was so ashamed. This was the doorman, and I didn't want him to see me like this. When I was with the boys, I had chosen them. It was on my own terms; I didn't want anyone choosing me. All the same, Mr Finnegan didn't let up massaging my arse, and I didn't let up pressing into him. I don't really know what I wanted, whether it would be better if Mr Finnegan sent him away, or to have him watch us, lust after me and fall masturbating in a heap in the corner. For one moment in my life, I wanted to be admired for my body as well as my brain. I wanted

191

to be respected for my fucking skills. Doesn't every woman feel this at least once?

I could see the bulge in his pants even from where I was. Mr Finnegan must have seen it too: he turned his finger inside my beaver so that he was massaging me with his nail.

'Do you like an audience?'

'No,' I lied, 'Mr Finnegan, you had better fuck me soon, or I am going to have to do it myself.' That wasn't feasible. I may have a vivid imagination, and I may orgasm easily, but not with just the pressure of thin air on my clitoris.

'Come on, come in: she doesn't mind you having a closer look.'

'No,' I whispered to Mr Finnegan. I shook my head violently, but I didn't shout. Funny how I didn't want to offend the doorman. For some reason, I really didn't want to hurt his feelings.

'Sally, you can hardly say no, can you?'

'Yes, I can. Don't you fucking dare!'

'My love, I know that you do it with anyone in trousers, or skirts come to that. Do you think he would like to hear all about that, or Ms Feather, or even Duncan?'

I don't know if he was threatening me or not. I fell silent.

Mr Finnegan came around the front of my desk, and, for the first time, he kissed me. It was a wet, slobbery, hungry-dog kiss, and then he entered my mouth with his tongue. He licked at my teeth. His tongue was swirling around in my mouth as I wanted him to in my pussy. Oh yes: I struggled for more, but he pulled back and bit my lip, and then kissed me again sweetly. I kissed him back, puckering up desperately. I needed his kisses. I wanted some warmth. He looked me in the eyes and said, 'You want him to watch, don't you?'

'No.' I couldn't admit to that.

I rubbed against the desk uselessly. I tried purring up at him, and then the doorman came in. I honestly don't know if they had planned it or not. Mr Finnegan was in his shirt and tie and no pants. And then, believe it or not, they shook hands, and there I was with my legs spread, one leg in Europe and one in America and my pussy – or my cunt, whatever you want to call it – begging for attention. We could barely look at each other. When our eyes met, he looked all hangdog, but his penis was like a stick in his pants: there was no way he could walk with that. I don't know how I didn't notice it before. All those days when I'd come to work, and he was hiding that in his trousers. Unless doormen have guns. You could tell he wasn't happy looking at my eyes. He too wanted to glory in one of England's finest views. He walked around behind me. He gasped, just quietly, but I heard him. I couldn't help putting on a show. I wriggled up at them. If they had undone my hands, I would have put them on my clitoris and rubbed my way to ecstasy, unpaying audience or not.

Mr Finnegan was whispering to the doorman. I felt like a fool: maybe they were laughing at me.

'You naughty girl, Sally! You do want to do it with this complete stranger watching.'

I shook my head vigorously.

'And I thought we were special,' he said with mock indignation.

'No, I don't.'

He slid his fingers around in my slippery cunt.

'You liar, Sally: you do, don't you?'

Found out. I closed my eyes, preparing to be humiliated.

'Yes, you do, you want to show yourself off in front of this man.'

If I closed my eyes, I could let Mr Finnegan take

193

control of the situation, which was what he wanted to do.

'She's very excited; do you recognise her?'

'I'm not excited.' I lied. I wasn't going to go down without at least some semblance of a fight.

'Yes, it's Miss Sally.'

I don't know where the Miss came from; he didn't usually call me that. But then I guess he didn't know the right way to address a fellow staff member who was lying on the desk like some fat piece of tuna on a bed of rice.

'Show us your pussy, darling,' Mr Finnegan said to me, as casually as if he were asking to see my latest project. I struggled to comply. I wanted the doorman to admire it, to see what he couldn't have. To be appreciated.

I heard Doorman say something appreciative. They were chuckling like two blokes at the counter of the bar.

'Yes, this is the office whizz kid. Here, served before us, is the girl who single-cuntedly saved our office from bankruptcy. Thanks to her, everyone with something to sell comes to us, and we've got to sell everything from dog food to candles to shoe polish.'

They stood back, as if they were admiring a car at a showroom.

Mr Finnegan put his hand into the lucky dip again, and I groaned, 'Don't take it out.' I couldn't hide my appreciation from him.

'I don't think I've felt a pussy as hot as this before.' Mr Finnegan was singing his approval.

'Yes, it's very nice, sir.' The doorman called Mr Finnegan sir! I could feel blood pumping down to my pussy, mischievous pleasures.

'Do you want to put your finger in there?'

'Yes, please.'

'No, he's only here to watch: he's only here to look,'

I shouted. Too late. His fingers felt different, but I liked it. They filled me up, and one of them moved inexorably towards my clit.

'Yes, the middle finger seems to be the most effective. Yes, you can see that she likes that: she starts moving up and down. Look at her go, my God.'

'It's like she's on heat,' I heard Doorman mutter.

Mr Finnegan laughed.

'Yes, look at her writhing around your fingers. I think she's going to come in a minute. Isn't she wonderful? She just doesn't care, does she? We used to call her the office mouse, but look at her, she's a tiger.'

What did my body know? Only that anyone's hands were better than no one's hands. It could be Will's hand, Marcus's hand, Mr Finnegan's hand, or the doorman's hand, as long as someone was feeling me up. I once had a fantasy of being in a crowded place – the January sales, or a rock concert – and someone would put their hand up my skirt and feel my pussy. I would look around but be unable to find out whose it was. I would desperately search for a frame of reference, a face to claim the hand that massaged me, that made me wet, but be unable to find one. I liked the anonymity of it. I tried to guess whose hand was which, and I wanted to orgasm impossibly quietly, so that only I knew the pleasure they were giving me.

They both had their hands in. Their fingers in pies. Two men's hands: I never felt so loved. I spread my legs as far as I could, to give them a better view, to give them a better hold. I was like a puppet, and they were controlling me with their hands.

'How does it feel?' Mr Finnegan asked the doorman.

'Wet,' he sighed.

They were talking about me as if I were a thing, as

195

if I were just a toy to play with. I had never felt so alive.

'I like this ridge here,' Mr Finnegan continued, giving the doorman a guided tour. 'She squirms around like hell when I go there. C'mon baby, that's better, wriggle for me. Look, she can't help herself.'

'Who is she?' I shouted out: I wanted to join in the conversation about my bits. 'The cat's mother?'

'No, she is the queen pussy,' he said and moved his fingers up and down the ridge. I bit down on my lip hard. My bottom was wobbling, and I wondered what they thought of the cellulite on my thighs, but they didn't seem to mind so far.

'Do you want to fuck our nice doorman?'

Actually, I was so turned on, I think I would have fucked anything that fitted. I didn't reply. I thought I was playing hard to get but, on reflection, I wasn't playing very well.

'He is hot for you, Sally baby: you should see his penis. What do you think of that?'

I opened my eyes, and there, reflected back at me, were two of them, standing up for attention. Two lovely boys with two lovely toys, flashing at me, one brown, one white, both as hard and long as the beacons the police use to direct the traffic. The doorman's won on bulk, he was wider, but Mr Finnegan won on length. It was the same rocket shape that I loved so much about Marcus. I saw that it was Mr Finnegan's hand on my neck; the doorman was doing all the under-the-bonnet work. Mr Finnegan's other hand was on his penis. I wondered if he still liked me. I wanted him to touch me, not the doorman.

I groaned in assent.

'Say yes: I want you to say yes.'

'Yes,' I said obediently. 'Yes.'

'Say that you want him.'

'I want him.'

'What do you want him to do?'

'I want him to fuck me.'

'Where?'

'Here,' I said, almost banging my head on the desk in my eagerness. Mr Finnegan laughed.

'No, which part of the body?'

'My pussy.'

'No, try again.'

I thought there was a limited choice. Armpits and ear holes weren't exactly my cup of tea. I may have a CV of different positions, a growing résumé of sexual experiences, but this was where I drew the line.

'My cunt?' I guessed again. He didn't like the P words. He was all hard cock and cunt, to my penis and pussy.

'Wrong again.' He lowered himself on to me. 'You want him to fuck you up the arse.'

'No, I don't.'

'I think you do.' He shook my arms.

'I don't.'

For the first time, I thought that maybe the game had gone far enough. Maybe he should undo me now. But I wouldn't interrupt. I did want to see what Mr Finnegan had in mind for us. He was famed throughout the advertising industry for his creativity, his daringness, and his ability to predict the change in opinion. I wanted to test him.

'Let's play some games first.'

I watched the doorman trot over to the desk where the box of candles was. We were supposed to think up a new way to sell them.

'No,' I shouted.

'Yes,' he said to me, pressing my head down so I couldn't see. Then he stuck two fingers up me, to shut me up. I gulped: I wished I wasn't so excited. I had no dignity. I wished fleetingly that I was like a princess from an icy land. How nice it would be to be glacial.

The doorman hesitated behind me. I could see his outline in the shadow, like some great god of darkness.

Mr Finnegan was instructing him to put the thin candle up my arse.

'No,' I pleaded. 'We have got to use those tomorrow for the campaign.' I tried to appeal to his professional nature.

'Ssshhh.' Mr Finnegan pulled his fingers out and looked at my arse. Suddenly he got down and bit into my cheek; then he slapped me a few times. It stung good and hot. Then he started massaging slowly again. He felt the puckered edge of my anus with his fingers, and then I felt the cold wetness of his tongue. I swallowed hard. I wanted to cry. I wanted him to tell the other man to go away, to make love gently to me. The doorman was waiting there with the candle.

'Have you ever seen a woman ejaculate? This one will.'

'No, I won't,' I hissed.

'Honey, I chose you because I knew what a hot lady you are.'

'I don't want it.'

'All right,' he said, amenably. 'We'll see. Let's just put the fat one in her pussy. That's it, see how she likes it. She loves it, doesn't she? God, Sally, I'm proud of you, my little hard worker. I'm almost coming just watching you.'

I wasn't looking. I don't know who was doing what. I think it was the doorman who started moving the fat candle in me, and I couldn't help myself: I was letting go, giving myself in to the motion. I still managed to muster up a desperate 'No.' I wanted romance and candles, but not like this. I was bobbing up and down on it, yet I was frightened that, after all my protesting, I was going to come.

'Yes, Sally,' he said, and this time he said it unequivocally. 'We're going to put the candle up your arse.' I shook my head wildly. 'Now,' he said to the doorman. I could feel the thin candle move forwards, making its road up into me. It didn't hurt! It slid in, and I let go: he was telling me to let go. But I felt stupid; I felt like a whore. I was fucking two candles in front of two men. It was like taking coals to Newcastle, or drinking instant when you had gone out and bought a coffee maker. They must have thought I was mad. I couldn't stop, and they didn't want to stop: they were working the controls, driving me easily as a driver drives the train. I was full up. One of them, I guess it was the doorman, was moving the candle in and out of me with fantastic dexterity, like a bell-ringer. In and out he went. I was becoming breathless. Mr Finnegan's candle was tickling at my clitoris. Flames of pleasure burned inside me.

'Look at yourself,' he commanded. 'Look in the mirror, Sally.'

I opened my eyes reluctantly, but even I had to admit it was a glorious sight. There was I, spread-eagled on Ms Penny Feather's desk; there were two candles sticking out of me, and there were two hard men standing to attention behind. I looked like a cactus or a prickly pear. Pricks, I gurgled happily. I wondered which one I would get to have first. I no longer pretended to myself that the doorman was just going to be doing the viewing. He was definitely a participant, and I was happy to go along with that. His penis was glowing, standing up impatiently.

They pulled the candles out. I was still rocking up and down, and I was getting anxious. If I couldn't come soon, then . . .

'This is going to be difficult, but I think she deserves it: you know she needs both of us at the same time.'

They were laughing about something. Yes, they were planning what to do. They were walking around me, poking, then in a huddle plotting.

The doorman levered himself on the desk in front of me. His penis flickered briefly in my face. It was stumpy, almost as wide as it was long, heavy and smooth. I didn't know how he would get it into me. His body was hot and warm. Mr Finnegan had to undo my legs to let him get in, and then he slid fully under me. Then we were tied together. Our skin met with a weird sensation. To be touched again was delicious; his warm, male flesh melted against me. His body was hot and round compared to the desk, and I sank against his chest gladly. His black, wiry hair made my forehead tingle.

Then I could feel him poking around me searching for his path. I shivered and moaned, and then he found the entrance. He drove in his thick wad of penis. It was such a relief that I started moving up and down on him almost immediately, my breath getting faster and faster. The top of his penis was rubbing my clitoris, and already my face was distorting. I could feel it: he had only been inside me a second, and I was going to come. He was so wide; I was locked into place. His cock bashed against my soaking wet lush. For a moment, I didn't know if I could move, and then I found I could, and I moved fast and hard. He was battering at my moist hole. I could glimpse my reflection. I was like a little koala gripping onto a eucalyptus tree. I could feel great clumps of my wetness welcoming him between my legs. I worked up to my own murderous rhythm, crunching up and down. He had his eyes closed in that adorable 'yes, yes' look that men have.

'Whoa, whoa little baby, what about me?' interrupted Mr Finnegan. What about him? It was his fault I was in such a state. He had shook me around and then insisted on sticking this great cork into me. I was full of fizz.

'I thought it was me you wanted, not him.'

'No,' I hissed. I was moving around the doorman. He filled me up. His cock was in my cunt, this stranger's dick was inside me, and I had never felt so out of control in my life. And I was so happy to be out of control. They would look after me, deal with me. I was chasing my orgasm, chasing something so hard, so big, so deep inside me. It must never stop.

'Stop, stop, stop,' shouted that bastard Finnegan.

The doorman stopped his movements, but I didn't. I wanted the friction to continue; I was determined to continue. But Finnegan grabbed hold of my hips and held me steady.

'Stop that.' He slapped my flanks and then pulled at my arse-hole.

'I want to have some fun too, Sally.'

'No, I don't want you.'

'Sally, how unfair, I brought you here to this position, and now you say that you have had enough of me.'

'I'm sorry.' I was working on the doorman. Perhaps if we both came quickly, then we could stop, but he was being an obedient sod and waiting for the master's orders.

Mr Finnegan put his finger in my back hole again and wound it round and round. He was talking all the while. I was wrapped around his little finger – literally.

'Sally, I have been fantasising about your fat arse ever since I met you. Don't deny me this pleasure: I'm sure you do it to your young men and women.'

I was embarrassed. He was just guessing, of course, but his guess was fairly accurate. I wanted to say that

201

it was sexual harassment; I felt like a frog must do when he is innocently mounting his mate and then a horrid person comes in and puts a firework up his backside.

'Get off,' I insisted, although maybe I wasn't in a position to insist. 'Afterwards,' I suggested cordially. 'You can fuck me afterwards.'

He pulled his finger out and, for a stupid second, I was relieved, but when I realised what he was going to do, I started squirming around him. I wanted to get away, but I was locked onto the doorman, and Mr Finnegan was enjoying my confinement.

'Look at you! Oh Sally, how you wriggle, but that just makes me even bigger and harder.'

'Don't!' I whispered, horrified. The worst thing, though, was that the doorman was itching to go off inside me, and I too felt like I was on the edge of orgasm. I couldn't resist jiggling around just a little to make his prick pound in my cunt. He mustn't treat me in this way; he must let me go. I wondered if Finnegan did this with his ex-wife. Or perhaps he had spread Ms Feather here too. Perhaps all their protestations were lies.

For a few moments nothing happened. Then I could hear the tearing of a packet, and the smell of rubber romped around the room. I heard the sound of a condom unravelling on his hard prick; I envisaged him pushing it down his erect shaft, pinching the end, the space for his come. And I waited.

Then Mr Finnegan gripped my arse hard. He pushed my cheeks wide apart and pushed himself inside me, the road less travelled. He was much bigger than the candle. I started to cry. I could feel him bruising the insides of my arse-hole. It felt so rough there, not smooth like the doorman was.

'Hush, hush, little baby: don't cry, we're not going to hurt you.'

'It hurts, though.' I was so embarrassed, and I was afraid. Things weren't meant to go up there. We kept still, our bodies sandwiched; the doorman's eyes were on me, his face close to mine. He was concerned. His expression was tender. My eyes had filled with tears of humiliation. The doorman's penis twitched around inside me: he was raring to go, but he was holding still for me. I liked him for that.

'You are so tight, Sally,' Finnegan murmured. 'You were a virgin here, weren't you, baby? Believe me, you're going to love it. I'm going to bugger you stupid.'

'Don't call me stupid,' I said, but his laughter made his body move, and that was agony.

I wasn't going to love it. I was crying. I was scared to let go, because I didn't know what would come out, and I hated Finnegan for putting his prick in me, and this stupid doorman, whose prick was hard up me but who wouldn't fuck me. I didn't want to be buggered. My mascara would run. Maybe I would die. The membrane there was too thin, too fragile. I felt like tissue paper. But I didn't want to be the one to stop it.

'Say that you want me to bugger you, Sally.'

I wouldn't speak: I couldn't. I was dribbling and holding my breath. I'm sure if I had tried to say anything that it would have come out as one long sigh, a release of steam. Then the doorman started to rock me just a little to begin with. It was a lullaby, or a small nudge. I was so sensitive, I don't think I could have taken any more, but I began nudging him back, feeling the beauty of his fine shaft, and I buried my face into his shoulder.

And then, gradually, I got used to it. Gradually, I suppose, I grew to accommodate it. I don't know how the metamorphosis happened, but one second I was begging them to finish, and then the next I was pouring over them, screaming that they must never, ever stop. I was sawing at them, clamouring for more, pressing against the doorman, and Mr Finnegan was pressing at me, rigid, up and down my arse, keeping it up. Chopping at me, a barrage, three bodies in motion, riding each other, clinging at each other. The doorman was moving me up and down, and Mr Finnegan was pulling me down and up.

I was shouting into the poor doorman's ear, 'Fuck me, fuck me up the arse, harder, harder, yes, yes, don't stop.'

I was liquid, wetness against their solidity. I felt my body spasm and contract, and my vaginal muscles clinging to something desperately. And I have no idea what I was saying or doing, only this riding on their shafts. Double shafts, twice as much come and, as I came thunderously, I caught a glimpse of myself in the mirror. I saw a collapsing creature with this beatific smile on her face, grinding her way to nirvana. When I came, it felt like I was being tossed in the air. I don't even remember what I howled, but I was howling so loud, we all were, and sobbing too.

Until then, I hadn't known just exactly what three bodies could do together. I had had my threesomes, yes, but it was as if there was always one hard worker. This time, we were a co-operative, a collective, all pursuing a joint goal. I had suddenly discovered an extra sense. I had my hearing, my sight, my taste, my touch, my smell, and now, I had my pleasure, a straight line from my cunt to my nipples. Now that I had found it, this was the one sense out of all of them that I could never give up. I felt as though I had found something I wasn't even looking for.

Mr Finnegan undid my bonds. There were red indentations on my wrists and ankles. Within seconds of the orgasm, everything that had turned us on so much before ceased to affect us. Everything that had seemed so sexual, so alive, had a different, more serious function. My legs, my bottom and my back were all sore. The doorman was glued to the desk. He picked himself up and shook himself down. We were all very mature about it, and then we all shook hands, and the doorman shook his trousers and went downstairs. I guess he was on the night shift, and that night he would have plenty of dreams to while away the time.

I sat on the black swivel chair and twirled around. I was exhilarated. I hadn't known I had it in me; I hadn't known so much could get in me. I was also a little frightened; I couldn't help thinking that maybe I would never enjoy sex as much again. How could I possibly equal that?

Mr Finnegan took me over to the leather sofa. He pushed me down roughly but then kissed me gently. He looked at my lips; he looked in my eyes. I hadn't made love face to face, as an equal, for a long time, and I was scared. But he made me feel beautiful. This time he paid attention to my breasts: he put his warm hands on them and squeezed. The nipples were still hard from before, like two little currants. He sucked them tight, rolling them around with expertise in his tongue. I stroked his hair; I felt peaceful suddenly. Mr Finnegan and I were having a harmonious moment. Caressing and mending like two old marrieds. But he wasn't going to allow me to relax. He made me keep my eyes wide open and watch his eyes as he talked. And how he talked: I would never have dreamed how much he could talk.

'Oh yes, your silky cunt: your cunt makes me want to come. Keep looking at me honey, I can't stop. Oh God, Sally, give me your arse and your cunt and your tits and your everything. I've fucked hundreds of women, Sally, but you know how to fuck: you do, don't you, Sally?' He just let go, whispering these hot obscenities in my ear. 'Don't shut your eyes, baby: look at me. I want to watch your face.'

He was the wildest man I've ever had. Again, I seemed to grow to accommodate him, just. He was long and still pulsating inside me, and I strained to get in to a position to make him go as deep as I could. With his fingers, he rubbed my clitoris, and he was still talking.

'Sally and the schoolboys! I would love to have watched you. Did they do you like this, Sally? Did they rub your little clit? Did they fuck you up the arse? Did they make you scream? I bet you fucked them all so hard.'

And I was like his echo, his Greek chorus, whispering back the words that turned me on the most.

'Harder, my clit, deep, deeper.'

He knew. He knew everything about it. I felt safe, and I was floppy in his arms. When his finger left the front of me, I took over and did it to myself, and he gazed at me admiringly.

'Good girl, Sally: come on, baby. I want to see you come, now, now.'

I felt myself sliding down a slippery slope: there was no mistake about that. I was opening up for him, feeling him fill me, feeling the ripples of an orgasm that was shortly going to turn into a great big stream. There was no turning back. But there was still a hole. The hole that he opened earlier was now gaping wide, aching to be loved. I was full of orifices and, now they were open, I wanted them all filled again. I didn't have to tell him. He knew. He got the thin candle and snuck it in around the back. I felt it slide in, and he jerked it in time with his own hard penis.

'Oh yes, baby, relax, relax.'

Usually I hate it when people tell me to relax. It's one of those one things you can't do on command, but with him I could. I threw myself into it. I was one hundred per cent relaxed, feeling his dick and the candle rubbing me so hard, so good, just how I wanted it. All doubts that I would never have sex to equal the time before were dispelled. I was going for it, madly going for it. I felt like I was blacking out or that I wasn't of this world. I was just a thing, just a cube of pleasure, just solid come. The exquisite pain of the penetration of my arse-hole, the insistent sweep of his cock inside me, and the labour of his fingers on my clitoris forced me to claw at his shoulders and made my vagina pump hard and fast. And I was fucking him uncontrollably with all my feelings of shame, of dirtiness, of love, of hate, of guilty, of victim, of mouse and tiger, and my body charged off into orgasm leaving my mind reeling, gasping to contemplate what I was doing. Seconds later, I was buckling underneath him, the final jolt of sweet energy, my legs swung up high in the air over his shoulders, and I was shouting.

'I love you, Will, I love you,' I screamed.

'Sally,' he said, when I had re-entered planet earth, 'who on earth is Will?'

'Will?' I said innocently. 'Oh, that: I mean Willie. That's what we used to call them – you know, dicks – when I was younger.'

He ruffled my hair and said something to himself. I'm not sure what he said, but it was something like, 'It's always the quiet ones.'

Then he turned into the professional again.

'We've got to do some work on the shoe-cleaner campaign. Now get your fat arse over here, and let's see if we can get some ideas that will show that Ms Feather a thing or two.'

'Was I better than her, at sex I mean?' I said, when he had got us coffee, and we were sat at the desks, looking every bit like two innocent office workers enjoying a bit of overtime. (Although I think that may be an oxymoron.) I fiddled with the candles: they were supposed to give us inspiration. They had managed more than that. I felt relieved that we had already finished the dog food planning. I couldn't resist asking. For all my noncompetitiveness, Penny Feather somehow brought out the very worst in me.

'I have no idea,' he said.

'But you – I thought you were together!' I said incredulously.

'Well, I've never done it with her. I don't even like her.' He paused, grinning at me. 'But who knows? You'll just have to ask our friend the doorman. He might know.'

'Mr Finnegan, I've just thought of our new advertising campaign for shoe polish.'

Chapter Eighteen

*A*ccording to some surveys, four out of every ten office workers have affairs at work. Until that week, I would never have believed it possible, but after that week I couldn't believe that the number was so low. The pleasures of our office romance were infinite: Finnegan and I giggled at each other in meetings, we wrote each other suggestive e-mails, and we sneaked off early to 'congress' in spare offices. He patted my backside when he shouldn't have, and I learned how to give a foot job: I got to be quite good at it. I also learned how to come in a room full of other people, without making a sound: an invaluable skill. We grappled each other in the lift, and although we never managed to do it in the stockroom, it wasn't for want of trying. We kept getting interrupted. We did succeed in making love once in the toilets while they were filming our 'waxy man' series of commercials, featuring candles sculptured into male shapes. Finnegan had slammed me against the toilet door (the ladies'). The lock dug a reminder into the small of my back. Then he was biting into my neck, pressing himself all over me, my skirt hoisted high, and my legs balanced precariously on the seat: the perfect position for penetration.

And if I ever said no (and I only said no to tease him) he would say that he would tell on me, he would get me in big trouble if I didn't. Only I didn't believe he would ever tell. I knew he was fond of me. Still, I didn't want him to know that I went with him willingly, although I guess he probably suspected it.

Other people in my shoes (or rather my suspenders – Finnegan had prurient tastes) might recognise the symptoms. I yawned when my co-workers talked; I doodled through the meetings I once prepared for. I no longer feared the disdain of my co-workers. I suppose I looked down on them. They were supposed to be creative, bohemian. Artistic? My arse. They were as conventional as a fax sent upside down. As radical as an Internet homepage about naturism. And none of them, not one of them, had ever had sex as good as I was having. Sometimes I even felt sorry for them.

After days of intermittent fore-foreplay, Finnegan and I met after work. He worked later than I did, and I used to wait for him in the café. Cream in my cup, creaming in my seat, drawing pictures of the night ahead. Sometimes, I couldn't help doodling little Kama Sutra sketches: ways we could get close to each other, ways he could come inside me, and other ways I could welcome him in.

I thought of Will. I spent hours trying not to think of him, blocking him out of my head, but he still came back, unrepentant. He was more habit that anything else. Forgetting him was like trying to give up smoking. And I hated myself for my weakness, and I would never admit it to anyone, not even Sharon, but the word 'destiny' did come to me late at night, did shake me awake and still leave me tearful. I thought of Marcus too, sometimes. But mostly I thought of Finnegan. I was loving being with Finnegan. I enjoyed my evolution from spineless amoeba to man-eating, hot-blooded mammal. (The only worry was that I would end up like the dinosaurs.) I spent several hours trying to guess his first name. I sensed it was something tremendously romantic, Roman possibly, or Celtic. I knew that when he finally told me, that would mean he trusted me as much as I trusted him.

One night, my lovely waiter with the bee-stung buttocks followed me from the café back to the office. I think he recognised the sexual hunger in me, the way they say a thief recognises another thief. However, when he saw Finnegan, on the way out of the stockroom with his arms full of recording equipment, the waiter turned and started walking off, his hands raised in defeat.

'I'm sorry. I made a mistake.'

'What mistake?' enquired Finnegan, putting the video camera down clumsily on the desk. I could see he enjoyed making the younger (and, frankly, more handsome) man squirm.

'I thought the lady was by herself. I'm sorry, mate.' He had light-brown hair draped over his eyes, and he had incisors like a vampire. I suppose, from his exceptionally smooth olive skin, that his parents or grandparents were from the Mediterranean.

'Why don't you ask the lady?'

The waiter looked confused. I, however, knew what Finnegan was getting at, and I couldn't see a reason not to. I knew that fucking was a particular skill of mine. The doubts that had dogged my sexual, or rather my emotional, career had deserted me that day in the alley with Marcus. I had no doubts about my sexual prowess any more. I could fuck, and, just as Beethoven didn't just play his symphonies for one person, and just as Picasso let more than one person see his paintings, so I was tempted to share my gift with the world.

I approached him; he stepped back warily, but then I kissed him.

'Don't go,' I said lightly. My lipstick left a red outline, like a bar code, on his cheek. I had stamped my ownership on him. I knew immediately that I didn't have to pretend with him. He knew my history: he had seen me dumped by Will, and had seen me dump Marcus. He had seen me with tears trickling down my face, and he had seen me come in some-one's face. I didn't think there was much that could surprise him. Or was there?

I touched his cheek, and it was damp. He looked away from me coyly. His Adam's apple cavorted up and down the slender throat.

Mr Finnegan had borrowed the video camera from the stockroom. He was always ready to experiment, always attracted to risk or danger. He was the opposite of Will, or perhaps, more precisely, the opposite of Marcus. Marcus was a wise old man inside a youthful body. Finnegan was a young boy kicking around in a middle-aged suit. Funnily enough, Finnegan was old enough to be Marcus's father!

The waiter's eyes lit up when he saw it and, for a moment, I was jealous as he went over to Finnegan and examined the equipment curiously, commenting on it. All men are geeks when it comes to technology.

'I want to film you,' Finnegan said decisively.

And so it was decided. 'Sally, the movie' was made.

I learned something about myself that night; I was a terrible exhibitionist. I went red in group meetings, but put a camera in front of me and the urge to perform was overwhelming. I don't know where the compulsion came from, but it came. Finnegan trained the camera on me, and I began by taking off my clothes. The lens caressed me; I felt the camera over my skin, and I wanted to show them everything. I opened my legs, and then, when I felt the angle wasn't right, I took the camera to do it myself. I was a woman in control. I made love to the whirring machine. I wanted the camera to capture my thighs, my pubic hair and my secret places. With one quivering finger, I felt inside my loins and showed the movie maker what I could do.

I noticed how the waiter's trousers stretched to accommodate the growing tension as he watched me. His cock was standing present and correct. I felt my way inside the pants, through the buttons. I could feel his cock jerk upwards, like a leg if you tap it on the knee. Yes, yes, you sexy sod. He was naked underneath his jeans, the cheeky fuck! I smacked his naked arse, and he nipped my breast with his incisors. I was going to show Finnegan what he wanted to see. I knew my tales of young men had excited him: now came the movie of the book. I wanted to screw for an audience.

I felt dirty. I was a bad woman, a seductress. I was on all fours, a bridge on the desk, waiting for the waiter to pull down my stockings with his teeth. His hands were tight around my bottom. He hissed words of admiration. I had high expectations of him: I had seen him at work. I had seen him pile up the plates on his arms, the way he remembered orders in his head, and how he maintained, at all times, a cool demeanour.

His hands were over my clothes, inside my clothes. His fingers stroked me, at first tentatively, then with confidence at my arousal, harder, straighter and more satisfyingly. Legs akimbo, pussy forming a big, gaping zero, knees so far apart that one was in Scotland, the other in Wales: I was a bridge on the desk waiting for him, his hands, his touch.

His penis was staring back at me. Mr Finnegan

murmured his approval, 'Very good, very good.' I knew that this was going to make a great film.

The waiter lay down on top of me, upside down. We swallowed each other. We were sixty-nining, but it felt like a higher number, a holier number than that. I felt as though I were encased in a giant ladybird. I wanted to pull myself inside out, so all those stingy, zingy points could be touched by him, him and his furry tongue and his sticky fingers. He worshipped me with his damp skin and his fruity tongue. I felt the camera lens trained on my face, so I performed. I pouted, and I licked my lips voraciously. I puckered up my face and squealed with pleasure. And I licked him, with my eyes open wide, staring into the peering lens, challenging the camera.

As they say in the Bible, the waiter and I 'knew each other', and we really did. I knew the swell and dips of his raw, meaty manhood, and he knew the way of my land. Within seconds, he had worked out exactly what I liked; within one minute, he had me panting, barely able to perform. The contours of my tight pussy were spread and stimulated. My engorged clitoris was treated like a queen. The camera moved down my body, and I knew that Finnegan had tightened the focus. He stood between my open legs, filming my open and engorged dip, with the waiter's tongue sliding methodically up and down.

I gave myself up to it. I came violently jerking, feeling the waiter explode inside me, feeling myself explode around him.

Later, the waiter blindfolded me so tightly that there wasn't even the space for me to open my eyes. I couldn't see what was going on and, although they say that your hearing develops to compensate for sight loss, the blindfold had partially covered my ears too. I felt vulnerable.

214

My loss of control made me excited, too. Within the restrictions, I was free. I knew I would see it all anyway on the replay on the video, and I knew I could trust Finnegan. As I waited for the men, without seeing and barely hearing, I felt an immense sense of liberation. I was doing well at work; I was indispensable to the team. I didn't feel like the odd one out any more, either at work, or indeed in life. The bad things I had anticipated weren't going to happen. There were only a couple of loose ends that I hadn't managed to tie up. Only a couple of things lingered to worry me; Marcus was one. And the other? A clue? It begins with a W.

I couldn't see what was going on. Someone opened me up with greasy fingers. It was jelly or something, cold and exciting. I rubbed against their soft, slimy fingers, wanting them to stay inside me. The fingers disappeared, and I was left alone on display. I could hear the camera whirring around, fishing around me. They were using me for their pleasure; I was being exploited.

'Fuck me,' I whispered. I began using my fingers on myself, but I wanted one of theirs. I tried rubbing against the table, but it was no good.

I strained to hear what was going on and was rewarded with the sound of a low whistle of appreciation. I sensed, I don't know how, that someone else was there. It wasn't just Finnegan and the waiter any more. I shivered. Who had been invited to my display? I knew intuitively that this person had been handed the camera and was now acquainting himself with the controls. There was a shuffle of voices, an exchange of ideas. People were whispering, jostling each other, pushing each other forwards, and deciding on an order or a position.

'I want to be fucked: who is going to do it?' I clamoured. At least my mouth was free.

Perhaps I should have said 'what'. The fingers came around. Something was inserted inside me, clipped up me. It felt cold and metallic.

They were still making no sound. The silence was desperately arousing. I wanted to fill the noise, fill it with my anticipation. I played with myself; I jerked the cold shape in and out and started groaning, for the camera, for the audience, for me. I liked the sound of my own excitement.

Something was tied to my nipples, and it was pulled tight, too tight for comfort. It hurt, somewhere between painfully and pleasurably, only more so. Suddenly I had an incredible burst of knowledge. It was Will. Will was back. That was why they were so silent, so secretive. They had brought him back to me. I felt the contours of the newcomer's shoulders. Yes, it was him. I gripped him closely. I was the best in bed, on the desk, anywhere he needed me. I bit into the little pointed nipple that was offered me. Yes. I wasn't the only one who could play rough.

'Owww.'

Will bit me back. Will, please, you came back to me! Now, do it to me! The metal thing was vibrating pleasantly inside me.

'Fill me up, fill me up, please.' I was groaning as loud as I could. Suddenly, something was stuffed into my mouth. Then I heard laughing.

'No.' I tried to speak; I tried to tell them. I was ready now. I didn't want any more play. I wanted to be fucked. I wanted to be screwed. I wanted a shag. I reached out to grab something.

'Bitch.' Someone else pinched my nipples roughly. I had become attuned to this, and my other senses were alert now, touch, smell, and taste. This was someone else's mouth. Pain mingled with pleasure.

'That hurts,' I screamed, but my words were muffled. One of them tied a piece of material around my mouth. My teeth clamped down on either side. I really was helpless now. My arms and legs were free, but I didn't think I could find my way to the door. And then what would I do? They could do anything to me: I had no control. No one would hear me: no one would know. But I felt, to my horror, my cunt inexorably jerking around with joy, a container looking for a content.

He – or they – tilted me back onto the desk. My sex was exposed at the edge. I felt vulnerable, sparrow-like. I had lost my powers of seduction, my femininity. The battle had moved on, and we were using force. I had lost. Someone got on top of me. They straddled my face. I felt their thighs around my ears; something was waving, dangling, over my eyes, like a hypnotist's beads. The silk gag was removed, and for a second my mouth was freed.

'What are you doing?' I roared. I felt like a bicycle saddle.

A cock was put into me: I was gagged again. I tried to work out whose it was. It was long and lean. I could feel my vagina, an embarrassing, twitching thing, waiting to be serviced.

'She's a filthy slag,' someone said, with glee.

I tried to speak, but the words came out muffled, and my head was pushed down. The owner of the prick wanted me to treat him well.

All the time, I knew the camera was there, watching me. I was going to put on a good show. I was going to be a goddess of the screen.

Someone opened my legs wide again. Fingers were pulling at me but, before I could adjust, I felt the beginnings of an enormous force pushing into me. I was unable to resist. I tried to shake my head, but the cock in my mouth reduced my mobility. I wondered if anyone had ever been suffocated by a man's penis.

Someone was holding my hand. Someone who

knew me well stroked the back of my hand. The pressure between my legs increased. I felt the throbbing penis make its way into me. I was so wet that it slid in as if it were skating home.

I didn't know if I wanted it or not; I wanted to know whose it was first. They weren't playing by the rules.

Then I heard Finnegan's voice. He just wanted to make sure.

'OK, Sally?'

I nodded, hangdog, because I was more than OK. I could feel my pleasure mount. I was foaming at the mouth for it. What was the matter with me?

'What did you do to those naughty boys?'

Not here, not now, Finnegan.

But the memory was exquisite and, once it started, it dominated me. It took over my mind, blotting out all else, even though it was wrong, even though it was dirty; I couldn't stop myself.

Andrew's face as he sucked William dry. What I had made them do. And that morning with Marcus, when we told each other we loved each other, tenderly. And that girl, her spread beaver, and that woman, that wet woman, with the nipples like closed roses, and the cunt like an open sunflower. My legs started jerking involuntarily; my pussy was alight, gushing, the way the first shower of the day comes down on your sleepy body.

For a moment, I was back there, back to the day I lost my virginity. Then I could see and speak, but I did neither. Now, I could do neither, and I wanted to more than anything else. If only to say yes. I gurgled and gulped at the slippery member in my mouth. Remember the camera, I told myself. I felt it slide in and out, in and out, in and out.

Oh God, Andrew's face as I tickled his balls. They were like small satsumas in a Christmas stocking:

tasty, ripe, and now available all year round. The woman, massaging my hair, the way that it turned me to jelly. The way Marcus groaned his orgasm. And Will, and Will.

The man in my mouth pulled out, leaving a sudden vacuum. Suddenly, I felt sperm spurt all over my face, white chocolate buttons. I gulped them down. The producer cried out: I recognised the cry. I focused on the one still inside me, feeling my pussy draw him into its core. I jerked against the dick that was manfully servicing my pussy. Surely deserving an award for long service – he had done his time, paid his dues – he now blocked me in, raising the friction further.

'Will, Will, yes.'

I couldn't wait to take the blindfold off. I couldn't wait to see him, to touch him. He would know how much I loved him. I had discovered I liked sex, but I loved Will. The evidence would be on video for all to see.

'I love you,' I whispered into his thighs, which were like two great columns around my ears.

I heard Finnegan's voice; he was next to me now.

He pulled up the blindfold, and I blinked into the light.

'Look,' he said triumphantly. 'It's your old friend the doorman.' The doorman's beaming face stared down at me. His pearly come was decorating my face. It was his hot-dog cock that had jammed into my throat.

I had to hide my disappointment, and I think I did that well. What an idiot I was.

'Thank you,' I said politely.

The waiter pulled out of me and came up to stroke my hair.

'Sally, you have just made three grown men very happy.'

There was a white tear of spunk suspended from

219

his penis. The French call it 'the little death'. I don't know why, but I felt something inside me die then too. I couldn't help shivering a little. When was I ever going to tie up the other end? Even Finnegan was a little quieter after that. He put his arm around me and snuggled into my neck.

Chapter Nineteen

*I*t was almost three o'clock in the morning by the time the waiter left. Finnegan and I stayed wrapped in each other. We caressed every part of each other, not just our genitals, but our stomachs, our arms and legs. I wanted to know every part of him, to feel each texture and to memorise each taste. He guided me over the map of his body. I learned which scars were from chicken pox and which one was from the snowball with glass in it. Then there was the one from the upturned nail. He also had a large pink scar on his thigh. He said it was from a game with air rifles when he was a kid. I felt a shudder of fear at the thought of him getting hurt.

I fell asleep on the settee. Finnegan must have put a blanket over me. I don't remember him getting up either, but he must have because, when I woke up about 7 a.m., he was asleep at the desk.

Finnegan was out of the office most of the morning, so I felt restless. I felt vulnerable amongst the others, and fearful too that someone would find out. I couldn't tell if it was paranoia, but I thought even Leanne looked at me uneasily. She wouldn't come near. I collected around me the tools of my trade and pretended that I was thinking great advertising thoughts. I squeezed the keyboard keys, and I punched the hole-punch. I pummelled plain sheets of paper into submission then slotted them into the hard-file. I pressed staples deeply into the paper, then leaned hard on the date-stamp. I thought I did everything, but it was not until five o'clock that I realised that I hadn't taken the video out of the machine. By that time, it was too late. Ms Feather had already swiped it into her sports bag. She was ready to go to the gym and work out to her Jane Fonda tape.

I was scared to tell Finnegan, but I had to. When I said it, he sat with his head in his hands. I stared at his heavy gold watch willing around the minutes.

'She may not watch it,' I suggested hopefully.

'Let's go and see,' Finnegan said steadily. He was calm the way people are when they are struggling to control their anger. I realised suddenly that he thought that I had manipulated it on purpose.

We crept behind the two-way mirrors in a small changing room area. We could see her, we had a glorious full-frontal view, but she couldn't see us: all she could see was herself.

Ms Feather had changed out of her work clothes into a black leotard. It was a surprisingly unostentatious and practical outfit, but then she was serious about working out and never missed a session. Even when she was sick, she struggled down to use the stationary bike.

I didn't think she was going to put on the video, and we watched for a while as she did her stretching warm-ups and bends. I couldn't bear the suspense, and I suggested that we left, but Finnegan wanted to wait. He clutched my hand very tight, and I thought he might break my bones.

It wasn't until she was halfway through her sit-ups,

with her feet firmly fixed under the supports, that she suddenly remembered the work-out video. She got up, switched it on, and started 'one and two-ing' her sit-ups. Then her eyes caught the screen again. Maybe she was aware of us, since she looked around: her eyes narrowed with suspicion, and then she lay again. The bench was at an angle, 45 degrees and, from where we were, she was lurching over us. I felt nauseous. I willed the machine not to work. I would have done anything for it not to play: I even would have given up the ghost of my hopes for Will, but the machine played.

The video started with my dance. We watched Ms Feather as I stripped and wiggled around the office on screen.

Ms Feather got up again. Her face was the image of shock, confusion. She moved slowly to the screen. Her finger touched the power button, but she didn't press it, nor did she move away. She was turning pink. Her face was brightening by the minute. I never would have dreamed it. It was like a rash on her. Instead of switching it off though, she waited. Her finger rested there. Then she sat back down on the bench, clipped her feet under the support, and watched.

I was on the screen. It was the bit where I was blindfolded. My face was groaning. It was my own pornographic video, with me as the main character. I looked alive, so alive. The memories flooded back, and I could feel the arousal, even though I was afraid, washing into me too. Now I could see what I had missed last night: the great size of their hard-ons, the waiter taking a sneaky wank near my breasts, Finnegan sweetly stroking my hand, and his face, his beautiful face.

I was clutching Finnegan tight, and he was holding me. If she wanted, she could go to Duncan, and even

Duncan's tolerance for Finnegan wouldn't extend to excusing this. She had the evidence there to make us or break us. There was only one possible way we could survive this: if she liked what she saw.

Ms Feather cast a glance around the gym again, and then she swiped the crotch of her leotard to the right side, and we caught an extraordinary glimpse of gaping pink skin. Holding the obstruction aside with one hand, with the other she entered her vadge.

I held onto Mr Finnegan. I felt a surge of relief run through me, and I know he did too. His shoulders slackened, and he sighed deeply. I could see drips of sweat had gathered on his forehead. On the screen there was a close-up of a huge cock. The sex apparatus filled the screen. It was a powerful and strong specimen with the baggage of balls crammed with cream. This was the doorman's pride and joy. The camera panned back to my arse. It was quite rounded, quite pert. I wondered what Will would do if he saw this. Will claimed he didn't like porn, but I had found magazines under his futon.

Ms Feather was flashing herself at us. Her legs fell either side of the exercise board, and we were both flashed the rare pleasure of her red slit, under a dark suggestion of fuzz. The more she opened her legs, the more the area was transformed from a single line to a glistening cave. I couldn't believe her plump lips were so inviting.

Mr Finnegan was now desperately swallowing his laughter. We were like two children playing the game sardines. I could barely stop giggling. We were squeezed up against each other. If we were caught now, it would be even worse than it already was, although that was bad enough. I was as glued to the vision in front of us as she was to the screen. Ms Feather was as efficient at masturbating as she was at everything. With one hand she clawed at her breast, and with the other she attacked her insides. She even masturbated better than I did (cow).

His comforting hands moved around to caress my neglected pussy. I felt his middle finger rub the wet skin of my vaginal cavity, and his thumb stayed outside to massage my clit.

On the screen the doorman had gripped me by the arse and was coming at me from behind. The camcorder was in my face; the waiter ejaculated in my face, and I licked around it. I was shaking. I was amazed how good I looked when I came.

I felt Finnegan wheedle his way inside my sex, and I sank back into his familiar security. At the same time, I was compelled to watch her. Poor Ms Feather, she had to do it by herself. I felt privileged. He fingered my clitoris, racing me: he wanted me to come, to come watching her, in his hands. I knew him so well: I knew he had a small mole on the finger that was oiling me.

She didn't know what we were doing; we were invading her privacy, but then she was invading ours. Invading: I longed to invade her properly, to show her a proper army, and to liberate her. I wasn't just a regular Peeping Tom. I wanted more than a peep.

Penny Feather's hand worked up and down ferociously. I could see the shiny pearls of whiteness on her fingertips. I remembered the fierceness of her nails. She was scraping at her walls. She started arching back. Her face was contorting with pleasure. Her legs were wide. I saw her looking around the room. She was searching for something, someone.

'Go to her,' I commanded Finnegan.

'No.' He looked at me pleadingly.

'Go to her; she needs you. I want to see what her face looks like when she fucks.'

I could see the distaste on his lips. He really didn't like her. I had to admit that I was happy about that.

'What about you?' he said. 'You go to her.'

'No.' I shrank back into his comforting arms; I wasn't going to leave this glorious place for the world. It's one thing to enjoy karaoke, quite another to get on stage.

She searched in her bag and produced her mobile phone. For a moment I thought she was going to stuff that right up her. She looked that hot for something.

She tried to call someone. She was wiping the sweat out of her hair. She dialled a number, snapped out a comment, and then leaned back again. As she waited, she fiddled with herself. Both Finnegan and I were enthralled. Our eyes were fixed on her treasure, enjoying her personal training session.

I couldn't believe it. The doorman came; he was right in front of her, on her. She didn't allow any touching, any warmth, nothing. He lowered his pants smoothly as an elevator on the descent, and his fabulous prick sprang out, as if pointing at her. Then he was climbing on top of her. Those claws of hers were firm on his buttocks, pressing him into her relentlessly.

We watched spellbound as he pumped up into her. It must have been the perfect angle for penetration. The passage sloped up at 45 degrees. It must have felt fucking amazing, to be taken hard against the rubber surface, the smell of sweat, and the smell of men, sport and come.

I felt almost jealous. The doorman threw himself up and down vigorously. He was a carnal athlete. His bottom soared up and down. I could almost feel the joyful sensations that his prick must be giving her.

She was squealing: her voice was high and girlish, the nails digging in. He was yelling, partly in pain, I guessed. She had hoisted him inside her. Just how could she endure him? I knew from experience that he was enormous. How could her sex contract and expand around him? She must be red at the core of her, like a flaming ball of fire.

Then her legs twitched crazily, like some zombie dance, and for a few seconds there was no movement, no sound. I realised Finnegan and I were also breathing really heavily. We could get caught, and I was nearly coming too. His fingers were working me so efficiently, and the vision of her was making me so horny. Finnegan pressed his index finger and his thumb over my G-spot and squeezed me tight. He bounced me on his knees and snatched at my nipples. His tongue darted in and out of my ear.

'Did she turn you on?' he hissed, knowing she did, knowing how much I loved to listen to him. 'Did you see the way she was when she watched you? How wet she was, just like you, baby: she wants you.'

He made me come. He made my body throb and spasm as I felt his hand controlling in my secret pocket, his breath, and his words in my ear. He could knock the nail on its head, every time.

'Get out,' Ms Feather barked to the doorman. 'I don't want to see you ever again.'

He laughed, his great white teeth flashing like headlamps on a dark street.

'I don't need you any more either.'

The leotard was pulled back into place, just a damp bubble betraying her exertions. She stroked back her hair. She started to do her sit-ups. She crunched up her tight stomach. I could see her lips moving, 'forty-one, forty-two'. It was as if she had never been away.

'Just who was that lady?' I asked. I couldn't believe she had just done that, and I couldn't believe we had watched.

'That was no lady: that was your boss.'

We sneaked away, chuckling like teenagers. I never felt giggly and open with Will. I was scared of annoying him. It wasn't always like that, but he was too image-conscious, too self-aware. I felt sorry for whoever was stuck with him now. She couldn't let herself be her. She would have to pander to his ego.

As we fucked later that night, I pictured Ms Feather's face. The way the arrogance had ebbed away and the delight flooded in. She looked human, not the ice queen she was in the office. Finnegan wanted to relax, so we did it 'mercenary style'. I swung around so that he was prostrate beneath me.

I was the lone soldier, straddling the enemy. I powered my way over him, and he moaned beneath me, begging me for more. I took no prisoners. I imagined what it would be like to do that with Ms Feather beneath me. To grind into her, to make her sweat and surrender. I knew I could make her come. I told Finnegan what I was thinking, and he said I was the most exciting woman he knew, the rudest, the dirtiest and the sluttiest. His words finished off what his cock had started, and I came jubilantly over him, feeling it to be true.

Chapter Twenty

The following day, Ms Feather leaned over my desk. She was wearing a tight skirt suit and high heels. Her hair was pinned back severely. If I hadn't seen her with my own eyes the night before, I would never have believed it.

'We need to have a meeting this evening to work out a new team-building strategy.'

'Do we?' I asked vaguely.

'Yes, we do. I think it's essential, don't you?'

She stared into her ring pad. She was doodling round blobs. I thought they looked like breasts.

'What are those?'

'Ideas,' she said and snapped the book shut.

I told Finnegan that I didn't want to attend the meeting, but he raised his eyebrows and said that it appeared that we had no choice. We were both as guilty as each other. We were both steeped in come so thick we could wade no further. No one cared about my adventures at St Matthew's any more: far more pertinent was our flagrant disregard of company rules, time and resources (although, if the President of the United States could . . .).

The exuberance of the previous evening disintegrated. I called Sharon and asked her to help me rewrite my CV. I was going to need it very soon. When she asked why, I was forced to invent a story about a mistake with a customer. I didn't want to shock her into premature labour. Then she told me that she was sure the baby was going to be a girl, and she was delighted, because 'girls are so much easier to control and so much less naughty than boys.' Even though I was depressed, I had to laugh at that.

Our company president, Duncan, arrived unexpectedly and Ms Feather stalked off self-importantly to his office. Finnegan and I waited tensely at our desks for the summons. I didn't want Finnegan to get fired. I suppose I had recognised that part of his appeal to me was that he was such a big, powerful man (except in my presence). I knew I would hate to see him unemployed or impoverished. It doesn't suit some men. But the dismissal never came. Ms Feather left the office and shouted at Janice about being on the telephone all the time, which wasn't true, and Duncan emerged some time later, looking quite pleased with himself.

At about six o'clock, just after Duncan left, the waiter turned up, self-invited, ready for the specials of the day. He looked surprised to see us all still at work. I went over to him and had to explain that we had an important meeting. I couldn't resist adding that, if he wanted, he was welcome to stay. It could be fun. Stroking his handsome chin, he slowly agreed. He was truly wasted as a waiter: he could have been an actor or a model, but in one of his few verbal moments, he explained that he lost everything, all his goals and ambitions evaporated, when faced with a 'hot' woman. He got fired from his last job because he was sleeping with the boss's wife in the storeroom. The one before that disintegrated when he and the daughter were found. 'We weren't even fucking,' he added, disgruntled, as if they should have been let off. 'Just mouths.'

'Just kissing?' I asked.

'No,' he said, pointing to his crotch, 'mouthy mouthy, the stuff you like.'

'No, of course I don't do that with the pretty customers,' he responded, aggrieved, when I jokingly suggested it. 'The manager found me once, and now I do that for her.'

'What's he doing here?' Ms Feather said. I noticed the worry lines on her otherwise smooth forehead.

'Ideas,' I replied, facetiously. What point was there in being nice to her, if she could get us sacked at a whim? I had already played that game with Finnegan: I wasn't going to start throwing the dice with her.

At the whiteboard, Ms Feather drew a mind map. In the middle, she wrote the word 'teams' and beside that she wrote 'communication'.

'What ways are there to communicate?' she asked. I realised she was nervous. Her lean hands were shaking.

'Meetings, memos, e-mails, faxes.'

The waiter put up his hand.

'Fucking.'

'OK.' She turned red, and primly wrote down 'sex'. Her high heels tapped viciously on the floor, but she seemed to have lost her spirit somewhere. She continued with her laborious explanations.

The waiter was bored with the lecture. He tapped me on the shoulder.

'Have you finished yet?'

I guided his hands under my white blouse and over my breasts. My nipples were already pointed. She could go to hell, she really could. If my professional career was over, then I was going to make sure my sexual career was only just beginning.

'We're just starting,' I whispered, looking intently and, I think, quite menacingly at Ms Feather. I didn't do menacing well, but I think I did a fair job then. She gathered her papers and took her cup over to her desk. Her skin was flushed, and she swapped her weight from skinny leg to skinny leg uncomfortably.

'I should go,' she said quietly. She clutched the file over her chest, hesitating again. What was she waiting for? She looked at me, and I stared coolly back. The waiter found out, to his surprise, that I was wearing a front-fastener. Exclaiming, he unfastened it, and my breasts tumbled free in the first of many glorious releases I anticipated for the evening ahead. She was still in the room though, probably wondering how best she could tell Duncan what an amoral crew we were.

'Why don't you stay a while?' suggested Finnegan, ever the gentleman. Finnegan, what are you saying? I wondered incredulously. This would all provide ammunition for the terrible denouement.

The waiter moved in front of me and dropped down to suck my tits. He was a breast man, a connoisseur. He rubbed my boobs together, swilling them in his mouth, pulling and pinching them. Then he started tugging at my skirt. I helped him unfasten my zip; I was already wet, as he knew I would be.

'No, I . . .' She began taking shaky steps towards the door, towards the sanity of the outside world.

'Wait,' said Finnegan. I gazed at him in amazement. This wasn't just a gamble: it was Russian roulette.

'I really must go,' she continued, although she stopped moving. I felt a surge of perverted disappointment at her words. We couldn't let her go now. I had realised too, what Finnegan had suspected all along: she wanted it. She wanted sex. Maybe she wasn't going to castrate us after all.

She looked like a frightened animal caught in the hunt. A frightened but aroused animal.

'Sit down,' I heard Finnegan say to Ms Feather. He used his most stern voice. They seemed far away, very distant, but when I raised my eyes I saw Ms Feather walk over to her swivel chair meekly. To see Ms Feather meek was a rare and unexpected moment, but I felt unsure, like an archaeologist must feel when he has just excavated an ancient monument, but is unsure whether there is a curse attached to it.

The waiter pulled down his trousers. As usual, he wasn't wearing any pants, and his penis whipped up in my face.

'Suck it,' he said to me. He was confident, as well he might be. He could have been the penis double for someone in a Hollywood movie. I couldn't hide how impressed I was. The balls hung low and pretty behind the massive shaft, like two friends hanging behind the leader.

I heard a whimper from over where Finnegan and Feather were. He was leaning forwards, his elbows on his knees, his chin in his hands, watching us. She was leaning back nervously, struggling in her seat. I kept my eyes fixed on her as I slid down the waiter's shaft.

She was biting her lip, and once again she got up to leave, but this time Finnegan whispered something to her. When I asked him afterwards what he had said, he explained he had simply asked if she were afraid of us. She could never resist a challenge to her authority.

I licked around his stem and rubbed my saliva all over him. He grazed my breasts with his fingers, little light touches that made me squirm with pleasure. I moaned my excitement and, although I told myself I shouldn't look back, I was like Lot's wife, and I couldn't resist. I didn't turn to salt, though, I turned to liquid.

She had pushed aside her shirt and slipped her fingers in her bra. She was swallowing hard; she must have been so turned on to give up in this way. Her underwear was exquisite. You can't help admiring a woman who dresses each day like she's going to get fucked. I mean, didn't the woman ever wear casual clothes? Or go out without her contact lenses? Obviously, from the sight of her panties, never. They were red and lacy, and the bra was a sit-up-and-beg. But underneath the bra I could see she was blessed with the perfect tits, a really magnificent rack. Her cups runneth over. Finnegan had said that to see but not to touch my backside was enough to make grown men weep: in that case, the forbidden promise of her upright titties would make them turn to Prozac.

Her skin was beautiful, straight out of the fashion pages. She was lightly toasted brown and covered in fine, gold hairs. She pulled off the shirt but kept on her bra. I would have kept mine on too, if I had spent eighty quid on it. She had slender legs that actually went in at the top, at the round of the thigh. I wanted them to hang over my shoulders. But not yet, not yet. Then I realised something strange. Under the arms there were tendrils of curling hair. That she didn't shave under her arms was such an unexpected thing.

The waiter dropped in front of me, nursing at my breasts and dampening my stomach with his tongue, but I couldn't take my eyes off her.

I called Finnegan over, and he approached, smiling. He knew what I wanted him to do. I wanted two on me and none on her. I wanted to show her who was the queen bee, and who was the drone. I was going to watch her every second.

'Lick me,' I demanded. They fell in together in front

of me, and I felt the sudden shock of pleasure of one tongue and then two inside my damp hollow. They had to spread me very wide to accommodate both of them. They were lapping like two cats. She might lose me my job, but who gave a fuck when I had two men eating out of my cunt, two men clamped to my gaping oval? (Old wives say two men in the bush are worth one in the hand, and they should know.)

'Oh yes, that feels so-oo good.'

Ms Feather's eyes were open wide, and her hand moved down to the edge of her skirt.

'Take your knickers off,' I said to her. She pretended to look offended, but how could she be with the shirt already off? She was playing with her firm, strawberry-red nipples. She edged her way out of the skirt. Her knickers matched her bra. The pubic hair wound its way up the sides of the cotton, nature making a bid for freedom. She looked at me, and I nodded. She slid them down to the floor. Her bush was hairy, a jungle or a rainforest to explore. I was glad. Who wants to play in a dry desert? I wanted to feel wild.

I couldn't stop watching her. I was glued to her face, as my body was glued to their fingers and thumbs. My two men were inside me. Tongues and fingers, fingers and tongues. Wills, Marcus, Andrew, Finnegan, the waiter. I didn't know who, and I didn't care. I had fucked more men in the last month than I had in my entire life before. Their thumbs worked me. My legs were open to a V and their shoulders were crunched up inside. Just the tops of their heads were visible. the waiter's thick, unruly mop and Finnegan's receding close crop.

I felt so hot there, burning with pleasure. Both of them were working as a team now, for the pursuit of their goal, and that goal was me. They lapped at my honey, and I pressed them closer to ensure that they wouldn't stop before I was ready.

It didn't take long. I had already decided I was going to come once, before everyone else. Why not? I was determined to get what was coming to me. I used my hands on my breasts. I was proud of the responsiveness of my nipples, enamoured with the shapes I could make as I pummelled and pushed my tits together and apart. My boss, my most hated boss, was staring at me with an expression of pure envy and desire. I didn't care what anyone thought. I jerked onto their faces, feeling an explosion of sticky wetness. As I came, on a pulsating raft of pleasure, I saw that her fingers were penetrating herself, telling herself a sweet lullaby. She was showing me her crack, showing off her special work to teacher. (She didn't know I had seen it the night before.)

The waiter was up first, holding his throbbing dick out to me like a peace offering, begging me to put it in.

'Please.'

'Sally,' added Finnegan, 'tonight we are all yours to orchestrate as you like.'

I shook my head. Not now. Then I walked over to Ms Feather. She was ready now. More than ready. At first, I wanted to have her in the same way that Finnegan had had me, but then I had a better idea.

'I know what we can do,' suggested Finnegan, the interfering bastard. I knew I could handle it. 'We can try –'

'You don't own me,' I shouted. I enjoyed seeing the look on his face: he looked surprised but, at the same time, pleased.

The waiter sat back in his chair. His hard-on mirrored his exasperation. He too was mildly annoyed at first, but I knew he would forgive me after what I was going to show him.

I had never touched her before. Even when we did those greeting kisses on the cheek, I knew she blew air so I did too. I put my hand on her shoulder and crept down her back. Her skin was damp, almost oily. I wanted to free her pointy breasts from the bra casing. I wanted to see her expression, but it barely changed from her usual set mouth.

Ms Feather's hair smelled expensive. It felt, not like feathers, but oily and wet. I was drawn to her underarms; I put my fingers there, the way you scratch a cat under the chin, and she sighed. It was a foretaste of what was to come. I moved my hands over her body. Her nipples were sharp little pieces of rock. Her stomach was flat. I realised who she reminded me of, the Tin Man in *The Wizard of Oz*. She had no heart. But I didn't care about her heart. I wanted the secret between her legs. Despite the rigid order of her stature, she was not a waxwork dummy, existing solely for display. Her tunnel was as wet and warm as mine was. Still she didn't move; her eyes were watching my hands, but her mouth was locked shut.

I opened her up and kept my hands either side of her, yanking her thighs apart. I hooked her over my shoulders to see her dangling redness. I stared at it, and then raised my eyes to her.

'What do you want me to do?' I said. I remembered her admonitions to me, her claim that I was inarticulate. 'Express yourself properly,' she had once said cruelly, scavenging over my words. She shook her head as if the cat had stolen her tongue. Her pussy was shiny, dripping invitingly like a garden in the morning dew.

'Say it.'

White discharge was clinging to the ends of her curly pubic mass. She was gushing with it.

She shrugged, trying to pretend she didn't care.

Her fingers, however, were sliding down over the flatness of her belly, sliding down to join my fingers.

'You have to say it.'

She looked up pleadingly. She was saying it with her eyes, but not with her mouth. Poor Ms Feather, she really was speechless.

'Say it, or I won't touch you.'

She sighed and then whispered indistinctly, 'Touch me.'

'How?'

'With your fingers.'

I moved my fingers towards the mound of hair. I was fascinated with it.

'Is that all?'

Her eyes were downcast.

'With your tongue.'

I covered her sex with my mouth. I washed around the insides of her. It was hard because of the hair barrier, but I liked its roughness on my cheek: I liked the naturalness. I stroked her slit with my tongue, sniffing in her fur. I felt my arousal growing crazily fast, like on a speeded-up film.

I climbed on top of Ms Feather, silencing her with my muff. I showed her no mercy. I sat down hard on her. She knew, she knew what to do. Her tongue slipped inside me, like a letter through the postbox, and her fingers arrived a second later, exploring my crevasses, searching for my holes. Soon she was lapping me up. We oral fucked, mouth to pussy resuscitation. She matched me, mirroring me swipe for swipe, wet sweep for wet sweep. I groaned, pulling her legs wider onto me. I pulled a cushion behind my head: I might as well get comfortable, we were going to be here for a while. She did the same. The cat hadn't stolen her tongue after all.

I felt her long nails digging into me; even there, on the sensitive labia, her nails scraped across me indelicately. It was so typical of her. If Marcus had been feline, he would have been a tabby; she was a leopard, put down for mauling. She sucked hard, but even there, between my legs, I could feel her petulance. She was a spoilt child, crying 'Me, me, me.' There was no love lost between us. My antipathy towards her excited me further. I shook my head inside her shapely thighs, working her expertly with my fingers.

We were sixty-nining on the desk. My audience was enthralled, coming closer to look. I liked being on top best. I could find my way into her, and I liked the feeling that I was almost suffocating her. I don't know how she could cope with it. My huge arse swallowing her, her tongue fixed into my clitoris. She knew what to do, though. Ms Feather learned quickly.

She was beautiful. Her buttocks were brown and tight, a faintly lighter colour than the rest of her. I was the more flared, the more sensual. I wasn't afraid of the comparisons any more. I felt beautiful too.

I dived in; I was rough but cool. I could dominate and, when the time was right, I could submit. I don't know how long we stayed like that, wrapped around each other's loins like two entwined flowers. We weren't chasing anything; it is different with men. You can feel their body desperately urging to their release, whereas with us, we didn't want it to end. The journey was equally if not more important than the destination.

I stole into her pussy, and then, when my jaw began to tire, I visited the back passage. I knew what she wanted. I wandered, my thumb heading towards Carnaby Street, the back door. She quivered slightly, but let me in, first with my fingers and then with my tongue and mouth. I was like a dog sniffing in the park. I couldn't get enough of her. I wanted her to do the same to me.

But she didn't.

'Do it, with your fingers,' I commanded. I felt I was almost coming. I wanted to penetrate her and to be penetrated.

She started doing the same to me. I felt her finger roar its way inside me, and I couldn't help myself. My groans got louder. Soon I was shouting. She was like an echo in a cave which shouted back everything I said, even louder. She wasn't Ms Feather to me any more. She was a slippery cunt: she was slippery in my cunt.

'More.'

'More.'

'Fuck me.'

I knew the men were watching us. I was going to put on the show of my life. I heard someone else, I was sure of it. It was the doorman, I suppose. I had to come up for air, and I saw the waiter had his huge stick out, a tear escaping from the end of the purple loneliness.

'Come here,' I said. He worked on the rubber, as easily as if it were thin air. I liked the way he did it. It said, right now, we're really going to fuck. No floating into sex haphazardly: we were prepared for this.

My anus was open and puckered ready for him.

'Come on.'

The waiter got on top of me. I had her head and his dick between my legs. I could accommodate them both. The waiter and I were old hands at this. He sank into my arse gladly. He was all man, all fucking man. I was sandwiched between them on the desk. I was the tuna, and they were the bread. I knew Finnegan wouldn't mind. He seemed to have no jealousy whatsoever. He was the strangest man I had ever met. He was enthralled, masturbating powerfully. His huge todge was erect and eager.

She didn't deserve the extra weight. She didn't

deserve the way I pressed on her clit. She certainly hadn't earned the release, not like I had. She had had years and years of selfishness. I had only hours. But they were going to be good hours. I loved it. She was licking his penis and me simultaneously. I was locked in heaven, two people working at me, me with my face in her muff. Heaven on earth. I suppose I could have invited Finnegan in at the other end to make a foursome, but I wanted myself to be the focus, the sun, and I wanted them to be the planets going around me. I was selfish, taking pleasure from them. I knew they were waiting for me to come. I was the boss, and they were my minions. Their pleasure depended on mine tonight.

I wasn't finished yet, although Ms Feather looked almost dead from the exhaustion of it, and Finnegan said that he was knackered just from watching our exertions.

Ms Feather still hadn't said anything. She sat behind me with her arms around me. My back pushed against her breasts, and her hands were cupping my breast. My skin flowed over her fingers. I remembered that more than a handful is a waste. I could feel the sweat dripping on her chest. Her skin was taut against the ribcage. The men and I chatted. I supposed the doorman was still spying on us, playing his little game, but no one else seemed to realise it and, since he hadn't come forward himself, I guess he was just happy taking care of security.

Ms Feather held her arms around me possessively. She seemed to think I was hers. I undid them and walked over to Finnegan, planning our next moves. He held up my chin and kissed me hard on the mouth.

'You are a wonderful woman, Sally,'

'Finnegan, by the way, what is your first name?'

He laughed. His teeth were even and white. The

total trust I had in Finnegan was a strange thing. It came through knowing him thoroughly. There was no rush to find out anything. I felt I knew him inside and out. Everything he did surprised me, yet nothing surprised me. I knew nothing about his home life. There had been the divorce and the child, but he kept that apart from me. I felt him beaming his encouragement across the room.

Ms Feather walked over. She was holding a shirt daintily to cover her breasts, but it was too short to cover the spread of forestation down there.

'Wasn't I enough for you?' she asked, but it wasn't her usual strident voice. It was simpering, dripping with embarrassment. I saw Finnegan turn away, laughing: he was so unfamiliar with insecurity that it made him laugh.

'What do you mean?'

'Why did you want him to do that?'

'I like it.' Suddenly, I felt a bit sorry for her. 'It's no reflection on you: I just wanted to, you know, get fucked up the arse.'

She looked shocked when I said that. The tongue that had been in my vagina only minutes earlier slid nervously over her lips. They looked bare without the usual coating of lipstick.

'I don't think that's very nice. It's distasteful.'

'It tastes very nice,' I said facetiously. She no longer scared me. In fact, Ms Penny Feather no longer affected me at all.

'No, I mean, it's disgusting.'

'Well, each to his own,' I tossed back.

'Sally,' she pulled me to the side, 'I want to be on my own.'

'On your own?'

'No.' She looked confused. 'On my own with you.'

'But that's crazy,' I said, and I shrugged her off. She irritated me. Then suddenly, just as I remembered that she had the power to send me scrambling for my P45, she said something that filled me with almost as much joy as the waiter's cock.

'I've resigned,' she said. 'My boyfriend has asked me to marry him, and he feels that I shouldn't work any more.'

I almost kissed her again!

'At the same time,' I told Finnegan. 'At the same time.'

I felt like I was a conductor about to conduct a great orchestra. I loved the symmetry of the occasion; me on him, him on her. I knew the doorman was choosing to play the voyeur tonight, and I loved having an audience for my efforts. I had always been the mousy one, and now I was the great entertainer. It was going to be a glorious finale: in years to come, people who weren't even there would pretend that they were, and the people who were there would write memoirs about it, and hint at it on cheesy talk shows.

I wanted us closer. We shuffled nearer together; we were side by side, close as could be. I mounted the waiter. Once again, his glistening shaft rode up me. I shivered, feeling the tremendous pressure of his arrival. I straddled him and, next to me, Finnegan got on top of Ms Feather. It was fitting that we were both on top. We were the same, he and I. We fucked hard, and we let them be fucked. We sat astride our conquests, grinning like idiots. Top layer and bottom layer, masters and serfs. I didn't care about the waiter; I didn't care about Ms Feather. All I cared was about bumping, humping, and coming, and Finnegan was the same too. We smiled at each other, surveying our conquered lands. I was being penetrated, and he was penetrating.

'Wait,' I said, cruelly. 'Stop.'

Finnegan pulled out of her, his rod shiny with her glorious wetness. He looked at me patiently. I felt a surge of affection for him, and felt my pussy wrap around the waiter appreciatively, the way a cat curls itself around a lamppost.

'She wants it there.' I pointed to the narrow line between her buttock cheeks. I wanted to see his cock disappear up her.

Ms Feather lay beneath him, frightened but impassive. The great lady was scared by her own impulses.

'Say it,' I commanded.

'No,' she said.

He clipped her legs neatly over his shoulders. He was such a fucking efficient professional.

'Show me,' I interrupted. I had to move up her buttock to afford the best view, and then I saw her shiny, wet oval, pink and vulnerable between forests of dark hair. He waited, poised to enter. His dick looked long and hard next to that. There were rivers of throbbing veins coming to meet the lush jungle of her pubes. The meeting of the male and the female. How fucking beautiful. How obscene.

'Say it, or you don't get anything.'

Suddenly it all came out.

'Take me, take me anywhere, my cunt, my arse, fuck me.'

Without hesitation, Finnegan moved his prick in. I watched as her tiny arse-hole was obliterated by his bullying cock, like Concorde flying into the clouds. I knew it must be exquisite agony for her. I looked up and knew that someone was watching us, and we were going to be fantastic to watch. She struggled, crying out as I knew she would, pretending to be shocked, pretending to be invaded, but loving it. She took it all in. The whole hot, shoving shaft of him disappeared up where the sun don't shine.

'Fuck me, more, screw me, there, there.'

People can change their minds.

'My hole, my arse, fuck me up the arse.'

The waiter, stuck on the bottom deck of me, could only listen to this glorious itinerary of exotic places. He reached around with his little finger, and carefully, while tipping his penis into my pussy, he opened my back door.

Finnegan took my hand. He kissed it, and he started sucking my finger; I could feel my vagina twist and dive in response, and the waiter beneath me smiled blissfully. He thought he was turning me on. Let him think that it was his dick that did it. But it was Finnegan whose mind was mine. I knew he couldn't stand Feather and was only doing this for me. He was fucking her for me, because I said so. He was hard for me. We started a rhythm. We were counting to see who was going to get to ten. I didn't think I would make it. I was going to come long before then. Who could hold out a whole ten seconds?

I let go of Finnegan's hand. I knew she had a space gagging to be filled too. I understood this. I crept into her soaking vagina; she was already squeezing and gripping, flexing with excitement. She wasn't going to make it to ten, that was for sure. She was so turned on. Everything she had said was a lie. She loved it. She loved it hard.

The waiter's dick was huge, and his fingers were wallpapering my clit, my passage. I felt totally taken care of.

'One,' I said, and laughed.

I watched Finnegan as he screwed Ms Feather. What a sight! He was vicious as a ram, and she was light as a comb. Each jab sent shock waves through her slender frame. Surely she couldn't stand the pleasure? I could hear her beginning to wail already. Lightweight, I thought.'

'Two.' Her groaning continued faster. She was

breathing like a marathon runner, heavy pig grunts in time with the stabs of his penis. I realised I was groaning too. It was not just Ms Feather: I was groaning and sighing, howling at the moon. The waiter had me covered. There wasn't one erogenous zone that wasn't being pleasured.

'Three,' we chorused. Finnegan had beads of sweat on his forehead; I wanted to touch his face. I jabbed my fingers into the recess of his mouth, and he gnawed at them gratefully. I looked down at the waiter. His eyes were fixed on me, on my breasts. I looked too, excited. They were swinging thunderously, like chandeliers in an earthquake.

'Four.' I missed the number, but the men roared it. Finnegan bit my hand as he said it, but I hardly noticed. The waiter put his hand and mine on my nipple and plucked it. Then he squeezed it again. My nipples were swollen and pink. His face was as hard as his grip. I threw my head back in pleasure, arching my spine. Ms Feather had started to shudder: she was coming soon, and I knew that if she came, Finnegan wouldn't make it. Her cunt would grip him uncontrollably, locking him in. Finnegan, my darling blackmailer, the one who forced me to do all this, he was going to lose it.

'Five,' we yelled together, just Finnegan and I. The waiter's face gave it away: his nostrils flared, he was close to ejaculation. His hips started jitterbugging, flipping out like a washing machine, but he didn't let up the pressure on my cunt. What a hero! I swooped up and down, arching back, leaning back as far as I could. I was happy with that angle. And how long and bendy his penis was! He held firm, his fingers crawling around my tender clit or brushing against my nipples in a way that had them clamouring for more.

'Six.' This time it was just my voice singing out

pure and true. Finnegan was in a trance. His eyes closed; he was concentrating on holding on, meditating. The waiter was just about coping with us all. He had outstretched one hand to play with Ms Feather's bullet-like nipples; the other stayed affixed to my throbbing clitoris. Finnegan was watching me, biting his lip, his pleasure a reflection of my own. Ms Feather was wailing to wake the dead. I was happy that I was on top, that I could control the body of traffic in my body. I swung forwards and back, according to how deep I wanted it. Ms Feather, however, was at the mercy of Finnegan's delving prick. It must have suited her though, because when we got to seven our three voices were drowned out by Ms Feather. She was screaming now, her body fitful. Her legs jerked, and I knew her clitoris had blown up to the size of a beach ball.

'Eight.' The waiter's voice soared alone. He flicked my clitoris, and I came on like a switch. I felt his dick suddenly triple in size; I was almost thrown off him. He pumped up his orgasm, and I couldn't stop hissing, 'Yes, yes.' I went up and down on him like a spring. It was a reflex. The waiter joined me, then he screamed, 'I'm coming, I'm coming.' I felt his cock pulsate around my insides, reaching up and out.

'Nine.' Finnegan's voice alone sang out. I was coming, riding on top of my frenzied stallion, holding Finnegan's hand so tight that he told me later that he thought I was going to break it. My knees smashed on the floor as I worked the waiter up and down, draining the spunk from the eye of his penis, not wasting a shudder or a drop of come. I was oblivious to everything: Finnegan, Feather, the waiter, and even the numbers. All I knew was that my entire being was amplified to a sensation of pure pleasure. Nothing else was important. I was spurting out juices like a great big orgasmic spray. I tasted heaven on earth. For once, I came silently, amazed at the strength of my own feeling, at the power of my body to make me do these things. It was a wonderful thing.

Then Finnegan came too with a tremulous roar, 'Ohhhh.'

'Ten,' I said quietly. Finnegan leaned over and kissed the top of my head tenderly, as though kissing it better.

'What about Wills?' he whispered. 'You didn't say it this time.'

'Wills, Wills!' It was a little mutter, more a sigh than a word, a small echo of Finnegan. Only it didn't come from me this time. It came from Ms Feather. Finnegan and I both looked at her, confused. The waiter wiped his forehead and examined the trail of slime I had left on his thighs.

We had collapsed in a heap, arms and legs wrapped around each other. Hearts beating together, I didn't know whose hand was whose, whose hair scraped against my cheek, whose knee was against my stomach. I was right. There was someone watching us. When we untangled ourselves, a man moved forwards out of the darkness. But it wasn't the door-man this time.

'I'm here.'

We all looked up.

'Penny, Sally. Hi.' It was Will.

Ms Feather was up like a cat, running across the room, picking up clothes. She couldn't find her skirt, so she put on Finnegan's trousers. They looked absurd on her. Finnegan, however, looked better with nothing on. He carried his nakedness with aplomb.

'I didn't know you knew each other so well,' Will said. The waiter gracefully pulled me off him and stood up. He put his jeans on and pulled on a top; he looked all ready to go, as if he had spent the last couple of hours getting ready for a night out. I stared back at Will, still confused. I felt Finnegan's hand in my hair, but I didn't want it there. Penny Feather was also looking at him, like I was. I walked over to Will. She did too.

'So, now you know,' he said.

'Know what?' I said. It's possible to be experienced and naïve at the same time. For a few seconds then, I was living proof of it. She put her hand soothingly on his arm.

'How do you know each other?' I asked. I felt bewildered. These two people from entirely separate areas of my life knew each other. I would have been less surprised to learn that the world was made of cheese.

'I told you to tell her. I told you!' Ms Feather shouted.

I swallowed hard. Was this, was this the one who had set Ms Feather alight, the one who she was so happy with? The one who had asked her to stop work? I couldn't believe it. I could see Finnegan's eyes were studying me carefully. He was concerned. Amidst all the chaos, I couldn't help thinking how considerate he was.

'Sally, I want to talk to you.' Will ignored everyone else in the single-minded way only he could. He pushed Ms Feather off him and held out his hands to me. He was wearing one of his suits, and he looked divinely handsome. I had fantasised about this for a long time.

'What about?'

He glanced sideways.

'Just the two of us.'

'I have nothing to say to you,' I said unconvincingly. 'It was you who finished with me, remember?' And you were screwing her, her of all the women in the world, you were shagging her and getting engaged to her, for fuck's sake!

'I didn't know you could be so uninhibited, so sexy.'

I noticed he had a hard-on. The front of his trousers strained awkwardly. I saw the outline of erect, earnest prick. I remembered kneeling before him once in his room. He had been wearing a baggy grey cardigan and black jeans, which he had unzipped for swift access. He was listening to his CD collection; he told me I rubbed too hard sometimes.

'It depends who I'm with,' I said grudgingly. Was she the one he made love to when I cried into his answering machine? I don't know how he had the gall to do it, to me or to her. He had asked her to marry him, and now he was holding out his hand to me!

'Sally, I miss you. Let's get back together.'

I remembered walking with him, a cold February afternoon, and he put my hand in his pocket, rubbed it and said what weenie fingers I had.

'You can't throw away five years.'

I remembered the last time Will and I made love. It was a Friday night two weeks before he dumped me. Will had gone out with his workmates and, when he came to mine, he was drunk and I was sleeping. He climbed on top of me, beery-breathed and heavy with curry sauce. As he came, he groaned in my ear. I remember thinking of water buffaloes.

'Four and a half,' I corrected him. 'And it's not throwing them away. What's done is done. I am what I am now because of that.'

Penny was clambering between us. She was furious in baggy Chaplinesque pants. She had heard everything. Even in that get-up she looked smooth, as if she had just got out of the beauty salon, not as if she had had three rounds. Not like me with my musty hair and animal smell.

'Penny,' he said, his hands palm upwards. 'What can I say?'

'Sod off, Will.' She turned to me and said, 'Sally, please, let's be friends. Come over to my house, and I'll cook you some dinner, and –'

'Sally,' Will interrupted. 'Let's go home. There's a song I want to play to you. It reminds me of when I first met you. And I want to take you to this hotel I know where they have four-poster beds in all the bedrooms.'

I liked Will. I had loved him, and I still liked him too much. He didn't only hold my hand, but he taught me how to love someone. However, there were other lessons to learn, and I wasn't going to get them from him. I was learning how to love myself. Besides, who wanted to fuck on a four-poster bed? It's not where you are, or even who you are with, but how you feel in your head and in your skin. For the first time I felt good in mine. And I had other fantasies to fulfil.

'Fuck off, Will,' I said confidently. I didn't care any more. Let them go: let it be. I had the perfect wedding gift for the pair of them: a video of me. May they spend ten thousand nights adoring my exertions.

Finnegan carried me to the car. I felt like a new bride being carried over the threshold.

'Its time I took you to my home,' he had said when they had left, the waiter back to his shift at the coffee bar, Penny Feather and Will arguing and jangling car keys.

Mr Finnegan still had no trousers on. He didn't care. He drove in his shirt, tie, and boxer shorts. His thighs were heavy, with golden hairs.

'Did you know?' I asked him. 'About Will and Ms Feather?'

'I suspected,' he said. I was glad he didn't lie. 'Do you mind?' he asked presently.

'No,' I said. 'I don't want him any more.'

'Sally, I only want you,' he said, 'but I like imagining you, watching you with other people. I want to be part of your life for ever. Do you mind?'

'No,' I said. That sounded good to me.

I trusted him driving. I liked the way he controlled the car, his power over the expensive machinery, like his power over me. I watched him make the gear changes, and I liked the way he endeavoured to drive smoothly. I could feel that Will was gone for ever, and the place that once was empty, my heart, was full again.

I had an idea for the new advertising for the big law firm.

'It's important to leave a Will,' I said, laughing as I spoke. 'Then you've got this woman, and she's walking out on this guy. And then we just say why, and I think you could say it's quite tongue in cheek.'

'I like that.' He stared at me admiringly. 'I really like that.'

I still couldn't stop chatting. Finnegan said that maybe I was overtired. 'I'm not sleepy,' I protested. 'Honestly, I could do it all over again.

'Tell me more about you. I don't know anything about you, your family or your hobbies,' I said.

'You'll find out from now on . . . Slowly.'

Some words, some silly words, just get you there. I loved the way he said 'slowly'. I felt damp and crinkly and couldn't stop smiling at my luck.

I started masturbating. I loved doing it on the road. We were driving fast, tearing past houses and parked cars and moving cars. What would they all say if they knew what was happening in my knickers? The traffic had been heavy there, too. The other headlamps brightened and then faded away. I wondered if they could see my road tax.

'Aren't you sore, baby?' he asked. He kept his eyes

on the road masterfully (except for once, when I caught them illicitly darting over to my thighs). 'You worked so hard tonight.'

'I'm still desperate for you,' I said, and it was the strange truth. Then I remembered why. I hadn't fucked him all night. It was like not eating dinner. I felt weird, as if our routine had been skewed. I felt like something was missing. I leaned back on the seat, my legs wider and more disputed over than the Suez Canal. I gave all the passing motorists an eyeful. I was going to be as loud as I could. I was going to shout my come into the motorway. He was going to have to press hard on his horn to cover up the sound of my orgasm.

'I can take you now,' he said, but his actions belied his words. He speeded up.

'You can't. You haven't got it in you: you're not so young. You're past it, you are.'

'Wanna bet?' His foot dipped the accelerator, and we drove faster, but Finnegan edged his hand inside his shorts. He delved in, hauling himself out. His massive cock, the other gear stick, popped up to see me.

What a darling. One hand on the wheel, with the other he wanked himself. I watched the flow of hand movements on his tool. It was like dick ballet. I felt full of anticipation, like the night before Christmas. His fingers gripped himself, and I exercised myself. It was lovely driving along like that with both of us pleasing ourselves. I couldn't stop myself: I was getting faster and faster. My fingers were covered with my juices.

'Oh, Jesus,' he said, when he cast a look over me, and the way he said it reminded me oddly of Marcus.

He swung the car on to the hard shoulder of the motorway. He undid his seat belt and turned towards me.

He tried to put his hand up my skirt, but I told him he could look, but he wasn't to touch. I was taking control. Other cars shot by, and I thought for a second that the hard shoulder of a motorway wasn't the safest place to be.

'Why not?' he said, amazed. 'Why d'you get me so excited?'

'For fun.'

'I'm so horny: help me!'

I giggled. He changed tack and started begging. That's what I liked about Finnegan. One minute he would be Mr Darcy, the next he might play Man Friday.

'No, you have to do something for me.'

'What? Please don't play games, I need you.'

'No, you have to do something for me.'

'Oh sweet Sally, let me rest, let me come inside you, that's where I'm happiest. Let me come home to nest.'

'All you have to do is tell me your name.'

'You know it, it's Finnegan.'

'No, your first name.'

'It's a secret.'

'Tell me your name, or you can't touch me!'

'I won't be blackmailed.' He was laughing.

'Then, my honey,' I said, leaning back to show him as much as I could, 'there is no room at the inn.'

I made my fingers accelerate up and down. I type at 60 wpm, and I masturbate even faster. I didn't need him. I didn't need anyone to tell me I was beautiful. I felt beautiful. I tilted the passenger seat back. My clit glistened, a small, shiny trophy in the sea of eternity.

'You are such an unusual woman, Sally.'

I grabbed the vibrator from my bag. It was going to feel so good. I switched it on, and it made the radio go funny. I smuggled it inside me, parting my lips. The dildo hummed against my clit. I stretched my arms over my head, tightening my taut fanny

254

muscles. The machine throbbed inside me, excavating my treasure, turning my private, tucked-away property into a public display.

'Oh, Jesus,' he repeated, looking at me.

It did feel good. I knew he liked watching, but I didn't care what he thought any more. Men come and go, but I have to live with me for ever.

'Come on, baby, you know you want me,' he said hopefully. He was still tugging his hard cock. It was red and manly, and I knew it would feel even better than the dildo.

'Nope,' I said. I was determined. 'You're the unusual one, anyway. Why on earth won't you tell me your name?'

'All right,' he said desperately. 'It's Norm.'

Before I could recover from the shock, he had whipped out the dildo from between my legs, leaving my cunt aching to be touched. I was already pulsating up and down, ready for him. He had his fingers on his dick, pushing back the wealth of foreskin. The crusading head was brighter than Superman.

'Sally, I'm coming in.'

He yanked my legs up and aimed his penis inside me. It sank into me, huge and hungry, and I gave a cry of exhilaration, as if I had just been launched from an aeroplane out into the cool sky.

Where the dildo was cold and smooth, his dick was hot, throbbing, and rugged somehow. It was the difference between seeing a photo of the Pyramids and taking a guided tour. It was the difference between a computer game of chess and feeling the actual pieces. Of course, I preferred the real thing. (But his penis was pretty good too!)

'Oh Norman,' I moaned. Oh, I was so happy now that I had a handle with which to wind him up.

'Please don't say that,' he hissed back.

I was jammed in the passenger seat. Gridlock. His

beige arse went up and down like a rutting pig. We must have been a strange sight for the other drivers. An exotic catch for the bird watchers. His knees were everywhere, caught in the window handle on one side, the gear stick on the other. We were both squirming against each other. It was a heavenly, abandoned squash. The tips of my nipples brushed against his hands. I felt the exquisite sensitivity of their peaks. Road sex is a better way to relieve stress than road rage. I heard the sound of passing lorries, felt the sudden brightness and then abrupt fading of their headlamps.

For a second, I thought about Marcus. I wanted to thank him. If it weren't for Marcus, I would never have found out there was more to me than the way I looked. I knew he wouldn't be jealous that I was thinking about Marcus. He didn't have a jealous bone in his body. For a second, I thought about Will, but only to notice that I hadn't thought about him before. Mostly I thought about Finnegan, and the way he screwed me like no one else in my life did but, at the same time, he managed not to screw up my life.

I came first. I couldn't stand it any more. He was pumping me harder and harder, and I swung back into him. I thrust upwards, jamming my clit against his skin, sawing at him until he bombed away. I felt his spurt, like an explosion inside me. His fist jammed on the horn of the car, and the noise accompanied his sighs.

It was a bonding fuck, a conspiratorial fuck. It was a friendly, almost neighbourly, late-night fuck, when no one else is looking. Afterwards, he did up the seat belt around me and buttoned up my shirt. I kissed each finger as it passed in front of my mouth.

'Go to sleep, my darling; you've had a busy day.'

When I was young, if I fell asleep on the settee, my parents used to carry me upstairs, undress me, and put me to bed. Sometimes, I would pretend that I was asleep just so that someone would take care of me. The worries of the day would disappear into the world of bed.

I fell asleep in the passenger seat. The car smelled of leather, football socks and our sex.

Chapter Twenty-One

When I woke up, I was naked in a room that I knew well. It was white, expensive looking, and there was a black piano in the corner. I was under a silk blanket on a leather sofa. Someone kissed me on the lips, and then kissed me once on each cheek.

'Hi, Sally.'

I sat on the sofa dazzled, trying to take it all in. Finnegan (yes, I would never call him 'Norm') put on some music and disappeared to make dinner.

His son's chest was bare, his small nipples uplifted to me. I wanted to touch him. Our legs found each other under the silk.

He leaned over to whisper something in my ear.

'Do you want to stay in my room or Dad's tonight?'

'Let's take it in turns,' I whispered back diplomatically, but Finnegan came running out of the kitchen. He was wearing a stripy cook's apron over his shirt. He still hadn't put on his trousers. The ensemble looked ludicrous. We both started laughing.

'What are you two plotting?' he enquired suspiciously. 'I'm making stir-fry.'

'He always makes stir-fry,' Marcus said and kissed my hand, like a gentleman would kiss a lady.

'I remember the last time I was near a Chinese restaurant,' I said. Marcus put my fingers in his mouth. I felt the wetness of his lips. He smiled at me sweetly.

'Wait till after dinner,' Finnegan said. But Marcus had already started kissing me. His lips were on me, singing his beautiful tongue into my mouth, his beautiful breath inside me. We didn't care.

'By the way, I'm taking you two on a long holiday.' Finnegan was behind me now; he ran his fingers through my short hair. 'I've been having these incredible dreams about having you on a beach.'

There was only one person I was worried about now: Sharon. When she found out about all this, I knew she was going to go mad.

BLACK LACE NEW BOOKS

Published in May

PLAYING HARD
Tina Troy
£6.99

Lili wrestles men for money. And they pay well. She's the best in the business and her powerful body and stunning looks have her gentlemen visitors begging for more rough treatment. Her golden rule is never to date a client, but when James Travers starts using her services she relents and accepts a date.

An unusual and powerfully sexy story of male/female wrestling.

ISBN 0 352 33617 X

HIGHLAND FLING
Jane Justine
£6.99

Writer Charlotte Harvey is researching the mysterious legend of the Highland Ruby pendant for an antiques magazine – a ruby that is said to sexually enslave any woman to the man who places the pendant round her neck. Charlotte's quest leads her to a remote Scottish island where the pendant's owner – the dark and charismatic Andrew Alexander – is keen to test its powers on his guest.

A cracking tale of wild sex in the Highlands of Scotland.

ISBN 0 352 33616 1

CIRCO EROTICA
Mercedes Kelley
£6.99

Flora is a lion-tamer in a Mexican circus. She inhabits a curious and colourful world of trapeze artists, snake charmers and hypnotists. When her father dies owing a lot of money to the circus owner, the dastardly Lorenzo, Flora's life is set to change. Lorenzo and his accomplice – the perverse Salome – share a powerful sexual hunger, a taste for bizarre adult fun and an interest in Flora.

This is a Black Lace special reprint of one of our most unusual and perverse titles!

IBSN 0 352 33257 3

Published in June

SUMMER FEVER
Anna Ricci
£6.99

Lara Mcintyre has lusted after artist Jake Fitzgerald for almost two decades. As a warm, dazzling summer unfolds, she makes the journey back to her student summer-house where they first met, determined to satisfy her physical craving somehow. And then, ensconced in Old Beach House once more, she discovers her true sexual self – but not without complications.

Beautifully written story of extreme passion.

ISBN 0 352 33625 0

STRICTLY CONFIDENTIAL
Alison Tyler
£6.99

Carolyn Winters is a smooth-talking disc jockey at a hip LA radio station. Although known for her sexy banter over the airwaves, she leads a reclusive life, despite the urging of her flirtatious roommate, Dahlia. Carolyn grows dependent on living vicariously through Dahlia, eavesdropping and then covertly watching as her roommate's sexual behaviour becomes more and more bizarre. But then Dahlia is murdered, and Carolyn must overcome her fears in order to bring the killer to justice.

A tense dark thriller for those who like their erotica on the forbidden side.

ISBN 0 352 33624 2

CONTINUUM
Portia Da Costa
£6.99

Joanna Darrell is something in the city. When she takes a break from her high-powered job she is drawn into a continuum of strange experiences and bizarre coincidences. Like Alice in a decadent Wonderland, she enters a parallel world of perversity and unusual pleasure. She's attracted to fetishism and discipline and her new friends make sure she gets more than a taste of erotic punishment.

This is a reprint of one of our best-selling and kinkiest titles ever!

ISBN 0 352 33120 8

SYMPHONY X
Jasmine Stone
£6.99

Katie is a viola player running away from her cheating husband. The tour of Symphony Xevertes not only takes her to Europe but also to the realm of deep sexual satisfaction. She is joined by a dominatrix diva and a bass singer whose voice is so low he's known as the Human Vibrator. After distractions like these, how will Katie be able to maintain her serious music career *and* allow herself to fall in love again?

Immensely funny journal of a sassy woman's sexual adventures.

ISBN 0 352 33629 3

OPENING ACTS
Suki Cunningham
£6.99

When London actress Holly Parker arrives in a remote Cornish village to begin rehearsing a new play, everyone there – from her landlord to her theatre director – seems to have an earthier attitude towards sex. Brought to a state of constant sexual arousal and confusion, Holly seeks guidance in the form of local therapist, Joshua Delaney. He is the one man who can't touch her – but he is the only one she truly desires. Will she be able to use her new-found sense of adventure to seduce him?

Wonderfully horny action in the Cornish countryside. Oooh arrgh!

ISBN 0 352 33630 7

THE SEVEN-YEAR LIST
Zoe le Verdier
£6.99

Julia is an ambitious young photographer who's about to marry her trustworthy but dull fiancé. Then an invitation to a college reunion arrives. Old rivalries, jealousies and flirtations are picked up where they were left off and sexual tensions run high. Soon Julia finds herself caught between two men but neither of them are her fiancé.

How will she explain herself to her friends? And what decisions will she make?

This is a Black Lace special reprint of a very popular title.

ISBN 0 352 33254 9

If you would like a complete list of plot summaries of Black Lace titles, or would like to receive information on other publications available, please send a stamped addressed envelope to:

Black Lace, Thames Wharf Studios,
Rainville Road, London W6 9HA

BLACK LACE BOOKLIST

Information is correct at time of printing. To check availability go
to www.blacklace-books.co.uk

All books are priced £5.99 unless another price is given.

Black Lace books with a contemporary setting

THE TOP OF HER GAME	Emma Holly ISBN 0 352 33337 5	☐
LIKE MOTHER, LIKE DAUGHTER	Georgina Brown ISBN 0 352 33422 3	☐
IN THE FLESH	Emma Holly ISBN 0 352 33498 3	☐
SHAMELESS	Stella Black ISBN 0 352 33485 1	☐
TONGUE IN CHEEK	Tabitha Flyte ISBN 0 352 33484 3	☐
FIRE AND ICE	Laura Hamilton ISBN 0 352 33486 X	☐
SAUCE FOR THE GOOSE	Mary Rose Maxwell ISBN 0 352 33492 4	☐
INTENSE BLUE	Lyn Wood ISBN 0 352 33496 7	☐
THE NAKED TRUTH	Natasha Rostova ISBN 0 352 33497 5	☐
A SPORTING CHANCE	Susie Raymond ISBN 0 352 33501 7	☐
TAKING LIBERTIES	Susie Raymond ISBN 0 352 33357 X	☐
A SCANDALOUS AFFAIR	Holly Graham ISBN 0 352 33523 8	☐
THE NAKED FLAME	Crystalle Valentino ISBN 0 352 33528 9	☐
CRASH COURSE	Juliet Hastings ISBN 0 352 33018 X	☐
ON THE EDGE	Laura Hamilton ISBN 0 352 33534 3	☐

------✂------------------------

Please send me the books I have ticked above.

Name ....

Address ....

....

....

.... Post Code ....

Send to: Cash Sales, Black Lace Books, Thames Wharf Studios, Rainville Road, London W6 9HA.

US customers: for prices and details of how to order books for delivery by mail, call 1-800-805-1083.

Please enclose a cheque or postal order, made payable to **Virgin Publishing Ltd**, to the value of the books you have ordered plus postage and packing costs as follows:
  UK and BFPO – £1.00 for the first book, 50p for each subsequent book.
  Overseas (including Republic of Ireland) – £2.00 for the first book, £1.00 for each subsequent book.

If you would prefer to pay by VISA, ACCESS/MASTER-CARD, DINERS CLUB, AMEX or SWITCH, please write your card number and expiry date here:

....

Please allow up to 28 days for delivery.

Signature ....

------✂------------------------